Haley's smile faded at the sight of the man in the doorway

"Can I...help you?" she asked, her gaze traveling over the man's strange clothes. In spite of the June heat, he wore a heavy coat and fatigue pants, and sweat dotted his forehead.

"You've been unfaithful to me, haven't you, Sabrina? Why didn't you answer my letters?"

Sabrina. Panic sped through her. She stumbled back and attempted to push the door closed, knowing instinctively who the man must be.

He stopped it with an outstretched arm. *I'm* the one you should be with, Sabrina. You have to love *me!*"

Haley swallowed hard as she watched him reach into his coat pocket and pull out a handgun. "Oh God, no," she moaned.

"Me! Me, Sabrina!" he cried. Then he leveled the gun and squeezed the trigger three times.

D0802690

Dear Reader,

Four more fabulous WOMEN WHO DARE are heading your way!

In May, you'll thrill to the time-travel tale Lynn Erickson spins in *Paradox*. When loan executive Emily Jacoby is catapulted back in time during a train wreck, she is thoroughly unnerved by the fate that awaits her. In 1893, Colorado is a harsh and rugged land. Women's rights have yet to be invented, and Will Dutcher, Emily's reluctant host, is making her question her desire to return to her own time.

In June, you'll be reminded that courage can strike at any age. Our heroine in Peg Sutherland's *Late Bloomer* discovers unplumbed depths at the age of forty. After a lifetime of living for others, she realizes that she wants something for herself—college, a career, a *life*. But when a mysterious stranger drifts into town, she discovers to her shock that she also wants *him!*

Sharon Brondos introduces us to spunky Allison Ford in our July WOMEN WHO DARE title, *The Marriage Ticket*. Allison stands up for what she believes in. And she believes in playing fair. Unfortunately, some of her community's leaders don't have the same scruples, and going head-to-head with them lands her in serious trouble.

You'll never forget Leah Temple, the heroine of August's *Another Woman*, by Margot Dalton. This riveting tale of a wife with her husband's murder on her mind will hold you spellbound...and surprised! Don't miss it!

Some of your favorite Superromance authors have also contributed to our spring and summer lineup. Look for books by Pamela Bauer, Debbi Bedford, Dawn Stewardson, Jane Silverwood, Sally Garrett, Bobby Hutchinson and Judith Arnold...to name just a few! Some wonderful Superromance reading awaits you!

Marsha Zinberg
Senior Editor

P.S. Don't forget that you can write to your favorite author

    c/o Harlequin Reader Service,
    P.O. Box 1297
    Buffalo, New York
    14240 U.S.A.

Dreams of Glass

Brenna Todd

Harlequin Books

TORONTO • NEW YORK • LONDON
AMSTERDAM • PARIS • SYDNEY • HAMBURG
STOCKHOLM • ATHENS • TOKYO • MILAN
MADRID • WARSAW • BUDAPEST • AUCKLAND

To Todd, my vision of love

Published August 1993

ISBN 0-373-70560-3

DREAMS OF GLASS

ABOUT THE AUTHOR

Brenna Todd's first Superromance novel, *All the Right Moves,* won the Golden Heart Award as well as kudos from reviewers and readers alike. Her second book, *Dreams of Glass,* is a worthy successor.

Brenna bases her stories on real-life events, then adds the magic "what if" and a healthy dose of romance for a recipe that leaves readers hungry for more. Her innovative approach and dedication to her craft make it certain that she'll be able to satisfy their cravings for a long time to come.

Books by Brenna Todd

HARLEQUIN SUPERROMANCE
474—ALL THE RIGHT MOVES

Don't miss any of our special offers. Write to us at the following address for information on our newest releases.

Harlequin Reader Service
P.O. Box 1397, Buffalo, NY 14240
Canadian address: P.O. Box 603,
Fort Erie, Ont. L2A 5X3

PROLOGUE

June 1990

HALEY RIVERS GLANCED UP from the script she was halfheartedly studying, glad for the distraction her roommate, Carolyn Kincaid, provided. She watched Carolyn edge into the apartment, then slam the door, effectively silencing the yapping of their neighbor's French poodle, Enchantée. Carolyn scowled, fanning herself with the stack of mail she held. "I'm taking out a contract on that dog's miserable little life," she threatened.

Haley chuckled and set her script aside. "I'll pay half." Carolyn strolled forward to the sofa where Haley sat and handed her a few pieces of mail, then went to the kitchen a few feet away.

Haley flipped through the letters and bills, hearing her friend open cabinet doors and the refrigerator, then clink ice into a glass. "You thirsty?" Carolyn called out.

"No, thanks."

She came back to the living room, holding an iced drink to her forehead as she made her way to the recliner opposite Haley. She took a sip of the cola, then pointed the glass at the letter Haley was frowning over. "I noticed that one was addressed to 'Sabrina,'" she said. "Another profession of undying love from your fruitcake fan?"

"Appears so." The handwriting was unmistakable. She had received too many of his letters over the past few months not to recognize the uneven scrawl and messy ink smudges. And, of course, the fact that it was addressed to "Sabrina Holloway," the character she played on the daytime soap "Forever and a Day," was a dead giveaway.

"When did he start sending them here? I thought you'd only been getting them at the studio."

Haley's frown deepened. Her eyes tracked from the Los Angeles postmark to the empty return-address space. "This is the first." Her gaze rose to Carolyn's. "Think I should worry about it?"

Carolyn shrugged. "I know Sy thinks you should."

Haley nodded. Her agent, Sy, had worrying down to an art. He'd wanted to turn the very first letter she'd received from this Jack Raymond Wharton character over to the police—his and several other fans' letters. Haley had thought that a bit extreme. After all, several of the other actors on "Forever" had received mail like hers. They'd all assured her that this sort of thing was a fact of life for a soap actor.

Wharton wasn't the only fan sending her letters. But he *was* the only one who sent them so regularly, a small voice in her head reminded her as she fingered the envelope. And now he had her home address.

Carolyn spoke up again. "Sy could have a point. Your number-one fan there might be unbalanced, but what do I know?" She shrugged and gave a short laugh. "I thought the woman in the pharmacy last week was certifiable, too."

"Oh, she was harmless."

"Yeah, right. Look, I'm no psychiatrist, just another out-of-work actor... but come on, the woman believes that the characters she sees on that little box in her living room every day are real-life people. She wasn't all there, Haley."

"I know it sounds that way, but really it's not. It's just that soap addicts get so wrapped up in the show. They get a little carried away."

Carolyn rolled her eyes. "She called you Sabrina, just like your letter writer, and wanted to know if the bottle of pills you were buying meant you had some serious disease or something. For Pete's sake, her voice was shaking."

"Bless her heart."

"Bless her pointed little head is more like it," Carolyn mumbled. She drained the last of her drink, then rose from the chair and took the glass to the kitchen. Over her shoulder, she added, "In my opinion, if you're not worried about someone like Pharmacy Woman, then you shouldn't waste time worrying about Jack Ray."

"You're probably right," Haley said, pitching the letter on top of the script she'd abandoned. "No, I *know* you're right." She also knew without reading it that Jack Wharton's letter would be filled with declarations of his eternal love and desire for Sabrina Holloway. Soap operas seemed to draw these types from the woodwork.

She put thoughts of the letter aside and looked at the phone for the hundredth time that day with a sigh. Why couldn't the damn thing ring? Why couldn't Sy just call and put her out of her misery....

When the phone rang, she blinked and her pulse jumped.

She dropped the rest of the mail at her feet. All thoughts of fans, unbalanced or otherwise, fled her mind. She hopped up from the sofa, but Carolyn raced around the corner from the kitchen and placed her hand on top of the ringing phone before Haley could move.

"Could this be it?" her friend asked dramatically, her eyes alight with mischief. "Might this be Haley's agent with the all-important news that she got the part? Tune in tomorrow, viewers, when we find out the answer—"

Haley gave a half groan, half laugh. "Answer the phone, you goof!" she demanded.

"Patience, patience." Carolyn lifted the phone to her ear. "Rivers-Kincaid residence. We work cheap."

Haley groaned again, then wrung her hands together like a nervous heroine in a B movie. Patience, as Carolyn damn well knew, was not at the top of Haley's list of virtues. In fact, it wasn't even on the list where this latest audition was concerned.

She'd first read for the part—one every other actress in town had also lusted after—three days ago. She'd made the cut along with five other lucky souls and had tested for the casting director a second time yesterday. After twenty-four hours on pins and needles, Haley was unable to concentrate on her "Forever" script for more than five minutes at a time.

Carolyn held her hand over the speaker. "It's for you," she said in a stage whisper. "Someone named Sy?"

Haley leapt over a coffee table and was at the desk in a heartbeat. "Give it to me," she demanded breathlessly. "Hi, it's me," she said into the receiver. "Whaddya got?"

"What have *you* got, you mean," boomed Sy's familiar voice.

"Does this mean . . . ? Did I get the . . . ?"

"You got it!" Sy said happily. "You, my dear, have star billing in next year's most talked-about movie!"

"Oh, God! I can't believe it!" She grabbed her friend's hand, squeezing it. "I got it! I got the part!"

Carolyn's smile was huge. She shouted "Yes!" then pulled Haley, phone and all, into a bear hug.

"I, of course, knew you would all along," Sy said smugly. "But I will caution you against burning any bridges at 'Forever.' I know you'll probably want to ditch the soap, but let's talk that over later."

"Right, right," she said, still thunderstruck. When she replaced the receiver minutes later, she locked gazes with Carolyn. They squealed in unison.

Carolyn was the first to calm down. "This calls for a celebration."

"Yes." Haley placed a hand on her chest and took slow, deep breaths. "Tonight. We'll go to . . . I don't know, anywhere that's expensive. Just you and me and—" she laughed happily and waved her hands in the air "—five hundred of our closest friends."

Carolyn's mouth spread in another smile, and she hugged Haley again. Only the tiniest trace of envy was detectable in her eyes. "It's taken you years, but it looks like you've made it, sweetie. Won't it be fun telling all those uppity Riverton relatives of yours that you have *arrived!*"

"Oh, you're right! I hadn't thought of that," she said as they pulled apart.

"And," Carolyn said, her gaze falling to the script and fan letter on the sofa, "no more loony-tunes soap fans sending you letters or freaking out in pharmacies."

Haley sighed with relief. Whether Sy felt the need for caution or not, she knew that she wouldn't be returning to the set of "Forever."

"YOU SURE you don't mind that I invited Don along?" Carolyn called out from behind the bathroom door two hours later.

"Of course I don't mind." Haley slipped into her dressiest heels, then checked her reflection in the floor-length mirror again. Dressed to the nines in black silk and pearls, she was impatient to get their celebration started. "Will he be here soon?"

"Oh, yes. It's the one thing I hate about the guy. He's always early."

"Good. I'm starving." She smoothed a hand over her sleek, upswept hairstyle, then straightened the belt on her dress. The beach, she thought, a smile dawning as she remembered the new restaurant that she and Carolyn had found a couple of months back. What more perfect place to celebrate than at the beach? It was far and away Haley's favorite thing about California.

When the doorbell sounded, Haley chuckled at Carolyn's loud groan. "I'll get it. You hurry up," she ordered as she passed the bathroom on her way to the front door.

"Hi, Don...?" Haley's welcoming smile faded after a quick glance at the man standing in the doorway. He couldn't be Don. Carolyn had described the fitness instructor as tall, California blond and tanned, and with a physique to die for. This man was short and a bit heavy, with dark hair.

"Can I... help you?" she asked, her gaze traveling over the man's strange clothes. In spite of the June heat, he wore a heavy coat and fatigue pants. His black hair was slicked back, and sweat dotted his forehead.

"Who's Don?" he asked angrily. "You've been unfaithful to me, haven't you, Sabrina?"

Sabrina. Panic sped through her. She stumbled back and attempted to push the door closed, knowing instinctively who the man must be.

He stopped it with an outstretched arm. "Don't be afraid. It's me—Jack," he said, backing her into the apartment. "I sent you letters. Why didn't you answer them, Sabrina?"

"I'm...not Sabrina. Please," she said as she backed farther into the living room. "You...can't come in here."

"I won't leave. I love you. Why didn't you answer my letters?"

"I'm...sorry." She hit the desk with her hip, knocking the phone to the floor.

"No, you're not sorry," he muttered, advancing another step. He looked her over, his black eyes menacing. "You're so beautiful in that dress...you're always so beautiful. But...you're going out with some other man...I knew there had to be another man. I'm not stupid! I knew when you didn't answer my letters." His features twisted in a grimace, and he dragged a hand across his sweaty brow. "*I'm* the one you should be with, Sabrina. You can't be with anybody else. Me! You have to love *me!*"

Haley's panic increased tenfold. The man wasn't simply an overzealous, starstruck fan as his letters had led her to believe; he was mentally ill. Pity joined panic, and she held out a shaky hand to him. "Please, Jack. You need help. Let me—"

"I don't need help! I need...w-want you to—" he screwed his eyes shut and tears squeezed out from the corners, running down his face "—love me, goddammit!"

She swallowed hard, fear swamping her as she watched him reach into the pocket of his coat. He pulled out a handgun. "Oh, God, no," she moaned, shaking her head. "No, Jack. Please don't do this—"

"Me! Me, Sabrina!" he cried. Then he leveled the gun and squeezed the trigger three times.

"Haley, what in the hell is going on out there?" Carolyn shouted as she ran into the room. "What's all the—" She saw the open, empty doorway, then Haley on the floor.

"Oh, Lord, no!" She fell to her friend's side, horrified by the sight of all the blood covering Haley's silk dress. "God, Haley...who did this? Are you—?" Her throat constricted, and she fumbled for the phone that lay inches away.

Haley moaned, opening her eyes, and tried to boost herself up on her elbows. It was odd, but she didn't hurt. She'd been shot...but she didn't hurt.

Shock. She was in shock. Haley remembered that from a part she'd played once, that of a gunshot victim. Shock came first...then pain.

Her thoughts blurred one into the next. *Gunshot victim...the letters...hadn't taken them seriously...he knew her address...the part, Sy said she got the part...they'd celebrate at the beach... victim...victim...victim...*

Pain tore through her chest and shoulder. She groaned. "Carolyn...it hurts."

The last thing she remembered before surrendering to an obsidian void was the sound of Carolyn crying and shouting hysterically into the phone. And the high-pitched barking of their neighbor's poodle.

CHAPTER ONE

October 1992

HALEY CLOSED the hated appointment book and slid it to the corner of the glass-and-chrome desk. She couldn't put it away in a drawer; the damn desk was too stylish for anything so useful as a drawer. She capped the MontBlanc pen her brother, James, had given her five months ago on her first day on the job, then set it—where else?—on top of the appointment book.

Planting her elbows on the glass and her chin in her palms, Haley imagined Carolyn breezing into this office. She would survey the room, taking in the dhurrie rug, the abstract paintings on the walls, the chrome-and-glass and blond oak furnishings. Then she would catch sight of Haley seated behind the desk—a *desk*, for heaven's sake!—and her eyes would widen comically. "What," she would drawl, "is wrong with this picture?"

Which was exactly the question Haley had been asking herself since shortly after her first week working in the position her family had created for her. Assistant to her brother, the general manager of the Tulsa Riverton Hotel. Five months ago the job hadn't seemed like such a bad idea. Five months ago she'd finally faced the fact that the career she'd dreamed of since childhood was no longer possible, and had come home.

Trying to resurrect her career had proven more painful than her year-long recovery from the shooting—the surgery, the rehabilitation, the plastic surgery—more painful than the next year she'd spent in therapy. The media had labeled her "stalker survivor," and the public had developed an insatiable appetite for articles and news reports about her and Jack Raymond Wharton. The soap had wanted her to come back, but the producer's requests, she'd felt, were based more on Haley's publicity value than anything else. That publicity had other offers flooding in, as well. Haley had grown more dispirited with each new role that required her to play a woman in peril. That, combined with the nightmares that had plagued her and the fear she'd never completely shaken, had made her agree with her therapist that her sanity was too high a price to pay for the dream.

She shook her head and pushed away from the desk, turning her back on it to walk to the full wall of glass that looked out on Tulsa's downtown skyline.

She was definitely what was wrong with this picture, she thought, regarding her designer-clothed reflection in the thick, smoke-tinted glass. And it was just as woefully wrong for her. She might have taken back the Riverton name in an effort to gain anonymity from the press—at her family's request she had forsaken the name to distance the career she'd chosen from their ultrarespectable life-style—but she was like a fish out of water here. And though she'd used every acting technique that ten years in Hollywood had taught her in order to play the part of hotel executive, appointment books, meetings with the huge hotel staff, dinners with Junior Leaguers and receptions for the mayor just weren't her style.

But after today she wouldn't have to worry about it any longer, would she? A smile curved her full lips. Today was her last day. Independence day.

"Miss Riverton, your brother is here to see you. He says he only needs a moment of your time."

Haley looked over her shoulder at the intercom on her desk and rolled her eyes. James rarely took "a moment." He'd been on a quest, after all, to transform Haley back into the Riverton daughter the family had thought they'd lost forever. Quests took time.

She left the window, seated herself in the high-backed swivel chair again, then depressed the intercom button on her phone. "Send him in, Donna."

"'Morning, Haley," he said upon entering. His brisk walk through the expensively appointed office had Haley wanting to roll her eyes again. There'd been a course at Princeton that had taught her baby brother that stride—she was certain of it. Executive Walk 101.

"James," she said as he took a seat in front of her desk, "what brings you by?"

"Just wanted to stop in for a moment before I meet with Father. That's a wonderful suit, by the way. Armani?"

"I'm . . . not sure," she answered, then frowned at him. "You have a conference with Dad?" She reached for the appointment book where James's manager doings were recorded, wondering why it had been so difficult to convince her brother what a failure she was at being his assistant. This was the third time in as many weeks that she'd forgotten one of his meetings. She flipped through until she found today's page and checked each line, unable to find a notation of the meeting.

"It's spur-of-the-moment. Won't be in the book."

"Oh."

"He wants to discuss problems we're having with the general manager in San Francisco."

"Problems with Thomas McElroy? I like him. He's...a fun guy."

James gave her an impatient look. "Being fun isn't one of the job requirements, Haley."

"I know. He won't fire Thomas, will he?"

"In my opinion, he should. But I imagine Father will review some options with him. Maybe the man will be better in a pencil-pushing job over at corporate. You know," he added, straightening in his chair and smoothing his slacks with his palms, "if you're interested, this could work to your advantage."

Haley caught her brother's meaning easily. With Thomas out, she could be in. But she wanted no part of that. And James knew it. She fidgeted with the oversize gold-linked bracelet that accessorized today's chic business suit. It felt too heavy for her wrist, and the clasp continually caught snags in her clothes. "James, I'm out of here as of today and you know it. You also know that I don't want—"

"San Francisco is a beautiful city," he said, breaking off her objection. "I would think that managing Riverton by the Bay would be enticing to you. You loved living in California once."

Haley ignored the edge of sarcasm in James's tone. She wasn't about to get into what he and the rest of the Rivertons considered her "checkered actor's past" on her last day. "James, I can't even handle this assistant's job. What on earth would make you think I might be management material?"

"You're intelligent. You could've handled this job if you'd wanted to. If you had concentrated a bit more and worked on keeping your head out of the clouds..."

"I like it in the clouds, James." She affected a faraway look in her eyes, knowing it would irritate the socks off him. "It's where I was born to live."

Sighing, he shook his head. "You were born a Riverton. Just like me. You should be managing one of the hotels, training to run the business one day. I thought you'd realized that after the..."

Haley let several moments of silence slip past, wondering if James would actually say the word—*shooting*. The fact that he didn't, couldn't, wasn't surprising. None of the Rivertons could quite bring themselves to say it. And though she knew the main reason was their concern for her health and well-being, the publicity surrounding Wharton's attack had been embarrassing to the family. It came in second only to the fact that she'd chosen a profession such as acting in the first place. Landing a role in a soap opera had been the most mortifying blow of all to them. "I thought so, too. But I was wrong."

James looked away then, muttering something along the lines of five months not being long enough to know.

Haley thought but didn't say that she'd given it four months and twenty-nine days longer than she should have.

"Look, I had another reason for coming by this morning. Father felt I should talk to you one last time about this . . . local theater business, the Tulsa Actors' Theater. We feel that you could be making a mistake by jumping back into acting—"

"Butt out, little brother."

James closed his mouth, and silence filled the office again. Haley held her gaze level with his, reminding herself that this was independence day. Independence from a job that seemed like punishment, hard labor for a crime she hadn't committed. And independence from a family who, for the second time in her life, had tried to inflict their wishes upon her.

His voice quiet, James said, "We're concerned that you'll want to go back to Hollywood. That you'll become bored with the local amateur stuff and want—"

"I won't." Picking up her career after the shooting might have been painful, but she supposed if she had persevered she could have accomplished it. But sitting at the hearing, listening to Jack Raymond Wharton's sick obsession for "Sabrina" spill out, had

cemented her decision to leave. It was a decision she
would never go back on.

James arched a brow skeptically. "You'll never be
entirely happy with it, Haley."

"I'll have to be, won't I?" Leaving her acting career, after all, had brought Haley a modicum of peace,
dramatically decreasing her fear...the nightmares. Her
eyes broke from his, and she stared at a streak of
bright scarlet on a Jackson Pollock print across the
room.

She caught James's nod out of the corner of her eye.
James rose from his chair, an emotion that resembled
regret shading the green eyes so like her own. He slid
his hands into the pockets of his slacks, then glanced
around the room and shrugged, looking almost boy-
ish when he said, "I took out all the antiques that were
in here before, you know. Thought the brighter colors and modern furniture would be less stuffy...more
you."

Unexpected pleasure stole over her, and Haley
studied his lean and aristocratic face, getting a glimpse
of the boy he'd been before he'd left for an Ivy League
school and come back ready for the corporate world.
She wanted to rise from her chair and cross the dhurrie rug to him. She wanted to wrap both arms around
him and breathe in the subtle scent of Grey Flannel as
she hugged him. She wanted to feel him hug her back.
But that would be inappropriate for the man who'd
returned from that Ivy League school. She knew that
and offered a warm smile instead. "You're okay,
James. You know that?"

He quirked a smile of his own. "Thanks." He stepped to the door. "Take care. And if you need anything..."

"I'll be sure to call."

He placed his hand on the doorknob, but glanced back before leaving. "I almost forgot. Mother wants the Riverton to host a reception for your theater in about three weeks. She'll expect to see you there. I just hope all the glamour won't make you homesick for Hollywood."

Haley grinned. "Hollywood's the least glamorous town I know of, James. You can stop worrying. I want no part of it anymore."

"That's good, Haley."

The door closed behind him, and Haley made her way back to her post at the windows. James's mention of the reception led her to thoughts of another "glamorous" event about to hit Tulsa. An old friend of hers, Ian Ferguson, would be directing a film that was to be shot by Madeira Productions there for the next few months.

And her friend Carolyn, she'd learned from watching "Entertainment Tonight," had landed the leading role in the film opposite some ex-football star.

Carolyn. Haley swallowed hard, and her gaze fell to Tulsa's outdoor mall below. She watched the people. Men and women in business suits with briefcases swinging at their sides, a UPS man pushing a dolly loaded down with boxes, shoppers entering and exiting the mall stores. Two women, obviously friends, sitting on a bench, talking and laughing.

She watched the women, her thoughts still on Carolyn. Her friend had moved out of the apartment and into her parents' home in Los Angeles after the shooting. Haley had taken a room at the Los Angeles Riverton. They'd seen each other from time to time before Haley had moved back to Oklahoma, but Haley had not spoken with her since. Carolyn had left a message with Sy for Haley to call a few months back. Haley hadn't returned the call.

ONE WEEK LATER in her office at the Tulsa Actors' Theater, or TAT, as it was commonly known, Haley was frowning as she paged through her new appointment book. The switch from hotel executive to director of the small local theater had been the right decision, because Haley was loving it. But she hadn't managed to escape the tedium of schedules.

Rehearsal schedules. Staff conference schedules. Schedules for costume fittings, for publicity interviews, for understudy and musician rehearsals.

After only a few hours into her new job, she had discovered that keeping track of James's appointments had been a walk in the park compared to overseeing the goings-on at the fledgling theater. Still, she loved it. This was her world. The small staff and the actors were her people, creative people who, like Haley, felt quite at home "living in the clouds." She woke up in the mornings raring to go, and left at the end of each late workday looking forward to the next.

Though she was working as she'd never worked before to get the new theater company off the ground,

Haley thanked her lucky stars that the opportunity had come her way. It had been in the form of a classmate, Dennis O'Kane, who had attended Tulsa's Holland Hall prep school with Haley. He'd been in drama class with her and had followed her acting career with interest as he'd pursued a successful career in business. Last year he'd purchased the old Blake Theater, which had been standing empty for years in Tulsa's Brookside area, and, finding out that Haley was working at the Riverton, had approached her with the offer of theater director. He'd dangled the carrot of directing some of the plays, as well.

Haley hadn't had to think his proposal over for longer than an hour. Maybe her days as an actress in television or on the big screen were over, but that didn't mean she had to give up the profession altogether. The director's position meant she could make a living wage while doing it.

Haley closed the appointment book with a sigh, knowing she should give it up for the day before she started doing damage. She had decided to approach Dennis and the board of directors today about allocating money for an assistant. Even if she were possessed of an organized nature, or a mind for schedules and details, the position of director was more than enough work without the added stage-manager duties that an assistant could handle better.

The phone rang and Haley reached across the cluttered desk for the receiver. She spent twenty minutes talking to a printer about the brochure that was to detail this season's productions. Then Haley talked to a painter who would be coming in to put finishing touches on the Blake's renovation, to the mother of a child who was interested in auditions for their upcoming production of *Oliver!*, and to the play service that had inadvertently sent TAT the musical score to *South Pacific* in the script shipment. Her last call was from her friend Dennis, who was not only the new owner of the Blake but also chairman of the board of TAT.

"Well, you ready to throw in the towel yet? Bet that job at the Riverton looks better and better every day, huh?"

Haley laughed. "Nope. I'm not certain I'll ever see the surface of this desk again for all the paper...but don't worry, there's not a chance in the world I'd go back to the Riverton now. I'm in my element, Dennis. Thank you again."

"No need to thank me, Haley. I'm just as thrilled to have you as you are to have the job. But in the event that the paperwork was too much, I've been checking into getting you some help. Could you use an assistant?"

Haley smiled, relieved that she wouldn't have to go begging now. "Are you a great boss or what? I was just thinking about asking for that very thing."

"Good. I've got a terrific prospect in mind, a friend, in fact, who's on the board of directors of TAT. If it's okay with you, I'll send him over this afternoon. His name is Brent Maloney. You must have met him when you met the board a few weeks ago."

"So soon! I thought you were just *checking* into getting me some help. I remember Brent. We hit it off really well," she said.

"Well, I think you'll need an assistant, Haley. I'm hoping you'll agree to direct the first play."

Her heart beat faster. "The first one?" she asked excitedly.

He chuckled. "That sounds like a yes."

"Oh, it is. It is definitely a *yes!*"

When Haley hung up the phone minutes later, flutters of excitement had taken up residence in her stomach. Directing! Starting in three weeks, she'd be directing for the first time! And it wasn't just any play, but it was *Oliver!,* the one that had first lit the fire in her to act so many years ago as a child. Haley took it as a good omen.

Her heart kicking a joyous beat, she automatically reached for the phone, then stopped when she realized there was no one to call. This wasn't something her parents or brother were likely to appreciate, and she hadn't made any close friends here in Tulsa yet. She frowned as her mind reached back to the old days when there would be any number of friends to call with news like this. She would race for a phone and stab out the person's number, then trip over her own tongue getting the words out. *Remember that audition I told you about? I got it! Or, I got the part! Everyone said this casting director was equal parts Attila the Hun and Hitler but he cast me in the movie! I think he's a saint! Or, you know that cattle call for the play I was telling you about? I got a call back!*

Most of the calls had been between Carolyn and Haley, and that remembered fact dampened her excitement even more.

No way, she thought, throwing off the slight beginnings of depression and hopping up from her desk. No way was she going to let her past slip in and cast a dark cloud over today's happy news. So what if she hadn't renewed old acquaintances or made new friends in Tulsa yet? There was still plenty of time for that. And so what if directing a local play wasn't on the same grand scale as working in film? The job Dennis O'Kane had offered her was salvation! And she was damn well grateful for it.

She busied herself clearing off the desk. Memos and receipts and letters were filed in drawers—thank God for a desk with drawers! Pens and pencils and emery boards and highlighters were stuck in the small pottery vase she'd picked up at a craft fair at one of Tulsa's malls. She replaced books in their empty slots on shelves and gathered the wadded-up sheets of paper that had fallen short of the wastepaper basket. It wouldn't do to frighten off her new assistant with evidence of her poor organizational skills.

The office straightened and looking as if a true professional was at the helm, Haley thought about lunch. She'd whittled her choices down to two nearby take-out places when the phone rang again.

"Tulsa Actors' Theater."

"Haley?"

The male voice wasn't immediately recognizable to her.

"This is she."

"Hello! This is Ian Ferguson."

Ian. At once she felt both pleasure and a strange uneasiness about talking with this person from her past. He'd been her first director on the soap. "Ian...it's..."

"I know. Weird to be hearing from me."

"No, not weird," she denied, and forced the uneasiness back. "Good. It's *good* to hear from you. How did you know where to call?"

"I remembered your family owns the Riverton. Called your brother the other night, and he reluctantly told me how to get in touch with you. I'm glad you've found something in acting this close to home," he said warmly.

"So am I," she said, and felt herself relaxing. Ian had gone on to do small, but critically well-received, films. From the press she'd heard on *The Loner,* the film he'd be shooting here in Tulsa, he'd now graduated from smaller films to semimajor ones. "How's it going? I'll bet you're up to your ears in preproduction."

"Actually, set construction's all that's left. Listen, I'm calling you to ask a favor. I know how you feel about the business these days, but don't say no until I've pleaded my entire case, okay?"

Haley's uneasiness sneaked back in. "W-what is it?"

Ian chuckled, and she could hear him take a drag off a cigarette. "Don't be so terrified. You sound like I'm about to ask you to audition for the movie."

That was exactly what she was afraid of.

"I'm only calling to see if you'll agree to give some acting lessons."

Her apprehension faded. Curiosity stepped in. "Lessons?"

"I've got a leading man who's...well, let's just say he's not exactly Sir Laurence Olivier. He's not bad, but could be better. Since there's a couple of weeks before filming starts, I was hoping you could help him...you know, brush up on his skills a bit."

"Your leading man. The ex-jock, you mean? The guy who used to play football?" Haley's eyes narrowed suspiciously. "Just how much brushing up are we talking here, Ian? You don't think I've forgotten about that baseball player who replaced Boyd Thornton on the soap, do you?"

"Now, Haley. Keith Garrison is a whole different story. He knows his lines and he'll show up for shooting on time. He minored in drama in college, and he's no stranger to a television camera."

"Done some after-shave commercials, has he?"

Ian chuckled. "Well, yes, but don't judge him so harshly until you've met him. Like I said, he's no Sir Larry, but he has promise."

He has promise. Haley rolled her eyes. It came as no surprise that Madeira Productions was willing to risk millions of dollars on an athlete with promise. It happened all the time. For some reason, having no acting skills whatsoever was perfectly fine if you'd made a name elsewhere. Like in sports or modeling.

She sighed. "Ian, not that I'm even considering this, but ... why me? Why not fly in a coach from the coast?"

"Number one, because you know as much as any three coaches in L.A. Number two, the producers aren't thrilled with above-the-line expenditures on this film. To be honest, you'll be saving me some money."

Haley shook her head, chuckling. "Ian, you are so cheap. So, I'll be saving you plane fare and lodging, huh?"

"That figures in. I've got producers who are even tighter than I am breathing down my neck. But the main reason is that I trust you. I worked with you too long not to be impressed with what you know, cookie."

"Thanks, Ian. That's a big compliment coming from you. But I'm afraid I'll have to turn you down. I won't have the time."

Ian groaned theatrically. "Two weeks, Haley. That's all I'm asking. A few hours a day, tops. Don't say no until I tell you how much the pay is."

"Ian, I'm sorry, but—"

He interrupted her with an amount.

Silence. Then Haley whistled. "Good grief, Ian. For two weeks' work you'd pay me that much?"

"Sy would have had a coronary if he'd heard you say that," he said, chuckling. "So how about it? Can I send him over tomorrow?"

Haley chewed her lip. She did need a new car. The one she had now spent more time in the shop than on the road. Ian's offer would cover something small and not too expensive. If she took him up on it, she wouldn't have to burden herself with a bank loan when she'd just started this new job.

Two weeks. She could squeeze acting lessons in between now and the beginning of rehearsals for the play, couldn't she? And the jock couldn't be that bad, could he? Ian would have refused the project if the guy couldn't act at all, right?

"Come on . . . say you'll do it, Haley."

How could she refuse? "Okay, yeah. I'll do it."

CHAPTER TWO

KEITH GARRISON PULLED the rental car to a stop at the intersection and laid his forearm across the top of the steering wheel. He ducked his head and squinted through the windshield, making out the letters on the green street sign: Peoria. His eyes darted to the map that lay beside his thigh on the seat, and he nudged up the aviator shades he'd donned in deference to Tulsa's bright October sun. He searched for the yellow highlighting on the page. Yes, Peoria was the street he needed. He made a right turn on the red.

Elm, maple and river birch lined the four-laned street, clothing it in beautiful autumn shades of russet and gold, with the older trees forming canopies overhead. Quite a difference from the brushy south Texas acreage Keith had purchased just months ago. And quite a surprise. He'd attended college at the University of Oklahoma in Norman, but had never set foot in this section of the state, the section known as Green Country. Having been raised in Texas, he'd always figured a state as small as Oklahoma must look the same geographically from one border to the other.

He'd assumed a lot of things he shouldn't have. Like the fact that his new career would go as smoothly as everything else in his life usually did.

He spotted a park to his right—Woodward Park, the rough-hewn wooden sign read—and turned in, deciding he should study the map a bit closer if he had hopes of ever finding the Tulsa Actors' Theater. He pulled the car to the side of the narrow road, shifted into Park and hit the automatic window button before killing the ignition.

Crisp, biting air that smelled of wood smoke from homes nearby drifted in as Keith removed his sunglasses and pitched them onto the dash. He checked the map again, then nodded, frowning. It figured. He'd been traveling the wrong way on Peoria, north instead of south.

He worried the back of his Super Bowl ring with his thumb, then, realizing it, stopped and placed his palm on his denim covered knee. His bum knee. The knee that had gotten him up at five o'clock this morning, aching like a son of a bitch. His own personal wake-up call, he'd thought, four aspirin and one cup of decaf later.

Not that he'd need a wake-up call for the next two weeks. Rehearsals had been postponed. The star of the film needed acting lessons.

MADEIRA'S LEADING MAN was late. Why didn't this surprise her? Why, for that matter, had she agreed to give lessons to some aging athlete who'd decided acting would be his next gig? The money, Haley reminded herself. If the money weren't so damn good...

She spread her arms across the theater seats on either side of her and dangled her wrists from the edges.

"Appears we have time to go through it once more," she called out to the young man and woman standing on stage. "Pick it up from Nancy's speech to Bill."

Haley listened as Nancy pleaded, hearing a bit more passion this time. But certainly not enough. Though most of the rehearsals for *Oliver!* weren't due to officially begin for three more weeks, Haley had wanted to get in a few extra hours with the principal actors who had already been cast.

One of the back doors of the auditorium opened with a scraping sound and a flood of light, and Haley frowned, closing her eyes to block out the distraction. She concentrated on the actress's rhythm, then opened her eyes and jotted a note on the clipboard in her lap. She let the scene go on for several more minutes, then called a halt.

"Okay, listen," she said loudly, standing and scooting out to the aisle. "You're on the right track here, but let me show you something." She walked to the stage and put her palms on the edge, then vaulted up.

At the back of the theater, Keith Garrison edged sideways and felt behind him for a seat. He tapped the rolled-up script pages that Ian had said his new acting coach wanted him to bring on the seat in front of him, watching as the actress on stage moved aside for the petite blond woman.

She spoke the same lines the actress had been reading when Keith had opened the door to the auditorium, but coming from her, the scene's emotional impact was heightened. He watched the woman with growing amazement. Her gestures were bigger, her voice louder than the young woman's had been, and the expression of intensity on her pretty face was quite visible even from where Keith sat in the back row of the theater. As the scene played out, Keith became caught up in her performance, wincing once when her voice rose to a shout, then smiling moments later when she deftly executed a joke meant for comic relief.

His enthusiasm grew. If the woman on stage was Haley Riverton, the former actress turned local theater director whom Ian Ferguson thought so highly of, then Keith had every reason to feel good about a brush-up course in acting.

She was very good. As he watched and listened to her, bits and pieces of his college drama course began to surface in his memory. Yeah, this was going to be great. He was rusty—he was the first to admit that. But he wouldn't be for long. Haley Riverton would whip him right into shape.

"Are you Garrison?"

Jerked out of his thoughts, he almost dropped the script. The scene was over, and the woman whose performance had entranced him was standing on the edge of the stage—the forestage, he remembered— with one hand shading her eyes, the other propped on her hip. The two actors she'd been coaching were leaving the stage together.

"Uh, yeah." He stood. "You're Haley Riverton?"

"That's right," she called back, then gestured him forward with the roll of one wrist. "Let's get this show on the road. We've already lost twenty minutes."

He trotted down the aisle, wincing once when a sharp pain sliced through his knee. "Sorry. I got turned around on Peoria Street."

She sat down on the edge of the stage, swinging her feet, encased in red leather Nikes. She reached out a hand, and Keith quickly put the script into it. Amusement lit a pair of the most beautiful almond-shaped green eyes Keith had ever seen as her gaze rose slowly from the script to him. "I was going to shake your hand," she said wryly.

"Oh." He grinned, took back the script and replaced it with his hand.

She grimaced, then turned his hand over. "That's... some grip you've got there, Keith. Some ring."

"Oh, sorry. Did I hurt your hand?"

"No, I'll live. Let's get going, okay? I've got an afternoon rehearsal starting in two hours."

"Okay. Just... tell me where you want me."

"Up here on stage," she said, then hopped to the floor. She wore an oversize sweatshirt with TAT on the front and back, and black tights covered her legs. "I want to conduct this first session like an audition, see where we're at here, see where we need to be. That's why I asked you to bring your sides."

"My, uh, sides?"

"Sides," she repeated, a touch of impatience shading the voice that had just moments ago executed a perfect cockney accent. "The lines you auditioned with? You did audition for this role, didn't you, Keith?"

"Well . . . no, not exactly."

"Not exactly?"

"I mean, no. Not at all."

"I see," she said curtly. Taking the script with her, she walked to the middle of the auditorium, where she'd been seated when he had arrived.

I see. The two words spoke volumes to Keith. His new coach had him pegged as an amateur. Well, she was way off. He'd minored in drama back at OU, hadn't he? And what about all of his product endorsements? Sure, most of them were print ads, but he'd made his share of television commercials. And most important, he thought smugly, he'd been Madeira's first choice for the lead in their movie. Audition or no audition.

"Any time you're ready, Keith. You can start with your first speech."

Nerves shot down his smug attitude, and Keith fought to remember his first line. God, what was it? Something to do with a threat. It was vitally important that he say the line before Haley Riverton fed it to—

"I believe you start with, 'You're not threatening me, are ya, Jackson?' "

Ah, dammit!

"Thanks," he muttered, then, of course, remembered the next line and launched into his character's dialogue.

Sliding lower into the seat, Haley amended her former thoughts about the money she was being paid by

Ian and Madeira Productions. It was not going to be enough. Not nearly enough.

She'd felt encouraged upon meeting Keith Garrison moments ago. His voice was perfect for the character he'd be playing, deep and strong with that charming Texas accent lazily riding the edges of his words. And his build would certainly work in his favor. He was large, but moved with a natural gracefulness that athletics had fostered. His rugged good looks, broad shoulders and slim hips would lend believability to his portrayal of a tough cowboy turned bounty hunter in the 1800s. The strong jaw was a plus, as were the dark eyes and mahogany-colored hair. Masculinity was seldom packaged so effectively.

Too bad silent pictures weren't still in vogue. Haley winced when Keith trounced heavily and loudly over another line of dialogue. Listening to him boom out his words and gesture to his imaginary gun belt with all the subtlety and finesse of a flashing neon sign, Haley sighed and rose from her seat. Not enough money, she thought again.

"Keith," she called out loudly, trying unsuccessfully to cut in. She shook her head, then shouted, "Keith! That's enough!"

He stopped and stepped to the edge of the stage, shading his eyes with one hand.

Haley groaned inwardly at the expectant look on his face, wrestling with the natural empathy she felt for actors. She had to remind herself that she wasn't dealing with an actor. Keith Garrison was a football player. Maybe he didn't play anymore, but he was still accustomed to taking criticism from hard-nosed coaches who weren't into mincing words or coddling egos. That was a damn good thing, because she had no time to coddle.

Striding down the aisle, she added steel to her attitude by thinking of the injustice involved in Keith Garrison's landing the lead role in a major motion picture. Talented, trained actors everywhere lived below the poverty line. They worked as waiters and waitresses and parking valets by night to fund days filled with auditions, lessons and disappointment. Mr. Star Quarterback had simply walked off the football field and flashed a dimple and that monstrosity of a ring, worming his way into a starring role.

"Well," he said, flashing that dimple now as he grinned, "not so hopeless, huh?"

She stood at the edge of the stage, her arms folded at her waist as she stared up at the man. "No. 'Hopeless' isn't the word I'd use." *Disastrous* was the word that came to mind.

"Well, all right. That's good."

"No, not good. Not good at all."

His grin wilted.

"Keith, we have no time to waste, so I'm going to be blunt."

"Okay, sure. Give it to me straight."

She nodded, then took a deep breath. "You had about a minute and a half of drama class in high school, didn't you?"

"No, it was in college. But it was more than a minute—"

"Because that would explain your obvious need to play to the balcony. Not this balcony," she added, flipping a hand in its direction. "Some other balcony three states away. Keith, the instant you bellow out that first line when filming starts, you'll have a deaf sound man on the other end of your mike."

"But I'm not miked now. I'm on a stage, and I just thought you wanted—"

"In two weeks you'll be miked, so you'd better forget all that high school drama crap."

"College," he corrected her.

"Okay...college." She began to pace. "Let me ask you something. In college drama, during those few hours a week when you weren't trotting around on AstroTurf, did your teacher ever mention a form of acting called stereotype acting?"

The AstroTurf comment jabbed at Keith's pride, but he ignored it. He trained his eyes on the thick blond braid that bounced against her back with each step and answered stiffly, "No. But it doesn't sound like something I should be doing. *Was* I doing that?"

She swiveled, looking up at him. Her hand went to one hip, bringing definition to the petite shape hidden beneath the huge sweatshirt. "Yes. It's like this, Keith. I'm sure you've got a basic knowledge of acting techniques somewhere underneath all that...that enthusiasm. But you're using it to imitate rather than to create. You're using other actors' gestures and expressions...even vocal delivery patterns. I saw at least three other actors' moves and manners just now. That makes your performance mechanical and predictable. Even worse, it lacks—" she placed a fist over her heart and thumped it lightly "—truth of emotion."

Predictable? Mechanical? Keith had known he needed help, but hell, he wasn't that bad, was he? Normally he wasn't one to get defensive in the face of criticism, but he squared his shoulders all the same. "Truth of emotion? It was a gunfight, not a love scene."

Her fist fell to her side. For several seconds the tight line of her mouth made Keith think she might jump up on stage and plow into him. Then she startled him with a short laugh. "Well, it's a damn good thing it *wasn't* a love scene! I'd hate to be the leading lady on the receiving end of some of your exaggerated gestures. One hug and I'd be in the hospital with broken ribs!"

Keith remained stone faced and silent as Haley vaulted up onto the stage.

"Look, I know I'm rusty," he said, "but—"

"No buts about it, Keith. I saw your 'Reach for the gun belt' business coming down Sixth Avenue! You played that scene like...like John Wayne on steroids."

Keith rolled his eyes and drew back one corner of his mouth in a smirk. "Please, don't hold back to spare my feelings," he muttered. "Tell me how you *really* feel."

She cracked a smile and swiped at several stray hairs that had come loose from the braid. Keith was distracted for a moment by the halo effect the stage lights created by dancing through the various shades of blond. He almost laughed aloud at his own observation. Halo effect? This woman was no angel.

"Okay. You asked for it," she warned, her smile turning grim, "so I'll give it to you. My real feelings are this. An actor who doesn't know that there's as much emotion involved in a hand reaching for a gun as there is in a man reaching for a woman *won't* deliver the performance that Madeira Productions and Ian Ferguson are looking for. And my feelings are that two weeks is not enough time to instill that kind of understanding in you."

With that, she walked to a nearby chair on stage that held a clipboard. Keith closed his eyes, wishing he'd kept his sarcastic remarks to himself.

She returned, the clipboard in hand and her pencil racing across the surface of a yellow legal pad. "Now," she said, not looking up from her scribbling, "the first thing I'd like you to do is rent these videos." She ripped off the page and handed it to him.

"I hesitate to do this, because I don't want you mimicking these actors. But I do want you to understand subtlety. Watch *Silverado* first. It's a modern Western."

"Modern Western?" Wasn't that a contradiction in terms? And speaking of contradictions, hadn't she just said she didn't think two weeks was long enough to get his acting skills up to par? Why was she giving him an assignment if she didn't think lessons would help in the first place?

"John Wayne was fine in his day," she explained, "but movies have evolved somewhat since then. Today's audience expects a modern hero with modern sensibilities, only in period costume. You'll understand what I mean after watching Scott Glen and Kevin Kline's performances.''

Keith watched as she compiled another list. She took a deep breath, then handed it to him. "I'm assigning you some reading, as well. We've got miles to go before we sleep here, Keith. I hope what I've said will impress upon you how serious the situation is. Madeira has millions of dollars on the line. This is a major motion picture we're talking about. Physical prowess won't help you now. It'll take concentration, *mental* concentration that'll make summer football camp feel like just that—camp.''

With that she'd stepped over the line, Keith decided. She'd made it sound as if mental concentration was completely beyond someone like him. "Look," he said, his irritation obvious, "if you don't think you can help me in two weeks, then why this?" He waved the sheets of paper in the air.

"I'm being paid to tutor you," Haley said evenly. "I'll just have to tell Ian Ferguson not to expect miracles. He probably knows that without me telling him.''

Keith's eyes narrowed, and he slapped the paper against one thigh. He felt his temper gather steam. "And why would he know that?''

Her gaze locked with his. "We don't have time to mince words, so I won't. Even you have to realize that you were hired for your name.''

Keith was normally a peace-loving, nonviolent man—off the playing field. He didn't rile easily or often. But right now Keith was as riled up as he ever got. Sure, he knew the main reason he'd gotten this part was because of his name. But Madeira wouldn't have approached him if they'd thought he couldn't do the job. Besides, he wasn't a complete amateur. And he did have that "minute and a half" of drama in college in his favor.

No matter what she thought, he was under contract to star in this film. And dammit, acting was what he wanted to do now that he couldn't play ball. It's what he'd always wanted to do, actually.

"What time do you want me here tomorrow?" he asked.

"Bright and early," she answered, then expelled a sigh as if the mere thought of these lessons completely exhausted her. "I have afternoon rehearsals. Make it eight o'clock?"

Keith gave a curt nod, then folded the papers neatly and slid them into the back pocket of his jeans. The one thought in his head as he walked up the aisle to the double doors leading out of the auditorium was that she didn't know just what a wonderful actor he really was. Because, unlike her, he hadn't expressed his *real feelings* before leaving. He hadn't wadded up the sheets of paper and pitched them at her feet. And he hadn't picked the woman up and hurled her into that balcony she'd accused him of playing to.

CAROLYN KINCAID TUGGED seat-belt straps from the
corners of her seat and glanced up at the attractive
blond flight attendant several feet away. She fastened
the belt, pushed several strands of newly permed hair
off her forehead, then settled back in her seat with a
sigh. When was it, she wondered as she watched the
woman smile and point out exits with beautifully
manicured nails, that flight attendants had become
younger than her?

Even worse than the stewardesses was the new crop
of actresses in L.A. They made the flight attendants
look like medicare recipients.

Rubbing at the frown lines between her brows with
her fingertips, she reached for a magazine. Her boy-
friend, Jonathan, would say she was being paranoid
again, but what did he know? He was a banker, not an
actor. He didn't run into those nymphettes at every
audition. He couldn't understand how impossible it
was to compete with gorgeous twenty-year-olds when
you'd just passed your thirtieth birthday.

"Ma'am?"

Carolyn looked up from the magazine at the smiling flight attendant. "Yes?"

"Tray tables in the upright position, please."

"Oh, right." She closed her magazine and folded up
the table, then secured the latch. *Ma'am,* she thought,
wrestling with a strong desire to put her foot in the
aisle when the woman came back with the drinks cart.

No matter what Jonathan said, time was pushing
forward faster than Carolyn could keep up with it.
She'd hoped to be better established in Hollywood by

age thirty. Instead, she'd been working like a mad-woman just to get steady work in commercials, voice-overs and bit parts on TV and in movies.

That's why she'd wanted the role in Madeira's movie. Wanted? She'd campaigned for the role like a politician, and had even resorted to nepotism.

Carolyn grimaced, recalling how she'd swallowed her pride and asked her parents to call in favors with the studio. She'd vowed never to ride on Dory and Edward Kincaid's influential coattails. But tough times called for tough measures. And, she supposed, sighing raggedly, for vows to be broken.

The plane taxied down the runway, and Carolyn turned her thoughts to the movie itself. The script was good, solid. Written by last year's Oscar winner for best screenplay, *The Loner* was a Western, and West-erns were getting better box-office returns these days. Keith Garrison in the starring role was causing a small stir of publicity already, which certainly didn't hurt. And, most important, a good performance could mean bigger and better parts. Her career—stunningly mediocre up to this point—could get the much-needed boost she'd been struggling for ever since Haley had been shot.

Carolyn felt her stomach lurch as the plane lifted in the air. She closed her eyes, waiting for the aircraft to level off and the slight queasiness to subside.

Minutes later, when the plane's initial steep ascent was over, Carolyn's stomach still felt the effects. Or maybe that was a product of her thoughts. She was never able to think of Haley and the shooting without some similar physical reaction.

Two and a half years. There were moments when it seemed as though it had happened a lifetime ago. And others when it seemed like only last week.

Carolyn shook her head and reached for the magazine again, wanting to escape the images that were certain to appear. She flipped through several glossy pages, sighing when she came to a picture of a model who looked a lot like her old friend.

Carolyn smoothed her fingertips across the page and refused to worry about the frown lines that were undoubtedly forming between her brows again. Against her will the images came. The sound of the three gunshots. The sight of Haley on the floor next to the toppled table. The blood.

Carolyn's mind had screamed in horror and disbelief for months afterward. Now sadness and loss had taken the emotional forefront. For just as surely as Haley had lost a promising career, Carolyn had lost a dear friend when Haley had left the West Coast for a saner life in mid-America.

Did Haley feel the loss as strongly? she wondered. Had she missed Carolyn and the bond they'd shared?

Carolyn gave her drink order to the attendant when she approached, then put away the magazine again. Should she look Haley up when she got to Tulsa? Both Jonathan and her therapist had encouraged her to do so, but Carolyn had objected, fearing Haley's possible rejection. She couldn't deal with rejection right now.

Thoughts of the movie drifted into her mind. The movie and the nude scene she'd consented to do.

God, she needed a friend.

IAN FERGUSON GRINNED, the corners of his eyes crinkling behind his trendy, round, wire-framed glasses. "So good to see you, Haley."

"You too, Ian." She smiled at him, not realizing until that moment how much she'd missed the man. They had remained friends after he'd gotten his first feature-film project, then later when his success had pushed him into the major leagues. She hadn't remained in contact with him after leaving California, however.

He motioned her through the door, then kicked it closed with the heel of one shoe. Taking her coat, he hung it behind louvered closet doors, then threw an arm across her shoulders and walked her through the hotel suite to a sitting area. Haley noted that Madeira was cutting costs by renting only one suite to house both their director and the production office; one side of Ian's suite was taken up by fax machines, copiers, telephones, stacks of paperwork, a television and a box of videotapes—for dailies. "You look great, kiddo," Ian said. "How're you doing?"

"Lots better than the last time you saw me," she said in a breezy tone. She sat down on a long sofa that was decorated in pale splashes of turquoise and coral. She propped her feet on the coffee table in front of her, careful to keep her Nikes several inches away from the Lalique vase filled with silk tulips that sat in its center.

Ian lowered to a chair facing her. He picked at the nubby, sand-colored fabric on the arm of the chair. In a quiet and hesitant voice, he said, "I wasn't too crazy about seeing you in that hospital bed."

"Just think how *I* felt," she said with a soft laugh that faded when Ian only gazed at her with a worried look. "I know, I know," she apologized. "Not funny. But don't look so worried about me. I must be better if I can joke about it, right?"

"Maybe. But you were never one to laugh things off with a smart-ass remark. That was more your friend Carolyn's way."

Ian's meaning was not lost on Haley. Carolyn was well-known in acting circles for her wicked sense of humor, her wisecracking mouth. And those who knew her best knew that her jokes and flip remarks were a protective veneer that hid a multitude of insecurities and hurts. The only child of two megastars whose egos allowed no room or time for nurturing their offspring, Carolyn had learned how to deny the hurt early. Ian's insinuation was that Haley had learned a bit about it, too.

Haley nodded. "I'm still affected by the shooting, I'll admit it. It's not something you get over in a day or two. I guard my privacy almost to the point of paranoia, and I'm less apt to open my door to strangers now, that's for sure. And I still have nightmares now and again." Like the one last night, she thought. The one with her standing at the end of a dark, closed-off tunnel. At the other end, prison doors swung open wide, and a man stepped through them. He had a gun. She had no way out. Haley held in a shudder. "But I'm not the walking wounded here, Ian. Time's done its job. Things are getting back to normal for me now."

Ian looked as if he were about to comment, then shook his head and reached for a pack of cigarettes on the coffee table.

"What? Tell me what you were about to say."

"Nope." He lit a cigarette and reached for an ashtray that was already overflowing with cigarette butts. "My New Year's resolution was to cut back on sticking my nose into other people's business."

Haley chuckled and nodded at the ashtray. "You'd have an easier time cutting back on cigarettes. Come on, get it off your chest."

He took a drag and blew it out in a straight stream at the ceiling. Squinting, he said, "Okay. It's that last thing you said—things are getting back to normal for you. Normal isn't working in little theater in Oklahoma, Haley. Normal for you is acting. In television or on film, on the stage. I'm sorry, but even with what happened to you, it's difficult to understand how and why you quit. You were just beginning to take off."

Haley felt a twinge of regret at Ian's mention of the career she'd given up. Yes, she'd garnered a certain amount of success up to that point. And the movie contract she'd lost because of the shooting would have probably led to more success. But her sanity and safety had been at stake. "Priorities have a way of changing when something happens to remind you of your mortality, Ian.''

"But acting wasn't merely a priority for you. It was your life."

Haley shook her head, then studied the tulips in the vase. "No. Maybe I felt that way at one time, but I was wrong. My life was what Jack Wharton almost ended that day. Acting was only my profession. Besides, I'm still working in that profession. Maybe not on such a grand scale. But I'm doing what I want to do."

Ian appeared a little reassured. He smiled, saying, "I thought I might have a chance to lure you back when I found out you'd gone into the family business." He glanced around the suite. "Your brother runs a class joint here, but I knew you wouldn't be happy as an executive for long. Then when I heard you were directing little theater...well, I knew my chances weren't as good."

"You're right. On both counts." Haley pulled her feet off the table, then leaned forward and tugged one of the silk tulips from the vase. She twirled it by its stem and chuckled. "You should have seen me, Ian. I was such a joke as a lady executive. Wearing those red-and-navy power suits every day drove me nuts after a while. It was like being in a bad horror flick— *Dress Code of the Living Dead.*"

Ian laughed and stubbed out his cigarette. "No dress codes in Hollywood, Haley..."

"Give it up," Haley warned good-naturedly. "Anyway, the suits were nothing compared to being cooped up in an office, doing essentially the same thing day in, day out.''

"Don't you mean playing the same *character* every day?"

"That's it exactly! Do you know that I actually tried to act my way through that job? I told myself, 'You can do this, just look at it as another role.'''

"I can't imagine a life other than one in this business," Ian agreed. "Living in the real world would drive me crazy inside a week."

"It took me five months. The theater director's position was a godsend. Salary's not quite as good as what I was making on the soap or at this hotel, but how does the old song go? 'You can't always get what you want...'''

"But you get what you need," Ian finished.

"Right." She stopped twirling the flower and looked up with a serious expression. "I *am* getting what I need, Ian."

"That's all I wanted to know. I won't harass you about getting your little butt back to L.A. if you're really and truly happy."

"Good. But you won't mind if I harass you about something else, will you?"

His brows drew together in puzzlement, then understanding dawned and his features relaxed. "Garrison."

"Yes, Garrison." She dropped the tulip on the glass table. "Ian, I'm amazed, simply blown away that you had anything to do with this guy landing a role—"

"Casting agent, Haley. Not me. She thinks he'll be fine. She says with a little work . . ."

"And you agree with her? Besides, how can she know that? She didn't even audition him for this!" Haley rose from the sofa and walked to the wet bar across the suite. "Do you mind?" she asked, holding up a bottle of imported beer.

"No, go ahead. Bring me one." Ian looked at her over his shoulder. "Keith called this afternoon. He told me things went badly."

Haley snapped off the tops with an opener and strode back to Ian. "Things went *very* badly. He can't act, Ian. Or at least not without lots and lots of work. I'm having a real hard time believing that a company like Madeira is willing to risk so much on Keith Garrison."

"They have faith in the casting agency." He took a swig from his bottle. "So do I, for that matter."

"I repeat, he can't act."

Ian merely shrugged. "I think he was just nervous this afternoon. He'll do okay with a little coaching from you. Look, I'm not usually one to go out on a limb. But my instincts tell me he's going to be great for this movie."

Haley shook her head. Ian Ferguson, one of the most demanding directors she'd ever worked under, thought Garrison would be great for the movie? "Ian, this is crazy. Civilization as we know it must surely be coming to an end. You think he'll be great? Looks-wise he might fit the role, but for God's sake, you yourself have delayed filming for him to take acting lessons!''

''Filming's delayed for several reasons, Haley, not just for him to take lessons. And I didn't say he's Oscar material. I said he'll be great for the movie. He has a certain presence—even you have to admit that. And his name is a big draw right now. The public's ga-ga for him. They buy every soft drink and athletic shoe he pitches, and they buy them in great quantity.''

Haley lifted a brow.

''Oh, don't give me that you're-selling-out look, Haley, because you know as well as anybody that the studios want a sure thing. And Madeira knew that Garrison's high profile would appeal to a major studio.''

Haley shook her head, taking a seat across from Ian again. ''What will the studio say when they see the film? The high profile won't help if Garrison can't act his way out of a brown paper sack.''

''He's not that bad. I know how you feel about him, but I've seen him act, too, and I'm not of the same opinion. He's just…a little rough around the edges.''

''Rough around the edges! Ian—''

''Just give him time, Haley. Will you do that for me?''

CHAPTER THREE

GIVE HIM TIME, Haley thought, sighing as she pressed the elevator Down button. She'd argued that she was no miracle worker. Ian had said that miracles wouldn't be necessary, only two weeks of lessons. She'd mentioned that she felt guilty taking Madeira's money when she couldn't guarantee the results. He'd smiled and assured her that he had all the faith in the world in her. In the end, excellent director that he was, the scene had gone his way. Haley had consented to continue with the lessons.

She punched the Down button again as if it might bring the elevator to her floor more quickly. Play practice had gone long, and she'd missed her late afternoon walk. Now evening was here, and she supposed the best place for it was in a mall. Tulsa's downtown mall, the Forum, was only two blocks from the Riverton and perfect for walking out the day's kinks.

"Come on, come on." She slumped against the wall beside the button and pushed it again.

"There's a convention in the hotel this weekend. Elevators have been really slow."

Haley glanced up sharply, her gaze connecting with the dark brown eyes of her acting student. She stood straight. "Hi," she said. "What are you doing here?"

"I live here. At least until the movie's wrapped."

"Oh. Oh, right." She stepped away from the wall and slid her hands into the pockets of her jacket.

"So," he said, rocking back on a pair of the highest-tech athletic shoes Haley had ever seen. "How 'bout you? What are *you* doing here?"

"I was here to see Ian."

Keith nodded, then checked the lit-up numbers above the elevator doors. "You...still going to coach me?"

A soft bell sounded and the doors slid open. They stepped inside the empty elevator car. Haley stationed herself close to the button panel, and Keith lounged against the back wall, his arms propped on the brass railing. He raised a knee and braced one foot on the carpeted wall behind him. When the doors shut, Haley pushed the Lobby button, then glanced over her shoulder at Keith with a questioning expression.

"Lobby for me, too. Well?" he prompted when Haley had faced front again.

She turned to meet his gaze. "I'm still your coach."

"I'm surprised. When you said you were visiting Ian, I figured you were there to beg off."

"To be honest, I tried. But Ian's a friend from way back. Even though I told him I'd be taking the money without being able to guarantee success... Well, I just couldn't turn him down."

Keith's ego suffered yet another blow. Now he wasn't merely a no-talent amateur: he was a favor for a friend. Geez! In all his years of amateur and professional ball he'd never run across a coach who'd made him feel this low. And he'd run across some sons of bitches in his time.

He couldn't keep his remarks to himself this time. "Well . . . that's big of you."

"Look, Keith, I'm sorry if I've damaged your pride, but I have to be truthful. I foresee big problems ahead. And I just think—"

"You just think . . ." he cut in, his voice hard. His foot slipped from the wall, and he stood straight. "How can you form any kind of an opinion after only one scene? I know I didn't deliver the most inspiring performance in the history of stage or screen, but it wasn't as bad as you made it out to be, either. And by the way, if you want my opinion, I don't think it's *just* my acting skills—or lack thereof—that you're critical of."

She raised a brow. "And what else would there be?"

"I'm guessing you have something against athletes."

Haley rolled her eyes and folded her arms beneath her breasts. "You're being awfully defensive, don't you think? Whatever gave you the idea that I have something against athletes?"

"Oh, I don't know," he said. "Think it could have been the cracks about AstroTurf and steroids? Or maybe it was the one about football camp and how I'll need mental, not physical, prowess?"

Coming out of his mouth, her remarks sounded much more cutting than she'd meant them to be. She'd been blunt to get her point across, but hadn't meant to be offensive. "I...guess I should apologize. If what I said about football offended you, then I'm sorry."

Well, don't knock yourself out, Keith thought, noting she wasn't exactly the picture of contrition. Would it have ruined her day to have been just a little more convincing? Especially since she'd ruined his. He leaned back against the railing again. "It's okay," he said quietly.

The elevator came to their floor, and Keith hung back, letting Haley leave before following her out. As they moved through the lobby she pulled a stretchy cloth hairband from her pocket. Then, lifting her elbows, she scooped up the mass of blond waves that tumbled down her back and wound the hairband around them.

He stopped her in the center of the lobby next to a huge brass planter filled with tall silk flowers. Though she'd apologized for her smart remarks, something inside him wanted more. "Look, I'm...curious," he started, then was distracted by the shorter strands of hair around her face that had evaded Haley's efforts to bind them. One stubborn strand still eluded her, and Keith was startled to see his own fingers reach over and brush it out of her eyes. She was startled, too.

"Oh, um, thanks," she mumbled. "You...were curious about what?"

"Um, right. You—" he chose a rose-colored flower in the brass planter over Haley's shoulder to stare at

"—you apologized for the football stuff, but you never said how much of your critique this afternoon had to do with me being a football player. I'm not looking for compliments, God knows I don't expect any from you at this point. I'd just like to know if I was as bad as all that."

It was difficult, but Haley held back a sigh. How was she supposed to answer that? With her apology, she'd as much as admitted to having been biased. But that wasn't the entire basis for the severity of her critique. He truly did need lots of help. She bit the inside of her lip, knowing she couldn't truthfully give any compliments. But maybe she could structure an answer that might buoy the confidence she'd damaged.

"Keith, I should explain that I get intense when it comes to acting. I spent ten years studying under some of the most respected names in the business, and I take what I do very seriously. I'll admit that I was a bit rough on you this afternoon, but that should make you feel better about me being your coach, shouldn't it? Haven't some of your more hard-nosed coaches in the past been the ones who got the better performances out of you?"

A moment passed with no comment from Keith. Then he shook his head, a rueful grin tugging at the corners of his mouth. "We're back to football again. Did you have a bad experience with an athlete in your past?"

"No. Really, it was just an analogy to—"

"Yeah, right. Tell the truth," he said. "You dated some jock who broke your heart, am I right? Probably had an ego three times the size of this lobby," he guessed aloud, gesturing to the large room with the sweep of one arm. "And you've decided all jocks need to be brought down a notch or two."

"No, Keith. I've never dated a jock. And no, I have nothing against jocks in general."

"Yeah, right," he scoffed. "Let me see your tongue."

"My...?" Haley's laugh was a sputter. "Excuse me?"

"Let me see your tongue," he repeated. "If it's black, I'll know you're lying."

She chuckled, propping one hand on her hip and giving him a skeptical look. "This is...something I've never heard before. When people lie, their tongues turn black?"

"You didn't know that?" His tone was serious, but the dimple that had come out of hiding belied it. "You must've gotten away with murder as a kid. Once my mother had me convinced of the black-tongue theory, I could never put one past her. She'd ask to see my tongue, and I would keep my mouth clamped shut, knowing it was blacker than sin. Pretty ingenious, huh?"

"It was. She used your conscience to keep you on the straight and narrow."

"Yep. So come on. Let's see it. Show me your tongue."

Haley laughed again, shaking her head. The obstinate strand of hair inched toward her eye again, but Keith was careful to keep his hands at his sides this time. Instead, his gaze followed her fingers as they reached up and combed it aside. She gave him one last smile, then clamped her lips shut tightly, much as he'd described doing as a guilty child.

"Aha! Works every time."

She nodded. "Okay, I'll admit it. I do have trouble with you having been an athlete. You're doing what so many other sports figures have done. You're trading on your name now that your career's gone south. I have the same trouble with models who get too old for print ads, then think they have all the training they need to be an actress simply because they're photogenic. It's an unfair advantage in my book."

If, as she had mentioned, she'd put so much time and study into her craft, he supposed it was only natural for her to feel that way. But she obviously didn't understand the other side of it. "I think it balances out in the end." He glanced down at the elaborate Oriental rug beneath their feet, then met her gaze again. "Think about the heightened expectations I have to put up with *because* of the name I've made for myself in sports.

"And by the way, it's not the greatest feeling in the world knowing you weren't necessarily hired with your skills in mind. This is the very first thing that I haven't had to work my butt off to get. To be honest, I've found that victory doesn't taste nearly as sweet when it's handed to you."

Haley realized that she'd been unfair. She hadn't stopped to imagine how he might feel about getting the part so easily. And she definitely hadn't considered the pressure he was under. Feeling petty, she grimaced and blew out a breath. "Oh, boy. I didn't help matters this afternoon, did I?"

"No, you didn't," he answered honestly. "But, hey, I can handle it."

"You shouldn't have to. I apologize again. We'll start fresh tomorrow morning, okay? I promise to keep my biases out of it."

"Thanks," he said quietly. Then, with a slightly off-center grin, he added, "It's not that I can't take the rough stuff. I just... needed to know that there was some hope before taking the risk of falling on my ass with this movie."

Haley realized in that moment what it was that the casting agent, Ian and the powers that be at Madeira had found so appealing in Keith Garrison. Yes, he had a certain presence; he had that rough-and-rugged look that was going to gain him hordes of female fans. But there was more to Keith than surface appeal. It was, plain and simple, vulnerability—a characteristic that would, if successfully captured on film, grab the heart of each and every member of the audience.

"There's hope, Keith. We'll do everything possible to see that you don't fall on your ass."

He chuckled and said, "Good. I've had this thing about it ever since the last time I fell and couldn't get back up on my own."

Haley guessed he was referring to a football story and politely chuckled along with him.

"Well, tomorrow's lesson is going to come early so I'd better be going," she said, starting off for the revolving front door.

"Yeah. Me, too."

"I'll see you, then."

"Right. Good night."

She stepped into a section of the revolving door, and Keith took the next one. When they hit the sidewalk, Keith pulled his keys to the rental car from his jeans pocket and was about to ask Haley if she needed a ride home. But the Riverton's doorman stepped up.

"Evenin', Ms. Riverton. Get you a cab?"

"No, thanks, Denny. I missed my walk today. I'm going over to the mall."

The doorman glanced up at the sky, and his brow creased in a frown. "By yourself?"

Keith watched Haley survey the well-lit but mostly deserted city street. Dusk had been crowded out by late evening's darkening sky. "It's just a couple of blocks. I'll be okay," she told the man blithely, then strode away.

Two thoughts occurred to Keith in rapid succession as he glanced at Haley's stiff posture as she walked. First off, the doorman had known Haley by name, the same name, Keith realized all of a sudden, as the hotel they'd just left. Secondly the doorman's concern wasn't misplaced. What was she thinking of, walking down a city street at night...alone? Tulsa might be middle America, but even a middle-American city street wasn't safe.

Keith pocketed his keys and trotted up next to her. "Hey, can I give you a ride?" he asked.

Haley stopped, gave him a polite grin and shook her head. "No, thanks, I'd rather walk."

"Oh...well, should you be doing that alone? I mean, it's pretty deserted out here and—"

"It's only two blocks to the mall."

"Well, yeah, but—"

"Thanks," she said, cutting him off, "but I'll be fine on my own."

There was a chill in the air, and Keith glanced back at the hotel, wishing he'd grabbed a jacket before he'd left. Getting out of the place for an hour or so had been a spur-of-the-moment idea. He'd needed to clear his head and do some thinking about the situation he'd gotten himself into.

He watched Haley as she marched along, the high ponytail quivering in the considerable breeze. He shook his head. There was no telling what or who might be waiting around the next corner. He made another impulsive decision.

Jogging up beside her again, he asked, "Does this mall you're going to have any fast-food places?"

"Yes, but the Riverton has room service, too. Don't you have some videos to watch? Books I assigned that you could be reading?"

"Yes, I do. But I've gotta eat, and I wanted to get out of the hotel."

She stopped again and peered up at him with a speculative look. "Are you really hungry or are you just worried about me walking to the mall alone?"

"Hungry. I swear."

"Uh-huh, I'll bet." The corners of her mouth twitched. "Let me see your tongue."

Keith chuckled, then closed his lips tightly as she had earlier.

Haley sighed. "It's only two blocks. Two well-lit blocks, for heaven's sake."

"With dark side streets branching off them, I'll bet. Come on, I really was going out for a bite. Why not just let me do the chivalrous routine here? All I'm offering is a little protection."

Protection. It went against the grain for Haley to accept his offer. After all, she'd been inching her way back toward independence for two years now. But Keith was only thinking of her safety. And no matter how safe Haley might feel living in Tulsa, no place was completely safe. "All right, you win. Walk me to the mall."

Keith had heard that evenings in late October could be downright cold in Oklahoma. Never mind that the daytime temperature had been in the high forties. When the sun went down, the wind kicked up. He, of course, hadn't known he would be out in the elements tonight. He'd thought he would be in his heated car. The lightweight sweater he wore was next to useless against the chill. Or maybe, he thought, two years of mild San Antonio weather had thinned his blood.

"Are you cold?" Haley asked, her hands still deep in the pockets of the jacket she wore.

"Nah," he said. "What about you?"

"No. I'm quite warm, actually."

They continued walking, passing a large, virtually empty parking garage, then a liquor store and an antique clothes shop that was closed. Keith pushed his fingers into his front pockets as far as they would go. Geez, what a wuss he'd become since he'd stopped playing football. He remembered a game once in Buffalo when the below-zero temperature had seemed like a mere annoyance compared to this. They passed a bank building with a lighted time-and-temperature sign. It hadn't even dipped below thirty-seven degrees.

"You're being awfully quiet," she said.

He glanced down at her. "Yeah, I'm a quiet kind of guy. Perfect walking companion, right?"

She laughed softly and agreed. "That you are."

They turned a corner and were suddenly in the middle of an open air shopping area. The walk was wide and brick lined, with trees planted at intervals in the center. The stores were mostly closed, and shoppers were few. Smart people, Keith thought, who knew when to come in out of the cold.

"This isn't the Forum Mall. It's up ahead," Haley mentioned.

Keith nodded, then slowed his pace enough to put Haley about a quarter step ahead of him. The maneuver placed his elbow just behind hers. It also made it possible for Keith to study her profile out of the corner of his eye.

He wasn't surprised to note that she was as attractive from this angle as every other. Strands of her blond hair lifted with the chilly breeze, a few of them fluttering across her eyes. She blinked and tossed her head to disengage the strands from lashes that were thick and incredibly long. The cold air had pinkened her fair complexion and made her breath a vaporous cloud at her lips.

Her lips. They were pretty, full, the bottom one almost pouty.

He dragged his gaze and thoughts away from her mouth and stared straight ahead, allowing the cold air to hit him in the face like a bucket of icy water. Being attracted to his drama coach was not a good thing. He would be spending several hours a day with her for the next two weeks in intensive study. And contrary to what she might have thought at first, he was extremely serious about learning all he could.

"Here we are," she said as they approached the mall.

He pulled a hand from his pocket and opened one heavy glass door. Haley stepped inside, and Keith followed behind her. The glass door fought against a draft to close while Keith rubbed his hands together and blew warm breath on them.

"You *were* cold."

"A little" was all Keith would admit to.

"You didn't need to come with me. I didn't want you to freeze on my account. Now you're going to have to walk back to your car and freeze again."

Keith shook his head. "Not for a while, I'm not. Come on," he said, grasping her arm, "let's walk around this place and warm up."

The mall consisted of three levels, and they had entered on the middle one. After walking past several shops, Keith glanced down at Haley. He remembered the coincidence of her name being the same as the hotel's and decided to ask about it, but a window display two stores down caught his attention first.

The window was in a shop that sold athletic shoes, and the display hawked the brand that he endorsed. Taking up a large amount of space behind the shoes was a life-size cardboard rendering of himself dressed in nothing but tight black shorts and the shoes. Keith winced. He didn't remember the shorts being that short. Or that tight. He sped up his steps. Maybe he could get them past it without Haley's noticing. Just what he needed...something to reinforce his image as the hotshot athlete.

Haley gave him a curious look and increased her speed to match his. "Are we late for an appointment or something?"

"What? Oh, no," he said, his gaze directed straight ahead. "I was just...hungry. Where are those food places you mentioned?"

"Food places." Haley slowed her pace, trying to remember. She'd only been in the Forum Mall once since moving to Tulsa. Her mall of choice was closer to her apartment on Tulsa's south side. But if she recalled correctly, the food court was on the first level with the ice-skating rink.

"Come here," she said, veering over to the railing. She leaned over to look. "I think they're...yes, they are. On the lower level."

He peered down, then said, "Good. Listen, do you mind?" He guided her away from the railing.

"No, I don't mind at all," she said, scrambling to keep up. "Boy, you really are hungry, aren't you. I mean—" Her gaze was snagged by stacks of running shoes in a store window. They were just like the ones Keith wore. And behind them—she stopped in her tracks. Behind them was... Keith Garrison. In living color. And with little-to-nothing covering him. "My, oh my," she said, amusement threading her voice.

She glanced up at him, then stepped slowly to the window.

"Aw, man," she heard Keith moan quietly from behind.

A smile creased her lips at his obvious embarrassment.

He tugged at her arm. "Come on. Let's go."

"No," she said, shrugging out of his grasp. "I'm looking at these shoes. The cross-training shoe for the serious athlete," she read from the sign. Shaking her head, she said, "They're certainly... serious looking. Masculine looking, too. Maybe my brother could use a pair."

He smirked at her. "You've had your fun. Come on, let's go."

"Nope." She turned back to the window. "Something about this display has caught my interest, made me want to buy. Effective advertising, I'd say."

"I'd say you're giving me the business."

She smiled up at him. Yes, she was giving him the business, but what he didn't realize was that she understood his embarrassment more than most people might. She'd done her share of print ads. She had posed for shots in everything from formal high-necked gowns to lace teddies, and had "made love" with her male lead in front of a daytime television audience that probably rivaled his viewers of Sunday football. She'd even done a suntan-lotion commercial dressed in a swimsuit that covered only a bit more skin than the shorts in his ad. There were worse things in the world than showing a little skin to sell a product. Like scars that prevented you from ever doing so again.

"No, really. It's a good display," she said, checking out his alter ego again. "You're in good shape. You should be proud of that."

"Think so?" He grinned, looking more relieved than embarrassed now, then scrutinized the cardboard cutout with her. "They airbrushed it like crazy. See? No scars on the leg."

"Oh?" Her eyes drifted down to muscled thighs, tanned and lightly furred with dark hair, shaped as beautifully as any male thighs had the right to be. There was no doubt about it. Keith Garrison was one finely formed man. And the perfect spokesman for the serious athlete. "I . . . guess you've had your share of knee surgeries, huh? Don't most quarterbacks end up with bum knees?"

"Yeah. But my knees didn't wear out. I got sacked my last season. Busted up my right leg but good a little over two years ago. I spent the better part of eighteen months in and out of surgery and rehab with it."

A little over two years ago. What a coincidence, she thought with an edge of bitterness. She had been in the hospital two years ago. And she'd known her share of surgeries and scars. "It . . . must have been painful."

"Oh, yeah. It was a bitch, all right. But the worst part was losing football."

Haley gave him a surprised look. "I thought you'd just retired from football because . . . well, I guess I thought it had been your decision. You mean you *physically* can't play anymore?"

"Not professionally."

She heard the regret in his voice and was struck by the fact that their lives were almost parallel in certain ways. She, too, had been forced in a way to give up a career. "That's . . . too bad. I'm sorry."

"Yeah. But, all things considered, I'm pretty lucky."

"Lucky?"

"Madeira. The movie."

"Oh. Right. The movie." And that, Haley knew, was where the parallels ended. His new life would be centered on the field she'd chosen to leave.

"Aren't you . . . ? Hey, it *is* you!" a voice from the doorway of the sporting-goods store exclaimed.

Haley swung around. A young man in jeans and a referee shirt came toward them.

"Garrison. Keith Garrison!" A huge smile was pasted on the boy's face, and Haley had to move aside to keep from being pushed when he reached to grab Keith's hand. He pumped it vigorously. "I heard you were in town making that movie, but man, I can't believe it's you! And you're standing here in front of my store! Well, it's not *my* store. I'm just *assistant* manager. But it's really you, man!"

"Yes . . . it's me," Keith said feebly, feeling self-conscious. He glanced down at Haley and saw that she'd turned away and was staring down at the stacks of shoes again.

"Man, I'm a huge Mavericks fan. And, hey, we've been selling your shoes like nobody's business!"

"That's . . . good to know." Keith extracted his hand from the assistant manager's.

"Yeah, they're probably our best seller right now. Hey, you wouldn't mind autographing your poster board, would you? Would that be way cool or what?"

Keith pulled his gaze from the boy's hopeful expression and threw another sidelong glance at Haley. She was still studying the display, a small frown creasing her brow. Was she put out? The request for an autograph wasn't a problem for him; he never refused them. But again he hated reinforcing his "athlete image" in front of her.

"Um, Haley?"

She looked up.

"Do you . . . mind?"

"Oh . . . no, fine. Go ahead. I'll wait out here."

"No, come in with me. Please." Keith reached for her hand.

"Yeah, it'll only take a minute," the assistant manager chimed in. "Hey, I know you, too, don't I? You look real familiar. Are you . . . somebody?"

Haley turned back to the window. "No, I'm nobody you'd know."

KEITH DRAGGED his wallet from the back pocket of his jeans and handed the girl behind the counter a ten. She gave him his change, then slid his order—a roast beef sandwich and coffee on an orange tray—toward him with a smile.

Haley had grudgingly accompanied him into the sporting-goods store and had waited patiently while he'd signed the board, then another poster the assistant manager had in the back room. She'd been silent on the way down to the food court, not frowning as she had at the display window, but not talking, either. Then she'd searched out a rather secluded place for them to sit and had refused his offer of anything to eat or drink.

He approached their table, searching her expression for signs of irritation. He saw only a trace of weariness.

He took a seat opposite her. "I'm, uh, sorry about all that stuff with the autographs." He unwrapped the sandwich he didn't really want, then took a bite.

"Don't worry about it. It goes with the territory, doesn't it?"

"Yes, it does. Happens pretty frequently." Keith watched her closely, noting an uneasiness in her light tone.

With her eyes still downcast, she said, "That'll be a plus for you."

"A plus?"

"You're used to it going into the acting profession. Loss of privacy is hard to get used to, as you already know. One minute you're so invisible you couldn't even get arrested, the next, you're...somebody, so to speak."

"You have a point there. But I can't help but think if I screw up with this movie, I do it in front of millions of people. That's why I'm glad to have your help. I might appear to be this supremely confident guy," he said with a self-deprecating grin, "but, like I told you, I'm shakin' a little here."

Haley smiled, watching him take a large bite of the sandwich. Her focus went to the auburn-hued lashes that lowered when he took a sip of his coffee and the fine lines that fanned from the corners of his eyes. "Now, don't start in on me about stereotypes, but most of you—athletes, that is—strike me that way. Supremely confident."

He gave a mock frown. "You're not suggesting that jocks have big egos, are you?"

It was exactly what she was suggesting, but she didn't say so. She said nothing, in fact, conveying her answer with a challenging lift of one tawny brow.

"Yeah, but there's a perfectly reasonable explanation, you know. It's all wrapped up in the 'winning mentality.' If you're going to make it to the top or even survive in pro ball, you have to be a winner. Having talent is certainly part of it, but attitude is important, too."

"A winning attitude."

"Yep." He wadded up his wrapper, with half the sandwich uneaten, and pushed it aside. He crossed his arms and rested them on the table. "I've known guys with natural ability who never make it off the bench because they lacked either determination or a winning mentality. And I've known those who don't have a snowball's chance in hell, but become superstars. Usually fueled by—"

"Ego," she supplied.

"Yeah, all right, ego. But it's a natural by-product. To be a winner, you have to convince yourself that you *are* one."

"You don't seem to have one."

His eyes widened. "I don't? Was that a compliment?"

She chuckled. "I just meant that you don't seem all puffed up with a 'winning attitude' over acting. And you weren't exactly fawning all over that cardboard cutout back there."

"Oh. Well, you've never seen me interviewed before a game." He lowered his voice and said out of the corner of his mouth, "Yeah, Howard, we're gonna take 'em down today. No doubt about it. I'm in the top physical shape of my career, my passing game's never been better."

Haley smiled.

"But I'm smart enough to realize that acting is a bit different. Attitude won't help if I don't have talent. I can execute a good pass with the best of them, but I'm not so sure I can bring a character to life on the screen."

"Then can I ask you a question?"

"Shoot."

"Why did you sign the contract? Why the movies?"

Keith nodded as if he'd asked himself that same question. "Mostly because I really loved acting in those college plays. But there's also the challenge. I was offered jobs as a sports commentator after I got hurt, and I've got plenty of contracts for product endorsements to keep me afloat for a while, but...I don't know, the commentating just didn't appeal to me. And the endorsements, they're more like time fillers than a full-time occupation. And maybe I'm just so used to the limelight..."

"If that were the case then you'd probably be more than satisfied with the endorsements and sports commentator offers. They're high visibility," she pointed out.

He gave her a thoughtful look. "You're right. Must be the challenge, then."

"I'd say so. And, for your sake, I hope you're up to it. You say those other offers you had seem like time fillers, but *they're* the more normal jobs, Keith. Acting, or at least the *business* of acting can make you crazy. Yes, it can be fulfilling," she said, her eyes lowering to the table, "if you're lucky enough and talented enough. But your spirit better be tougher than any linebacker you've ever faced."

Silence bled into the air around them, and Keith wondered how much of the speech had been for his benefit. Ian had said that Haley had acted in Los Angeles for several years, then moved back to Tulsa, her hometown. The director hadn't offered more detail than that, and Keith hadn't been curious for more. He was curious now.

Watching her fiddle with a lock of tawny hair, he quietly asked, "Did something...or someone... break your spirit, Haley?"

She glanced up quickly. "I was...talking about, you know, the business in general. And I meant—"

"It's none of my business," Keith put in. "You don't have to give me your life history or anything."

"I know. It's just that—" She sighed. "Let's just say that I picked a career that had my family in spasms for years. It wasn't the career for me, they insisted. I wouldn't be able to handle it. But I knew that I could prove them wrong. In the end...well, they were right."

So, he thought, she hadn't been able to hack it. "Your family. Any connection with the Riverton hotel?"

"They *are* the Riverton hotel. After I came back to Tulsa, I worked there for a while. I lasted for about fifteen minutes as assistant to the general manager, my brother, James."

He couldn't picture her with a briefcase or wearing one of those blazers with a hotel emblem on the pocket. Sure, he hadn't seen her in anything but the sweatshirt, tights and red running shoes, but the look seemed to work for her. It worked really well. "Somehow I just don't see you behind a desk doing paperwork."

She laughed and admitted, "Neither could I. I quit in time before I went completely mad."

"Is that when you took the job at the theater?"

"Yes. TAT. And I—"

"Ah, dammit!" From the corner of his eye, Keith noticed a woman approaching, a pad of paper and pen in hand.

"What?"

"I try not to get annoyed, but sometimes people can have the worst sense of timing," he said in a low voice, leaning close. "I don't want to be rude, but I think I'll politely refuse to be interrupted this time."

"Interrupted?" Haley glanced around, saw the woman walking toward the table, then faced front quickly, lowering her eyes.

"Hi," the woman said as she stopped at the table's edge. She smiled hesitantly. "I was wondering if I could get an autograph."

Keith summoned a cordial expression. "If you'll tell me where you're sitting, I'll be glad to give you one when my friend and I are finished with our conversation. You don't mind waiting for a few minutes, do you?"

"Oh." The woman's smile faltered. She looked from Keith to Haley, then back again. "Well...I don't mind waiting, but I was wanting Sabrina's autograph, not yours.''

Confused, Keith said, ''Sabrina's?''

''Yes.'' She looked at Haley, the hesitant smile blooming into one of excitement. ''All my friends and I just love you. We can't wait to see you back on 'Forever' again. They're not going to replace you with a new Sabrina, are they? I mean, it's been a long time, but you have a good excuse for being gone. And I just can't see anyone else being Sabrina but you. You're just—''

''I'm...not Sabrina,'' Haley said, her words on the curt side. She looked nervous suddenly, her face a bit pale. Taking the pad and pen from the woman, she quickly signed ''Best, Haley Riverton,'' then handed it back.

''Oh, you know what I mean,'' the woman said, her smile still beaming. ''You were just so good you made me believe you're Sabrina. You're her. Sab—''

''No, you're wrong. I'm not her. My name is Haley Riverton,'' she said abruptly, scraping her chair back, then standing. She swiped strands of hair off her face with a jerky motion. ''Look, uh, thank you for all the nice compliments, but Sabrina was a *character* I played. You understand that, don't you? A character, not me.''

With that, Haley turned on her heel and walked away, leaving Keith and the woman staring after her in tense silence. The woman glanced up at Keith. ''Well, that's gratitude for you. I've been a fan of that soap for years, and I am—make that *was*—Sabrina's number-one fan!'' She pitched her writing pad in a trash can before striding indignantly back to her group of friends.

CHAPTER FOUR

THE SHOP WINDOWS WERE a vague blur of color as Haley sped away from the food court. Her heart pounded an angry beat when she stepped onto the escalator that would take her to the mall exit. The urge to scale the steps of the moving stairway met with a quick flash of common sense. She couldn't trust the state she was in. With her luck, she'd trip and go head over heels down the thing. And wouldn't that make a sensational headline? Actress Who Was Stalked And Shot Meets Tragic End on Mall Escalator.

She gripped the handrail hard and pressed her fingertips to her lips, hoping to stem—what? Hysterical laughter... or tears?

Sabrina. God, when would people forget? How long before they stopped approaching her, stopped demanding these little pieces of her as their right? Hadn't she paid enough? She'd given up everything, left it all behind and moved as far from the world she loved as she could. How much further would she have to go?

She got off the escalator, her first step wobbly, her heart still slamming in her chest. She struck out for the door, but stopped when a loud voice registered in her brain. She heard the shout again.

Keith.

She hadn't even thought of him as she'd bolted from the table. Glancing over her shoulder, she found him looking up at her from the lower level.

"Haley! Hey, hold up a minute!"

He vaulted up the escalator, his long legs taking three stairs at a time. In the few strides it took him to reach her once he'd hit the upper level, Haley noticed his favoring his injured leg. She felt a sudden stab of guilt.

"Keith. Your leg..."

"What?" He glanced down as if he hadn't realized he'd been limping, then back up at Haley. "It's okay. Best workout it's had in a while. Are you all right?"

"You...shouldn't have run after me." She toyed nervously with the strap of her shoulder bag, watching him massage his thigh and flex his leg at the knee a few times. "Now, see what's happened...you're hurting."

"No, I'm fine," he said. "But you're not."

"No, I just..." She pinched the bridge of her nose and looked away. "You're right. I'm not fine. I get really crazy when that sort of thing happens," she explained. "I... don't handle the fan stuff as well as you do."

Apparently not, he thought, noticing how her hands shook as she twisted the leather purse strap. Apparently she couldn't handle it at all. Her breathing was erratic, as well. Then, out of the blue, she struck out for a bank of pay phones a few feet away. Once there, she dug around in her handbag.

Keith frowned and walked over, his leg sending out
the message that he shouldn't have taken that escalator with such enthusiasm. "What are you doing?"

"My car's in the shop. I'm going to call a cab."

Her complexion hadn't regained a bit of color, and
her mouth still trembled noticeably. A protective instinct that Keith preferred to think of as chivalry made
him take the receiver from her, then cradle it. "No, I'll
take you home. I have a car two blocks from here, remember?"

She shook her head. "I appreciate the offer, but I've
already taken too much of your time tonight."

"You're riding with me," he insisted, then took the
purse from her and looped the thin leather strap over
his shoulder. His action brought a wavery smile to
Haley's face. She shook her head again, sighed deeply,
then gave in.

She allowed him to take her arm and steer her to the
door. "You look ridiculous with that purse, you
know," she said.

"Make fun of my purse," he warned, his voice low
and gruff, "and you'll ride on the luggage rack,
woman."

The levity Keith had aimed for by swiping Haley's
shoulder bag didn't last long. The temperature had
dropped several degrees. By the time they made it to
Keith's car, both were all but frozen. Haley was biting her lip, her fists buried deep in her coat pockets.
Keith was both cold and curious as hell. It was one
thing to be put out with autograph seekers, but a

whole different story to run away as if she'd been frightened the woman would chase her.

He slid his car keys from his pocket, then unlocked the passenger side, holding the door for Haley while she got in. After positioning himself behind the wheel, he fired up the engine and quickly reached for the heater buttons. The air that flooded out around their feet was like an arctic front. "Damn!" He fumbled for the buttons again, reducing the blast by half. "Does it always get this cold in Oklahoma?"

Haley chuckled softly. "It's just late fall, you know. Are you going to be able to handle it when winter gets here?"

"That depends. How cold will it get?"

"It can get pretty chilly at times. Of course, I've only been back for five months. Ten years in California made it difficult to adjust again."

I've only been back for five months. He drove the car out of the underground parking garage, remembering what the woman in the mall had said. Haley had a good excuse for being gone from the soap. What had that meant? Glancing Haley's way, he said, "Do you like living here?"

"Yes," she said, but her wistful tone betrayed her.

Keith glanced at her again, then asked, "By the way, exactly where am I going here?"

She gave him directions to the Broken Arrow expressway, then seemed deep in thought, staring out the passenger window.

Keith guided the car through the quiet streets and took a stab at small talk again. "Not much traffic. Downtown's dead this time of night, isn't it?"

"Um-hmm. Tulsa's more suburban than most cities this size. Very few high-rise condos or apartments downtown."

"So I see." He made the next three lights, then found the expressway she'd mentioned. The conversation he'd hoped for was deader than the streets. As he accelerated up the entrance ramp, he tried again but met with failure when Haley answered his next two questions in monosyllables.

She started chewing her lip again. Seconds later her foot began patting a soft but nervous rhythm on the carpeted floorboard.

This was none of his business, he told himself. He'd only known her for one day. And up until an hour ago, he'd had real doubts that he could ever come to like the woman. Besides, they were only going to be teacher and student for the next two weeks, nothing more personal than that. And if she needed to talk about what happened back at the mall, he decided, she should be the one to bring it up.

He concentrated on driving and tried not to think about that patting red sneaker or Haley's poor lower lip. He watched illuminated green exit signs go by, taking hers when Haley pointed it out. Still hugging her side of the car, she added that her apartment complex was only five or six miles away.

They traveled down Lewis Street, passing older, stately homes set back on beautiful, well-kept lawns.

"You know what's so amazing about the whole thing?" she asked abruptly. She didn't look at him, just continued gazing through the front windshield. "It's that they can't seem to understand that you're just an actor, not the *fictional* character you portray."

Keith took his eyes off the road to look her way. "You mean the fans? Soap-opera fans?"

"Make a right turn here."

He flipped on the blinker, keeping her profile in his peripheral vision.

"Yes, the fans," she said, veering back to his question. "That woman back there. To look at her you'd think she was harmless, right?"

"Well . . . yeah, I guess so. Wasn't she?"

"You just can't know that. You can't trust . . ." She shook her head, then gestured to a complex up ahead.

He slowed the car and turned into the apartment drive, darting more sideways looks to see if Haley would add to her last mysterious comment, but she wasn't forthcoming. Her only words were "I'm the third building on the right." Then she dug through her purse, coming up with a set of keys.

His mind buzzing with the strange conversation Haley had started and ended so unexpectedly, he stopped in front of her building. Seconds from now she'd go in, leaving him to wonder about it all night.

She turned on the seat to face him. "I hope you'll be all right," she said.

Keith blinked. She hoped *he'd* be all right? "What do you mean?"

"Your leg."

"Oh, yeah. Don't worry about it. It feels fine now. But—" he reached over and touched her arm lightly "—are you going to be okay? You seemed really shook up back there."

"Yes, I was." Haley sighed and glanced away for a moment. When she glanced back, her eyes looked tired. Keith's heart went out to her even as he struggled to understand. "It's been more than two years. You'd think I'd stop overreacting to those kinds of situations by now, huh?"

Without further explanation, she opened her door, letting cold air drift in as she scooted off the seat and out of the car. "Thanks for the ride. I'll see you tomorrow morning."

HALEY THREW her purse on a chair, then stood in front of her answering machine while she listened to the three messages on it. The first was from Dennis O'Kane, wanting to discuss next season's playbill. The second was from her brother.

"This is James. I'm surprised you're not at home at this hour. The reason I called is . . ."

James told her in detail about the reception her mother was planning to celebrate the opening of the theater. Remembering the many receptions her mother had hosted, Haley rolled her eyes. Formal attire, Tulsa's society crowd, media coverage. She sighed as she took off her jacket and walked to the closet. Publicity. Just what she needed.

The third message was from Carolyn. Haley's hand froze on the closet doorknob, and she looked back over her shoulder at the machine.

"Hi. I, um, I'll be in town for a few months and...well, I just thought..." There was silence, then, "Look, maybe calling you wasn't such a good idea. I mean, I think I understand your reasons for not staying in touch. I'd probably do the same if it were me. I'll leave it up to you. Call me...or don't. I'm at the Riverton."

Haley closed her eyes, upset by the pain in Carolyn's voice. Dammit, why did things have to be so hard now? It wasn't fair that someone else had to be hurt by what had happened to her.

I'll leave it up to you. Call me...or don't.

Haley couldn't *not* call her. Carolyn was her friend and didn't deserve to be pushed aside. Haley's peace of mind would have to go on the back burner for a while. It might hurt to hear Carolyn talk about the career that Haley could no longer have, but that was a price Haley was willing to pay. Yes, she would call her. But not tonight, she decided. Not in the frame of mind she was in.

Her frame of mind wasn't conducive to calling James, either. It was the last thing Haley wanted to do right now. She wanted to take a hot shower, then crawl between the sheets of her bed and lose herself in television or a book. But she knew he'd only worry if she didn't. So she called him and listened to the plans he and her mother had for the reception they wanted to hold two weeks from now at the Riverton. As theater director, she was in charge of publicity for TAT, and she knew how foolish it would be to turn down the free press. So she agreed to be there. He ended the call in much the same way he did all of his calls. "So you're...okay?"

She assured him she was, then said goodbye and hung up the phone, wanting things to return to normal. She wished that after more than two years her brother could stop worrying when she was out at night. And that the thought of her face on television or her name in the newspaper would stop causing her so much anxiety. She also wished that the simple pleasure of someone asking for an autograph hadn't been taken away from her by Jack Wharton.

Haley pulled her sweatshirt over her head and tossed it on the bed. Moving to her dresser, she took out a nightgown. Before donning it, she gazed at her reflection in the dresser mirror, and the cotton gown slipped from her grasp.

She should have been used to the sight of the scars by now. But she was always surprised to see them. She lifted her hand and traced the one that had come closest to killing her, the one that had missed her heart by millimeters. Then her fingertips traveled slowly to her shoulder and slid her bra strap aside, uncovering the other two. She closed her eyes, her index finger still touching the puckered star-shaped skin, and the memory, still sharp and hellish after two years, made her throat convulse.

You're always so beautiful. Me! You have to love me!

Haley turned away from the mirror, took off her bra and quickly pulled the nightgown over her head, then made her way to the front door and checked the lock. Locks. Thanks to her brother, who had insisted she install two dead bolts in addition to the one already there, not another door in the entire apartment complex could boast of so much hardware.

She shot all three locks home, remembering how she'd argued with James over the extra security measures. "He's locked away in a hospital in California. I don't see why I have to live like a prisoner behind my own walls...half a continent away in Oklahoma," she'd said. James had been adamant, telling her that if she had taken more precautions two years ago, the shooting might never have happened in the first place.

Haley went back to her bedroom, switched off her light and slid beneath the covers. James might have been right about precautions preventing the attack, but Haley didn't think so. She had reread Jack's letters since the shooting, and there was nothing in them to indicate that he was anything more than an eccentric fan. His letters had made him seem no less normal than the woman in the shopping mall had appeared to be. His background, Haley had found out after the fact, was ironically similar to Haley's own— he'd been raised in a well-to-do family who had given him every advantage in life. So how was Haley supposed to have protected herself against someone no one would have guessed would be a threat?

She rolled over and punched her pillow, readying herself for what would probably be a torturous night.

Invariably on days when Wharton and the shooting occupied her mind, her dreams were replaced by nightmares. Nightmares in which she was hunted down by Jack Wharton.

Dear Sabrina,

The doctors here think they'll help me by pounding things into my head. But it only makes me angry. Angry that I'm here, angry they're always trying to crawl around inside my head, angry that they can't see there's nothing wrong with me. And they don't want me to talk about you. They say it's *me* they want to know about.

My thoughts, my past, always *me!* What they don't understand is that to know about me, they'll have to hear about you.

I've seen you, you know. Pictures, at least. In magazines or on TV in reports about what I did. It hurts to see it, but I deserve to hurt, don't I? Don't think I don't feel guilty. I'm remorseful. How could I not be, loving you like I do?

And how can I pretend that you're no longer a part of my life to these doctors? How, when we're connected to each other for life now?

All my love,
Jack

Pleased with the letter, Jack Wharton set down his pen and read it over again, checking to make sure there were no ink smudges on the page. One of the magazine articles about him and Sabrina had said that his words were always scrawled and smudged with ink. Scrawls and smudges! The jerk reporter hadn't even paid attention to the content of the letters; he'd just singled out Jack's mistakes.

Just like his parents, he thought sourly as he got up and paced the room. Just like them, the reporter had been quick to point out where Jack had screwed up, but had completely ignored his skillful writing, all the beautiful phrases. He gave a harsh laugh. How stupid he'd been to think he could escape all of their goddamn expectations of perfection! He'd thought that moving away from his family to California would ease the pressure, but now he found himself under even more scrutiny. Perfect! Everyone demanded he be perfect!

Except Sabrina.

At the thought of her, Jack's anger faded. Sabrina had never expected more of him than he could give. She was sweet and loving...forgiving. Never impatient or demanding. She was the one person, the only person for whom he wanted to be perfect.

So he wouldn't send this letter to her agency, he decided as he sat back down and picked it up again. He would go over it several times more, until there were absolutely no mistakes. Then he would keep it until he could give it to her himself.

Of course, he would have to write another, less personal letter to send to her agency. He didn't want Sabrina to worry that he'd forgotten her.

KEITH HELD the black comb under a thin trickle of water, then shut off the faucet and shook excess moisture from the comb. He raised both elbows in the air, combing with one hand and smoothing with the other, then watched his expression in the mirror as he repeated the line of dialogue for the tenth time in as many minutes. *"I'm not a gambling man, but I'd place odds against you slipping the noose this time, Stuckey."* Frowning, he set the comb down next to the sink and gave the line a little more snarl. *"I'm not a gambling man..."*

No, that wasn't right, either. He added a squint and a smirk, propped one hand on the beltless waistband of his jeans and drawled, *"I'm not a gamblin' man, but Ah'd place odds against you slippin' the noose this tahm, Stuckey."*

Yeah, he thought. That was better. More drawl, more squint and smirk. He tried the expression again, then turned to the side and angled a look at his profile. Facing front again, he experimented with lifting one brow, then the other. He leaned closer to the mirror. *"...Ah'd place odds 'gainst—"*

The phone rang and Keith jumped, banging his hip on the edge of the counter. Damn, that was the loudest phone! He reached behind him for the extension on the bathroom wall.

"Hello."

"Good morning, Mr. Garrison. This is your 6:00 a.m. wake-up call."

He thanked the woman, hung up the phone and turned back to the mirror. He shook his head, laughing at himself when he remembered the time his twin sister, Angela, had caught him posing in front of a mirror. It had been in junior high, the day before football pictures were to be taken. He'd been snarling and smirking at his reflection that day, too. Not to mention flexing muscles that had yet to develop.

Angie had razzed him mercilessly, had stuck him with the nickname "Heartthrob," and to this day, when they saw each other after long separations, she would greet him with a hug, then squeeze his upper arm and pretend to swoon.

But for all of Angie's ribbing, Keith had to admit as he left the bathroom and shrugged into a long-sleeved shirt, she'd pretty well hit the nail on the head. Since birth, he'd been the ham-it-up, attention-seeking twin, and Angie, the shy, quiet twin, had been his built-in audience. He'd kept their parents in stitches with his constant showing off, had been leading man in all the neighborhood backyard plays and an enthusiastic church choir member—even though he couldn't carry a tune in a bucket. Then football had come along. With it came bleachers full of cheering fans, not to mention adoring high school girls.

Keith slipped a belt through the loops of his jeans, then stepped into a pair of loafers, wondering if he might have gone for an acting career had sports not come so easily to him. Thinking back, all the indicators were there. He'd been a movie junkie, seeing as many as his allowance and part-time jobs had afforded. And in college he'd chosen drama for an elective.

He pulled a sweater on over his shirt, then straightened his collar. Pretty serious stuff to mull over at six o'clock in the morning, he thought wryly as he picked up his script from the night table. But then, ever since his injury, he'd seemed to become more serious about things. He'd finally seen the wisdom in his parents' advice to invest in a house and had bought ranch property outside San Antonio. And unlike the scared kid he'd been when he'd opted for pro ball after college, he'd pushed his insecurities and fear of taking a risk aside and signed Madeira's contract. Even so, Keith had spent last night clear into the wee hours alternately studying his script and one of the books he'd been assigned to read. He'd awoken at five, anxious to get back to it.

That alone, he thought, if not solid evidence supporting the seriousness of his commitment, was at least a testament to his powers of concentration. It had been difficult as hell getting Haley's last words out of his mind so he could pay attention to the script and book.

You just can't trust...it's been more than two years...you'd think I'd stop overreacting...

Keith shook his head and lay down across the bed on his stomach, paging to the scene in his script where he'd left off last night. Odd that she just assumed he knew whatever it was that had happened to her. Odder still that more than two years later she was still so affected by whatever it was.

AT THE SOUND of the car horn outside her apartment, Haley took one last swallow of coffee, then grabbed her bulging canvas briefcase and headed for the door. She switched on the porch light, knowing it was going to be another late night for her, then locked up and walked to Brent Maloney's car. She opened the door and slid in, plopping the case on the wide bench seat between them.

"Good morning." He didn't look up from the radio station knob he was turning this way and that. A small frown played between his brows.

"'Morning. Thanks for the ride, Brent. Surely my car'll be out of the shop someday." But that wouldn't really matter, though, because she'd have the money from the lessons for a new one soon. "What's wrong, can't find your station?"

"Hmm? Oh, yeah. I lent the car to my son, Josh, last night. Do you know how much fun it is to start the car at seven-thirty in the morning and be blasted in the face with Nirvana?"

She grinned. "Nope. How much fun is it?"

"Not much." He found a classical station, smiled at the more mellow sounds emanating from the speakers, then put the car in gear. In moments they were on their way to the theater, his off-key humming filling the car.

Humming off-key was the only fault Haley had found in Brent Maloney since Dennis had sent him over yesterday. A local dentist with a sideline interest in acting, he had downsized his practice for the very purpose of devoting more time to the theater.

And devoted he was. As well as organized. He'd jumped right in yesterday, saying the stage-manager duties sounded fun.

She eyed Brent's briefcase, which sat next to hers on the seat, and sighed. Burnished cordovan leather with shiny brass locks and monogrammed initials in one corner, it made a mockery of Haley's casual canvas model with papers always getting caught in the zipper.

"What's the matter?"

She leaned her head on the headrest and glanced his way, watching as he straightened his already-straight tie. "Just thinking that I'd like to be you when I grow up," she answered wearily. "I am *the* most hopelessly disorganized cookie."

"You couldn't be. You haven't met my ex-wife."

"Is that why you're divorced? Oops, that's probably none of my business."

"No. It's okay to ask. My being a neat freak and her being *very* relaxed about things was only a minor irritant among many." He chuckled wryly and stopped the car at a red light. "The reason I'm divorced is that I'm going through my mid-life crisis."

Mid-life crisis? Brent? He didn't fit the type. Haley cataloged his conservative clothes, from the business suit and tie to the argyle socks and wing-tip shoes. She noted the silver at his temples, which blended nicely with his silver wire-rimmed glasses, and judged him to be the correct age for mid-life crisis. But age was the only factor that might suggest one.

"So," she asked, amused, "where's your red Corvette?"

Brent shrugged, signaling for a turn. "According to Carol, acting is my red Corvette."

She laughed. "No, really?"

"Oh, yes. She thought I'd lost my mind when I caught the acting bug. She said I'd become someone she didn't know anymore. I was no longer dependable, levelheaded Brent. I was some middle-aged teenager all of a sudden who wanted to try out for plays and waste time on the board of directors. That, along with several other things, was finally resolved in divorce court."

Haley's amusement with the situation faded. "I'm sorry."

"Yeah. Me, too." His fingers stopped tapping along with the Mozart concerto, his expression becoming thoughtful. "She was right, you know. I have changed. I didn't buy a sports car or trade in my wife for someone younger and blonder, but I did do some major priority shuffling."

Seeing his frown, Haley said, "That isn't a bad thing, Brent. People are doing it all over the place. It's more a trend of the nineties than a mid-life crisis, wouldn't you say? And it's not as if you sold all your worldly possessions and struck out for Hollywood. Local theater is as sane as running a mom-and-pop grocery store, Brent. Hollywood can be a real circus."

"Suppose you're right. I shouldn't be second-guessing myself. I feel guilty about it sometimes, but

I've been happier since the divorce than I have been in a long time.'' He pulled into the smallish lot behind TAT and parked in one of the spaces reserved for board members.

He opened his door, and Haley followed suit. She waited at the back of the car for Brent to lock up and join her, then they strolled to the theater together. At the door he stopped her, touching her arm.

"You look tired, Haley. Maybe you need to hand more of the paperwork over to me."

"No, I just had trouble falling asleep last night." And when she finally had, she'd found no peace there. The nightmare had returned with a vengeance, and even when she woke up, she'd had the lingering feeling that Jack was out there somewhere, waiting, watching.

She shook her head and gave him a wan smile. "You know that circus I was telling you about?" she asked in a tired voice. "Sometimes I feel as though I'll never be completely free of it."

CHAPTER FIVE

FROM HIS CAR, Keith watched the man take hold of Haley's shoulder, then give her a gentle squeeze. Seeing the sweet smile she gave him and the expression of affection on his face, Keith wondered if a kiss would come next. When it didn't, Keith let out the breath he hadn't even realized he'd been holding.

He rolled his eyes at that, then gathered up his script and books and hustled out of the car, telling himself that his acting coach's personal life was none of his business. Oh, his interest in her was explainable. She was an extremely attractive woman. And Keith seldom let the opportunity to flirt and otherwise get to know an extremely attractive woman pass him by. But explainable or not, an attraction would only get in the way of the business at hand.

He opened the back door and waited a second for his eyes to adjust to the dimly lit back hall of the theater. When they did, he saw a doorway several feet ahead that was lighted and from which came two muted voices, one female, the other male. The aroma of brewing coffee was overlaid by the pungent odor of paint and turpentine. Against one wall leaned a rickety old ladder with rusty bolts and two rungs missing.

There were two backdrops next to it, one a rendering of a sunset, the other, the wall of a living room.

He made his way forward, sidestepping two extension cords. Graffiti on the wall nabbed his attention, and he grinned when he read it. Someone had penciled "Out, out, damned spot!" next to a water stain.

He grinned again when he got to the doorway. On the wall next to it were two signs. First there was Haley's nameplate. Beneath it was a handmade sign that read Director Babe.

Haley and the man she'd arrived with were standing next to a large, cluttered desk that took up most of the small office's space. They were searching frantically through stacks of file folders, magazines and paper. Two of the drawers were open. Haley pulled open another and lifted a stack of folders out of it. "Oh, where is it?" she groaned, then shoved a stack aside, knocking over a small vase full of pencils and pens. The noise made Haley and the man look up, and they noticed Keith. It was unnecessary, but he rapped on the door frame.

Haley waved him in, giving a brief smile around the pencil she was holding in her teeth, then continued her search. Her companion smiled broadly at Keith. "Keith Garrison!" He scooted around Haley, his hands, Keith noted, brushing over her shoulders in the process. He held out a hand and gripped Keith's hard as they shook. "Haley told me about the movie you're making in Tulsa. It's a pleasure to meet you."

"Thank you. And you're...?"

"Oh! Sorry. Brent Maloney." He pumped Keith's hand some more. "I'm Haley's assistant."

"Who'll probably kill me if I can't find those press releases," Haley mumbled around the pencil.

Brent grinned at her over his shoulder, then winked at Keith. "She's got this idea that I might get hostile if things get misplaced."

"I just don't want to take any chances," she put in, opening yet another drawer and shuffling through it. She looked up at Brent, shuddered and affected a look of fear. "Hey, I saw *Marathon Man*."

Addressing Keith's puzzled expression, Brent explained with a chuckle, "In my other life, I'm a dentist."

"Oh..." Keith responded with a chuckle. "Oh, right."

"I'm also a big fan of the Mavericks, though not as big as my son, Josh."

Inexplicably Keith's mood lightened. "Bet that doesn't sit well with your wife."

"You're right, it didn't. But we're divorced now, so it's not a problem."

"Sorry to hear it."

"Yeah, well..." Brent glanced down, spotted something of interest on the desk and picked it up. He smiled, then waved the paper at Haley. "Voilà."

Her mouth dropped open and she reached for the paper, snatching it from his hands. Her eyes lit with a smile. "You are a genius! Where'd you find it?"

He circled around the desk to her side and pointed. "Right there on top."

"Oh, for heaven's sake!"

She laughed and Brent shook his head with an indulgent expression.

Keith regarded the couple with a polite smile but felt uneasy with their familiarity. He glanced away. Why should he care one way or the other? Why should he care if Brent and Haley rode to work in the same car together, or traded dentist jokes, or were so...*familiar* with each other?

He shouldn't.

Noticing a time-worn sofa against the wall opposite the desk, he strolled over to wait there while Haley finished the business at hand. Setting down his script and books, he occupied himself by looking around the room. The walls were covered in old playbills and posters. Shelves over the desk held photos from days gone by of cast members in costume from various productions. On the floor were two large spotlights.

"Keith, I'm almost ready here, okay?" She circled around to the front of the desk and hunted through a stack of folders.

"Sure. No hurry."

He crossed an ankle over his knee, his gaze lifting to the thick blond hair she'd piled atop her head. She wore an oversize sweater in shades of autumn leaves, and black stretchy pants with a seam up the front. On her feet were metallic gold flats.

When she'd found her folder, she leaned across the desk to hand it to Brent, and the sweater rode up in back, revealing just how clingy the pants were. And just how nicely curved his acting coach was. He thought about looking away but he didn't. Looking was no crime.

"Well, I'll be back later today," Brent said, snapping the locks on a pricey-looking briefcase before heading for the door. "Great meeting you, Keith."

"Uh, yeah." Keith returned Brent's jaunty wave. "You, too, Brent."

"All right," Haley said, shutting the door behind Brent. She moved back to the desk and started foraging through a canvas briefcase until she came up with a copy of Keith's script. Then she dumped the briefcase in the chair and circled to the front of the desk again. After boosting herself up to sit on its edge facing Keith, she said, "Are we ready to start?"

"Now. REPEAT after me. Lazy, lily, lacks, loo."

"Lazy, lily, lacks, loo."

"Sid, salary, silly, Sue."

"Sid, salary, silly, Sue."

"Good. Now say lastly, lovingly, lowly, languishing."

"Lastly, lovingly, lowly, languishing."

"Very good. Now, watch what I do." Haley pointed to her face with both index fingers. She stuck out her tongue as far as it would go, then pulled it back into her mouth. Next she thrust it out again and repeatedly touched both cheeks with it as quickly as she could. "Now you," she instructed with a nod. "Five times."

Keith followed her example, unable to keep from laughing at the end. "I look ridiculous doing this stuff, don't I?"

Still perched on the desktop with her little gold shoes swinging, she smiled. "Yes. But do it, anyway. It'll improve your diction."

"Next are lip exercises. Open your mouth, spread your lips in a wide smile and say eeeeee."

"Eeeeee."

"Good. Now round them and say oooooo."

"Oooooo."

"Fantastic. Now, breathing. Stand up and put your hands on your sides at the base of your ribs...yes, like that, only—" she hopped off the desk and took his hands in hers "—with your fingers just touching in front."

It was human nature, Keith told himself, that made his muscles tense at her touch. If the scent she wore, a subtle blend of wintry spices, seemed more compelling than most, it was because he'd deemed a flirtation unwise. If her hands, satin soft and warm on his, made him wonder how they'd feel on other parts of his body, it was because such an idea was foolhardy. He was like any other man: the forbidden held special appeal.

"Relax," she said, and Keith made a gargantuan effort to do just that. "Good, now inhale... Right, feel your chest wall expanding? Your abdomen pressing out? Look down at our hands."

He forced his gaze down, hoping that this exercise would be over soon.

"See? The greater the expansion, the farther apart the fingers are. Now, exhale and watch how your fingers meet as the chest wall and abdomen contract."

He watched, but he knew he should be paying more attention to his fingers than hers. He shouldn't be thinking of the striking contrast her smooth, ivory-colored skin made to his darker, rougher-textured skin. He should have been concerned with learning to improve lung capacity, not wondering about the significance of the plain gold pinky ring she wore on her right hand.

"You'll need to do this exercise every day for a minimum of fifteen minutes. Inhale slowly... good, now hold for a count of ten. Right. Now exhale slowly, evenly for a count of fifteen. Great, just like that."

She stepped back, and Keith's muscles relaxed.

Checking an old schoolhouse clock on the wall, she said, "Whoa, did you realize we've been at this for four hours?"

"No, I didn't."

She walked behind her desk, rotating her head this way and that, then massaging her neck with one hand.

He hadn't imagined that he'd been on that lumpy sofa that long. Amazing that his leg hadn't protested a couple of hours ago. But until this last exercise, he'd been so caught up in Haley's lesson that he doubted he would have noticed if a Mack truck had driven over him.

She was something else. He'd found that out a half hour into their lesson as they'd tackled one of the scenes in his script. Keith had figured they'd start by going over his lines, then Haley would jump in with her critique, pointing out ways he could improve his diction, gestures and the like. But he'd been wrong. Instead, she had set the script aside and asked him to analyze his character's actions in the scene. Keith had made a stab at it, giving what amounted to some very surface reasons for his character's actions. That's when Haley had gotten serious.

They'd spent the next hour dissecting his character. She'd engaged him in fantasizing about the character's past, in deciding what might have happened in his childhood to shape the man. And they'd talked about life in the bounty hunter's time, even outlining what a typical day would have been like for him. Entering his character's soul, she had said, was the only way he would bring the man to life on the screen. And finding out everything about the man, from what he might have eaten for breakfast to his opinions on the politics of the day, was just the first step. The next three hours had been devoted to the mechanics of voice and speech—quality, resonance, pitch, power, tempo and delivery.

"Well, I don't know about you...but I'm starving," she said. "Why don't you grab some lunch. We can start again in say...forty-five minutes?"

Keith nodded. He started for the door, then stopped and looked back at her. "Would you...like to go somewhere with me? I saw several places along Peoria that looked interesting."

She appeared hesitant, then shook her head. "Thanks, but I brought a sandwich."

"All right. See you in forty-five, then."

Keith ignored the small flicker of disappointment he felt and left the theater. He reminded himself that theirs was a working relationship, one he was damn fortunate to have. He couldn't allow soft skin and a compelling scent to distract him from his real purpose. No matter how much he liked the shape of her legs, no matter how much he liked the curves beneath her sweater...

HALEY PUSHED stacks of paper aside, then swung her feet up onto the desktop. She leaned back in the ancient, creaking swivel chair, wadded up the cellophane sandwich bag and tossed it toward the wastebasket, missing. As usual. With a sigh, she closed her eyes, her thoughts about the morning's session bringing a smile to her lips.

Had this been the same man who had read for her yesterday? The same one who had scoffed at her suggestion to display more emotion in a gunfight? She'd been worried that she would have to chisel through a concrete wall of macho attitude before she'd be able to teach him anything. She'd thought that he would balk at the need for character analysis or think basic voice and speech lessons beneath him.

But he'd been as open and eager as Haley had been ten years ago with her first acting coach. She might just accomplish what Ian had hoped for. Keith might turn in a better-than-decent performance his first time out. She'd marveled at his enthusiasm all morning, but had marveled just as much at his heartbreaking good looks, appreciating Madeira and the casting agency's savvy more with each minute. She'd made mental notes all morning, as well.

If his lopsided grin had charmed her, it would charm an audience. If she'd felt a tug of feminine awareness when he stretched both arms wide over the back of the sofa or raked a hand through his thick russet hair, then women in theaters would feel it, too. If her pulse had quickened when she'd caught him checking out her legs, then he would garner that same reaction from other women. It would be great if he could incorporate those male gestures and expressions, she thought, if he could project his personal charisma through the character.

She sat up and searched the messy desktop for a pad to make notes for Ian. Anxious to scribble down the many looks and body movements she had observed, Haley was surprised when she found them difficult to describe. She chewed on the end of her pen. The grin. Saying that it was lopsided wasn't descriptive enough, because more than just his mouth was involved. There was the one dimple to think of, and the way his eyes crinkled at the corners and appeared to become a warmer shade of brown. And his arms stretching across the sofa—Haley thought about the way the movement had made his shoulders seem broader, more powerful.

Frustrated, she set down the pad. Then her mind cleared and she blinked. What was she thinking of? Ian didn't need a detailed description from her, not when the camera would catch the color of his eyes and his dimple and the breadth of his shoulders.

She leaned back in her chair again, wondering if his handsome face and killer physique had affected her on more than a professional level. Yes, her pulse had sped up a couple of times this morning. And yes, she'd felt little zaps of awareness here and there. But she'd been putting herself in an audience's place, hadn't she? She'd been feeling the responses moviegoers would feel when they watched him on the big screen. Right?

Wrong.

So she was attracted to Keith Garrison. Nothing unexplainable about that. He was an appealing guy. Even through her initial anger yesterday, she'd recognized that. And considering the fact that she hadn't dated in more than two years, it would have concerned Haley more if she *didn't* find the man attractive.

But it was ridiculous to speculate. Sure, she'd caught him looking at her legs, but that didn't mean anything. And he was only going to be in Tulsa for a few months at most, her student for only two weeks.

She propped her feet on the desk again, this time closing her eyes and focusing on the scene they would be reading through after lunch.

"HALEY? Are you . . . asleep?"

"Oh, no. Just resting—" Haley sat erect and opened her eyes. Looking at the clock, she realized she had indeed drifted off. When her gaze connected with the woman in the doorway, her eyes widened.

"Hello, Haley."

The last vestiges of fuzzy-headedness cleared in an instant. "Carolyn?"

The woman brushed back a strand of wavy black hair and gave a strained smile. "Right the first time."

"Carolyn."

Carolyn stayed in the doorway. "Ian told me you're a theater director now," she said, her words quick and her tone overly bright. "I see it's no different here than in Hollywood. You're not a director, you're a director babe."

A slight frown wrinkled Haley's brow, then she remembered the sign one of the more juvenile male staff members had made. "Oh, you mean the sign. I decided to have a sense of humor about that."

"Yeah. Wastes too much energy being a feminist, anyway."

Haley smiled, the shock of waking to find Carolyn Kincaid in her office beginning to wear off, only to be replaced by tension. Tension that kept Haley glued to her chair much as it seemed to keep Carolyn planted in the doorway. Did Carolyn understand why Haley had not returned her call? Did she realize that not keeping in touch hadn't been something Haley had *wanted* to do, but what she'd needed to do? Breaking all ties with her life in Hollywood had been the most painless way for Haley to deal with her choices. Giving up her career had been agony enough. Keeping in close contact with someone still in the business would have made the agony tenfold. On edge, Haley said,

"You're...here for the movie. Congratulations on landing the part."

"Thanks. They decided it would be cheaper to hire me than pay to have me removed from the premises every day. Very effective, chaining oneself to the casting agency's front door."

Haley chuckled, quickly cataloging the differences in her friend since they'd last met. Carolyn had cut her beautiful waist-length hair to shoulder length and had it permed. And she looked as if she'd lost weight, maybe five or ten pounds.

But there were things about her friend that hadn't changed. Her clothes—tight jeans, T-shirt and unstructured jacket—were the same casual style that Carolyn had always been most comfortable wearing. And her flip manner when something was chewing at her, that was the same, too. Haley wanted to go to her and hug her tightly. She hadn't thought it wise for them to see each other, but God, how good it was to see her now.

"You'll be a great Sarah, Carolyn." Haley meant it, but wondered if Carolyn would consider her sentiment insincere.

"You always were my biggest fan, Haley," she said with a nervous laugh. "What am I saying? My *only* fan."

"Not true. But if it were, this movie would change that."

"Thanks. It's a great role. I'm really excited about certain aspects of the movie. Other aspects I'm not too fond of, but—" Carolyn's words broke off, and she sighed loudly. She threw her head back and gazed at the ceiling tiles for a moment, then looked at Haley again.

"Listen to us. Did you ever think things would be this awkward between you and me? We haven't seen each other since you left L.A., yet we're standing here just ...*chatting!* Haley, we've never chatted. Not even the day I answered your ad for a roommate, and we were complete strangers then."

Carolyn was right; they'd hit it off as friends from the very beginning. And they'd supported each other through good and bad, more like sisters than mere friends. Haley stood. "I don't want to chat, either. I want to apologize for—"

"No, no. I'm not asking for an apology. I understand how difficult it must have been. You wanted out, you got out, but still you had to listen to me talking about auditions and agents and ... Well, anyway, you did what you had to do. I promise I didn't take it personally for more than six months."

It was Haley's turn to laugh nervously. "You're still neurotic."

"I know. You gotta love me, huh?"

Haley came forward then, meeting Carolyn halfway for the hug they'd both been dying for. For long moments they simply held on to each other. One grateful that her friend had a forgiving heart, the other relieved that she'd found acceptance and not rejection.

"I do," Haley said. "I do love you."

"Me, too. I was afraid, you know," Carolyn admitted. "I had this major internal tug-of-war over coming to see you when I got to Tulsa. It'd been so long since we'd spoken to each other, and I was worried that the sight of me might bring back memories of that day."

"No, no. Here, come over and sit down." She led Carolyn to the sofa where Keith had been all morning, then sat next to her friend. "I didn't stop calling you because you were a reminder of that day. You were a reminder of... I don't know, everything I had to give up. I... should've considered your feelings, though. I feel guilty about—"

"Don't feel guilty," Carolyn said, taking Haley's hand and squeezing it. "Guilt, I've discovered, can be expensive. I've spent several sessions and lots of money with a therapist trying to get past the guilt I feel about that day, Haley."

Haley was amazed. In the two and a half years since she'd been shot, Carolyn had never mentioned feeling guilty. "What in the world would you have to feel guilty about?"

"Well, I wondered if things might've been different if *I* had answered the door instead of you. Maybe he wouldn't have... Maybe if he'd seen me and not you, he would've hightailed it out of there. Maybe... if I hadn't laughed off his letters, if I had understood them for the threat they really were..."

Haley shook her head. "I didn't realize what a threat they were, either, Carolyn. And if you'd answered the door that day, he might have hurt you."

"No, we both know better than that." They were quiet for a moment, then Carolyn smiled.

"What?"

"You're better now, aren't you? I mean, you would never talk about it. Not in the hospital, not after that when you were trying to get your life back to normal."

Haley returned her smile. "I was a basket case, wasn't I? But you're right. I'm better now."

"Good." She hugged Haley again. "You know that internal tug-of-war that I told you about?"

"Yes. What made you decide to take the chance and come see me?"

"Finding out that you weren't working for your family anymore. When Ian told me you were directing little theater, I had to smile. I just knew you couldn't give up acting completely."

Haley nodded, grinning. "No, I couldn't. I can't go back to L.A. but—" Haley caught sight of Keith out of the corner of her eye. He was standing in the doorway, trying his best to remain inconspicuous. "Come on in, Keith." She and Carolyn stood. "Keith Garrison, this is Carolyn Kincaid, your leading lady in *The Loner.*"

"Well hello, tall, dark and athletic." Carolyn, ever the extrovert, strode forward with her hand outstretched. Keith clasped it in his, a bashful smile on his lips.

"I'm, uh, glad to meet you."

"Oh, not half as glad as I am." Haley couldn't hold back a grin as her friend gave Keith the once-over. She shot a glance over her shoulder at Haley. "And here I was dreading the love scene."

"Carolyn, you're bad." Haley detected a hint of color creeping up Keith's neck.

He cleared his throat. "Did...Ian send you over to meet me?" he asked.

"No, he told me this is where Haley works. We're old friends."

"Yeah?"

"Yeah, ex-roommates, as a matter of fact." Carolyn aimed a smile at Haley, one that said she was glad she'd made the decision to come today. "He did tell me Haley was coaching you, though. You're damn lucky to have her."

Keith nodded.

Carolyn picked up her purse from the sofa, then hugged Haley again. "When can we get together? Do you have any free time these days?"

"I'll make some," Haley reassured her friend.

"Remember, they've put me up at some fleabag called the Riverton," Carolyn reminded Haley.

Haley shook her head. "Get outta here."

"I'm going." Carolyn moved to the door. "Listen, Keith, I heard you're at the Riverton, too. Don't hesitate to ring my room if you need any extra help with your lines."

Keith answered her flirtatious smile with one of his own. "I'll do that."

When she'd left, Keith turned to Haley. "She's a real character, isn't she?"

Haley took her place at the front of the desk, boosting herself up. "She's terrific. And, you'll be glad to know, a very good actress."

He sat on the sofa. "She looks just like I pictured Sarah."

Haley considered that. "Yes...she does, doesn't she?"

Haley thought about the two actors together. They would complement each other perfectly. Especially in the love scenes.

Out of nowhere the idea occurred to Haley that maybe the two might complement each other just as well offscreen. She allowed herself just a smidgen of healthy jealousy at the notion, then came to her senses. The smart thing to do in this situation, she thought, would be to encourage Keith to take Carolyn up on her offer.

She opened up the script and flipped to the scene she wanted to go over with Keith. "Okay, tall, dark and athletic. Let's get to work."

He rolled his eyes. "I can tell your friend is a bad influence on you."

"Yeah. You gotta love her."

CHAPTER SIX

KEITH STRODE nude from the bathroom, toweling his hair dry and whistling. He tossed the damp towel on the bed and pulled a pair of bikini briefs from a drawer. Stepping into them, he remembered the clause in his contract with the underwear manufacturer promising him a lifetime supply of briefs. All he'd had to do was pose in the underwear and be plastered on billboards across the country, in magazine ads and on television.

He put on a scruffy sweatshirt and shorts, preferring not to recall how scandalized his mother had been the first time she'd seen one of the ads. Thank heavens he wouldn't be doing *those* anymore, she'd said when the movie offer had come through. He had to admit that posing for the ads and acting in the commercials hadn't been his favorite way to earn a living, either.

After ordering room service, he whistled his way to the premier room's spacious sitting area.

He plopped down sideways on a plush chair, his legs dangling over one arm of it, and flexed his bad leg. It was amazing how good the leg felt. It hadn't bothered him all day, though he'd spent hour after hour sitting on that old sofa. Of course, maybe it had, and he just hadn't noticed because of his good mood.

Psyched. It felt good to be so psyched. Yesterday's apprehension was nothing but a bad memory now. Today, after spending some of the most intense, grueling hours he'd ever spent without full pads and cleats on, he was on top of the world.

Things were looking better and better for him. Not that he didn't have lots of work still ahead. But if eight short hours of lessons from Haley Riverton had made such a difference, then Keith was anxious to see what two full weeks with her could do.

He closed his eyes and thought about the smile she'd given him after he'd delivered his last line of dialogue for the day. He couldn't remember a woman's smile ever meaning so much. He'd looked up, praying she thought he'd done a passable job, hoping for at least a smidgen of approval. Her smile had started in her eyes, a mere sparkle at first. "I don't think you'll be falling on your ass with this, Keith," she'd said.

His mouth had quirked into a smile. "You mean it? Really?"

"If you work hard for the next two weeks."

God, how relieved her words, and the look of praise in her eyes, had made him feel. Flying with the emotions of the moment, he'd had the urge to grab her up in his arms and swing her around in circles. It had been an instinctive, from-the-gut urge. One he'd shut down quickly.

He reached for the TV remote, deciding he'd catch the news while he waited for his food. Switching through the channels, he found it was too early for the evening newscasts. His only choices were a game show, two talk shows, cartoons and a tabloid newscast. Since the newscast had a report later about star stalkers, Keith set down the remote, leaving it on that channel. One of his teammates, Griff Patterson, had been stalked by a woman a couple of years ago.

Keith sat through a lurid, sensationalistic report on a serial killer in Oregon, distaste making him wonder if he shouldn't have chosen "Tiny Toons," after all. Then the anchor announced a commercial break, leading into it with a teaser on the stalker story. His friend's picture flashed on the screen, followed by one of David Letterman, Jodie Foster and two other actresses, Theresa Saldana and Rebecca Schaeffer. But Keith got the shock of his life when the last photo in the group appeared.

He bolted upright in the chair. Haley?

The anchor called her Haley Rivers, not Riverton. But still, she could've changed her name. Many actors did. Keith shook his head, stunned.

The knock on his hotel-room door cut through his thoughts, and Keith jumped up, realizing room service had arrived. He sprinted to the door, opening it quickly. He wanted to get the room-service guy out of there before the show resumed after the commercial. Then it suddenly occurred to him that this man had probably known Haley when she worked at the Riverton.

"Evening, Mr. Garrison." The uniformed young man strode past Keith, placing his order on a table.

"I'm so pleased to meet you. I've always been a big fan—"

"Thanks." Keith shook the man's hand, quickly spotting the name tag pinned to his chest. "Listen, Michael, can you tell me something?"

The young man glanced down at the hand Keith kept gripped in his. With a quizzical look, he said, "Sure, I'll . . . try."

"Haley Riverton. Do you know her? Were you working here when she was assistant to the manager?"

"Yes. Her brother, James, is still the manager. Did you need to speak to him, Mr. Garrison?"

"No, no. I just need to know about her. She was an actress before she came to Tulsa, right?"

"Well, yes. Why do you need to know?" Michael cast a suspicious look at their clasped hands again.

"Oh, sorry." Keith let go of the young man's hand. "I just saw the beginning of one of those tabloid news shows. It was a report about her. It said she was stalked by some . . ."

Michael nodded. "Yeah, you didn't know about that? A crying shame, huh? She was real popular on that soap. You know, 'Forever and a Day.' Then this sicko starts writing her letters and shows up at her apartment one day. I still can't believe he got off. You can't tell me the jerk needs to be in a hospital more than he needs to be behind bars."

Hospital? Behind bars? God, what had the man done to Haley? Had it been as bad as it had for his friend Griff? "What happened?"

"Well, he was lucky. His parents are like the Rivertons—well-to-do. They hired a bunch of high-powered attorneys who got him off on a plea of insanity."

"No, I meant what did he *do* to her? You said he showed up at her apartment one day...."

"See for yourself." Michael nodded at the television, where the report had begun. Haley's story, it seemed, was to be first.

Keith walked to the set, his heart pumping faster as several publicity shots of Haley flashed across the screen. One was of her and a group of smiling young men and women. The caption beneath it read "Cast of 'Forever and A Day.'" Haley's face was highlighted. Another was of her in period costume on a stage. The last was a black-and-white still. Under different circumstances the photo would have made Keith's mouth go dry. Haley was beautiful, a real stunner in the black strapless dress, with diamond earrings that spilled to her bare shoulders and long blond hair cascading down her back.

Then came a videotaped clip. Keith's blood ran cold as the camera panned to a large dark stain on a carpeted living-room floor. Beside it lay a small table on its side, and a phone was nearby.

"...and shot her three times in the chest here in the Los Angeles apartment she shared with roommate Carolyn Kincaid, daughter of Hollywood royalty Edward and Dory Kincaid...."

Keith blocked out the rest of the reporter's words when the video switched to the next scene. Paramedics were wheeling Haley, who lay unconscious on a gurney, out of the apartment to a waiting ambulance. Holding Haley's hand, Carolyn walked alongside her. Tears stained the woman's face, and she appeared to be in shock.

"Haley...*shot*."

"Yeah."

Keith's gaze jerked to Michael. He'd forgotten the man was still in the room.

"And that's him." Michael pointed at the screen. Keith got only a quick look at the man who was sitting in a courtroom. He noted jet black hair, a weak chin and a half grin, half sneer on his face.

The camera panned to Haley testifying from a witness stand. Keith's heart clutched at the sight of her. Her eyes were downcast, her complexion winter pale. She looked fragile. Weary. So different from the vibrant, healthy, beautiful young woman in the publicity photo of just moments ago.

The report changed focus to another star, and Keith reached forward, switching off the set. A tangle of emotions swirled in his gut.

"You say you just met Miss Riverton?" Michael asked.

"Right, two days ago. She's coaching me for the film I'm in."

"That right?" Michael grinned. "Well, she's great. Of course, we here at the Riverton are just a little prejudiced." He shook his head, the grin fading quickly. "No telling where she'd be now if that nut hadn't shot her." He glanced at his watch. "Better get going. They're going to wonder where I am."

"Oh, right. Wait here a minute." Keith hurried across the room and came back with a five he'd fished from the pocket of his discarded jeans. He handed it to the man.

"Thanks, Mr. Garrison. Enjoy your meal. And tell Miss Riverton 'hi' from Mike next time you see her."

"I'll be sure to. And thanks... for everything."

The man nodded, closing the door behind him.

Keith left the sandwich where Michael had placed it, his appetite ruined, and crossed to the chair, where he slumped down.

He thought about the woman in the mall who'd asked for an autograph last night. Haley's reaction made sense now. As did the odd statement she'd made when he'd dropped her off at her apartment.

You just can't know... you can't trust...

Keith stared at the blank TV screen, remembering how Griff Patterson had suffered. The letters, at first merely filled with sexual innuendo, became outright obscene toward the end. The phone calls all hours of the day and night had gone from pleas for attention to threats of violence. By the time the woman was locked away for breaking into Griff's home and holding his wife and children hostage at knife point, Griff's personal life had become a nightmare. His performance on the field had gone south, his once-solid marriage had dissolved in divorce, and his children had ended up in therapy.

The publicity photo of Haley surfaced in his thoughts again. There'd been something about her in that picture that was missing now, he thought. Her looks hadn't changed. She was just as beautiful without the dramatic makeup, the jewelry, the glamorous dress. But something was different. Her eyes.

In the two days he'd known her, Keith had seen a myriad of emotions flash in Haley's eyes. He'd seen her angry after his first reading, amused when he'd joked with her, nerve-racked and afraid when the woman asked for an autograph. But he hadn't seen an expression close to the one that had radiated from her eyes in that picture.

In that picture she had seemed supremely confident ... absolutely convinced that any dream was hers simply for the taking.

HOURS LATER the phone rang, waking Keith with a start. He sat up, still half-asleep, and groped in the general direction of where the receiver should be. Finding nothing, he blinked, looked over at the bed where he should have been sleeping, and came to the conclusion that he'd fallen asleep in the chair watching a video Haley had assigned. He dragged a hand over his face and yawned, then ambled toward the bed, grabbing the receiver.

"'Lo."

"Keith?"

"Um-hmm."

"This is Angie. Did I wake you?"

"Hi, Ange. Yes, you woke me up."

"Oh, I'm sorry. I didn't think you'd be asleep before nine. I'll call back—"

"No, it's okay. I'm awake now." His twin had never completely outgrown her shy childhood demeanor, even with him. Keith propped both pillows beneath his head and reclined on the bed. "What's up?"

"Well . . . I'm calling to ask a . . . favor."

Keith grinned at Angie's discomfort. "This is a first."

"Don't tease, Keith. You know how I hate this sort of thing."

"Yes, I know, but you shouldn't. What do you need?"

"Your house."

"My house? Geez, Angie, you don't ask for favors often," he joked, "but when you do. . ."

"I don't want it forever, just for a little while. Garrett's going overseas for a few months to demonstrate a new computer system at the company's Italian branch, and I wondered if you'd mind the boys and me staying at the ranch while he's away. Until this trip came up, we'd been looking at houses to buy, but now we'll have to wait, and we're all so tired of this small apartment."

"Of course I don't mind." Keith rubbed his eyes and yawned again. "I'm surprised you're not going with him, though. Getting tired of all the traveling? Or are you afraid the hellions would stir up trouble at the Vatican?"

Angie chuckled. "Keith, I wish you wouldn't call them that. They're not *that* bad."

"Yeah, right." An image of Angie's redheaded twin boys doing swan dives off the headboard of his water bed came to mind. That had been last year, when they were three years old.

"I'll make sure they don't destroy anything, Keith."

"I'm not worried about anything in the house. Actually, with Garrett gone, I like the idea of you guys being there instead of in an apartment. It'll be safer for you."

"Yes. That's Mother's opinion, too. She says you had a sophisticated alarm system put in."

"Um-hmm. Hired a security guard to make rounds a few times a day, too. I'll give the alarm company a call and tell them you'll be in the house for the next couple of months."

"Thanks, Keith. The boys will just love it. I've promised to teach them how to swim in that indoor pool."

Keith chuckled. "Just so long as it's in the pool and not on my water bed."

"I promise I won't let them inside your bedroom." Keith could hear the amusement in his sister's voice. "It's you they take after, you know. Garrett and I were both model children."

"Hey, they're your kids. Don't try to blame me."

"How's the movie going?" she asked, changing the subject. "Are you loving it as much as you thought you would?"

"Well, so far, shooting hasn't begun. The director felt I needed some acting lessons to brush up—"

"Acting lessons? Keith, you're a natural. You don't need lessons. Your director should have seen you in your college plays."

Keith grinned. "Thanks, Ange. It put me off at first, too. But it's been a few years since those college productions. And besides, my coach is great."

"Oh . . . well," Angie said, her tone grudging, "as long as you're okay with it. So, are you gonna have a case of big-head now, or what? Hollywood hunk with his own personal coach flown out from California to the set."

"No," he said, laughing. "She lives here. Name's Haley Riverton. She's the director of a small community theater."

"I see." There was a pause, then Angie said, "Haley Riverton . . . why does that name sound so familiar?"

Keith remembered the report he'd seen earlier that evening. "You're probably remembering her from a soap opera she was on a couple of years back."

"No, I don't watch soaps."

"Then it's from news reports. She was stalked and shot by a fan. He'd written her letters and—"

"Oh, that's right. I remember now." Angie sighed. "Just like Griff, huh?"

"Yeah," he said, distracted as images from the report came back to him. The publicity photo. The bloodstain. The sneer on the stalker's face as he sat in that courtroom. "Just like Griff."

S & J Oyster Company was one of several eateries located down the street from the Blake Theater on

Peoria, and it catered to a yuppie clientele. It was modeled after a New Orleans-style café, with lots of black-and-white ceramic tile and glass brick. Neville Brothers music was piped out over the sound system. After Carolyn and Haley were led to a booth and their orders were taken, Carolyn glanced around at the nearly empty dining room.

"Pretty deserted for nine-thirty at night," she commented. "Are you sure the food's good here?"

"Um-hmm. Tulsa's on a different clock than L.A. The late news is on at ten, not eleven." It had been one of the many small adjustments for Haley when she'd first moved back. "Restaurants don't come alive at nine here—they're pretty much closing down."

Carolyn grinned and tore open a little blue packet, adding the sweetener to her iced tea. "So. Tell me all about it. Are you loving the job at the theater?"

"I am. Of course, my schedule will be a bit tight for the next few weeks. That's why this meal had to be so late. I'll be spending all day coaching your leading man and pushing papers, then early evening will be taken up by play practice."

"My leading man," Carolyn said with a sigh. "I like the sound of it."

"Pretty proud of yourself, I'll bet." Haley remembered the euphoria she'd felt the day she'd landed such a plum part. Of course, she'd been unable to take the role.

Carolyn sighed again. "Too early for pride. Let's just say I hope to be proud of the finished product."

"Come on. You know you'll be great. You should be celebrating the fact that you got the part. Like we used to do." She took a sip of her water. "You're not worried about playing opposite Keith Garrison, are you?"

"No, I'm not worried about him. Or at least that's not my major concern right now."

"What is your major concern?"

Carolyn broke eye contact and reached for her spoon. She rubbed her thumb over the base of the utensil and said quietly, "You've read the script, Haley."

"Um-hmm. I think it's excellent, don't you? I mean, it has everything going for it. There's great action scenes, dialogue I would've died for on the soap, poignant romance..."

Carolyn's gaze shot up.

"What? The romance? What's wrong with...? Oh, the love scenes. The love scenes have you worried?"

"Bingo."

Haley chuckled. "Carolyn, I'm surprised at you. You're no amateur, you've done them before. They're no different from any other scene, and you know that."

"When was the last time you played a death scene or a chase scene or any other scene in the buff, my dear?" Carolyn asked with a smirk.

"Ian wants a nude scene?"

Carolyn nodded. "And I agreed to it. I would've agreed to get paid in Hershey's bars and silk stockings if it had come down to it. I wanted the part that badly.''

''But...'' Haley was shocked. The topic of nude love scenes had come up plenty of times in conversation over the years. Carolyn had always been adamantly opposed to them. ''You said you'd never do a nude scene. You asked Ian for a body double, didn't you?''

''Ian says a body double won't be possible with the way he plans to block the scene. It was either agree to the nudity or get another actress, one who could shed her *inhibitions*.''

Shed her inhibitions, Haley thought sourly. As if stripping and making love on screen were as easy as simply telling oneself not to be embarrassed.

''And, of course, the old double standard is alive and well,'' Carolyn continued, a bitter aura circling her words. ''You can bet your SAG card that Keith won't be showing more than a bare chest.''

The image of Keith, shirtless and entwined with Carolyn, was vivid and immediate. And vaguely disturbing. Haley blinked the picture away and concentrated on Carolyn.

''Will you be able to do this, Carolyn?''

''I'll have to, won't I?''

''No,'' Haley said quickly. ''No, Carolyn. When did you decide that you had to set your principles aside to work in this business?''

''I . . . haven't done that. I simply made a decision. One I'm not particularly thrilled with, but I'll live with it.''

Their waiter arrived with a plate of *shrimp étouffée* for Carolyn and red beans and rice for Haley. When he'd left, Carolyn picked up her fork and made a great display of digging into her food. "Mmm. This *is* good. I'm glad you recommended it. How's yours?"

"I...haven't tasted it yet." Haley glanced down at the plate, then slowly lifted a fork full of rice to her mouth. The Cajun spices swirled over her tongue, providing only a momentary distraction from Carolyn's words. The Carolyn she'd always known would never have compromised herself this way.

Haley took another sip of water. "Why this movie, Carolyn? Why did you want the part so badly?"

Her friend gave her a look that suggested Haley had taken leave of her senses. "You know why. You said it yourself—the script is tremendous. The whole project from director to leading man has success written all over it. I'd have been a fool not to take it. And by the way, I didn't simply *accept* the part—I campaigned for it."

"But there's always another movie. One you can keep your clothes on for."

Carolyn's exasperation showed clearly in her eyes. "I wonder if you would have turned down a certain part two years ago if the director had demanded you show some skin, Haley. And there's not always another movie. You remember how tough the competition was when you left? Well, it hasn't gotten easier. If I'm going to make it, I'm going to have to lose my puritanical values."

Haley struggled to keep from gaping at Carolyn. "Are you listening to yourself? Your values aren't *puritanical*. Besides, self-respect is what we're really talking about here. What in the world has happened in the past two years to make you care so little for self-respect?"

"Now you sound just like Jonathan."

"Jonathan?"

"He's the man I live with. I love the guy, but he makes me nuts sometimes. He's always thrilled whenever I get a part I've auditioned for, but on the other hand, he complains constantly at how hard I push myself." She rolled her eyes. "Good thing he doesn't know about the nude scene, huh?"

Haley nearly choked on her food. "Doesn't— Carolyn, why would you keep this from him? He's going to know about it sooner or later. You're headed for disaster. You know that, don't you?"

"What I'm headed for is the career I've always wanted. I want to be A-list, not B or C anymore. I want feature films, not commercials or guest shots on sitcoms. I want the same thing you always wanted, Haley. The same thing you would've had if not for Jack Wharton."

Carolyn's words sent a jolt of pained remembrance through Haley, and she was unable to reply. Moments passed, then Carolyn sighed audibly.

"Haley, I'm sorry. I shouldn't have mentioned—"

"No, it's okay. You're right. I did want all those things."

"But I didn't have to bring it all up again." Carolyn set down her fork, then sighed again. "So much for worrying about being a reminder of that day."

"Don't feel guilty. Not mentioning his name won't erase what happened."

"I know. But still...I'm sorry. It's just that I'm tired of defending myself for wanting to give my career a boost. Ever since that day, I've felt more determined, more ambitious."

Haley took another bite of rice. "Since that day? You mean the day I was shot?"

Carolyn nodded, then looked away for a moment. "You know that voice-over on the commercial for cross-training shoes, 'Life is short, play hard'?"

"Yes."

"Well, it's true, Haley. Life *is* short. You and I know that better than most, don't we? And I refuse to simply tread water, hoping that a break might come my way. These days I make my own breaks, and yes, I've had to make a few sacrifices. You can understand that, can't you?"

"Yes," Haley said reluctantly. And she did. She'd sacrificed her personal life for ten years at the altar of her career. And since Jack Wharton, she'd done a complete turnaround, giving up her career for sanity and the personal life she'd ignored. "Be sure it's what you want, though. And be sure you can handle it, Carolyn. I thought I could."

Carolyn looked at Haley for long moments, then a small frown appeared between her brows. "You handled it pretty damn well for ten years. If you're talking about after that...you never got a chance, Haley. Wharton took care of that. How can you say you weren't able to handle it?''

Haley set down her fork and dabbed at the corners of her mouth. ''I'm not the only one in Hollywood or public life to have been...in this situation. But I'm one of the few to have completely dropped out after it happened. I couldn't handle it when it got tough, Carolyn.''

CHAPTER SEVEN

Dear Sabrina,

I have good news for you. One of the doctors said today that I'm making progress. What a joke! Because I'm no different today than I was when I came here. I'm still as much in love with you as I ever was. The important thing is that *they* believe I'm different.

I've just learned to say the things they want to hear. And make sure not to say the things they don't want to hear.

It's all in knowing how to work them. Believe me, I've had years of practice at knowing how to say the things people want to hear, acting the way they want me to act. It hurt inside, because I wasn't good enough simply being me, but it got them to leave me alone. Sometimes, anyway.

So with the doctors, I'll just keep quiet about you and be who they want me to be. It's the only way I'll get out so we can be together, Sabrina. And don't feel like it's a lie, what I'm doing. I know that someone like you, someone so honest and good, might get the wrong idea about what I'm doing. But really, it's only a means to an end. And if that end is something as important as the two of us being together, then it's the only thing I can do. Put that way, you understand, don't you?

All my love,
Jack

JACK READ OVER the letter again, nodding at the crisp printed letters. His penmanship was getting better and better. He sealed it in an envelope and placed it in hiding with all the others that were meant for Sabrina's eyes alone. Then he got out a sheet of paper and wrote another letter, one he would send to her agency. He knew that the first letters he'd sent to the agency had been read, then sent back to the doctors here. Some of the things they knew about his relationship with Sabrina had been taken from those letters.

He got angry just thinking about it. They thought they'd outsmart him, thought they'd use his *private* thoughts and emotions against him. But he'd been telling Sabrina the truth when he said he knew how to work people. One of the ways he was doing it now was continuing to send letters to the agency, but these were filled with everything the doctors wanted to hear.

THE AD WAS large, eye-catching. It featured the silhouette of a young woman in a hat that threw shadows over her face. She had long, thick, wavy hair. The picture could have been of anyone. It teased the reader with the idea that it could have been Haley. But the copy beneath the picture assured Keith that it wasn't her. It read, By Popular Demand! Sabrina Returns!

The newspaper advertisement went on to announce
the date of the character's return, the soap's network
and time slot.

Keith slapped the pages of the newspaper shut and
shoved it across the table. He reached for his cup of
coffee and took a sip, discovering with a grimace that
it had cooled. How long, he wondered, had he been
staring at the ad? As long as he'd stayed awake last
night after Angie's call thinking about Haley? As long
as thoughts of Haley's attack had torn at his gut after
waking this morning?

He scraped back his chair and went for his jacket
and script, thinking about the lesson ahead for today.
He and Haley were slated to read through a scene involving Carolyn's character. She would play the sister
of a woman who had been murdered, and was hiring
him, the bounty hunter, to track down the killer.

When Keith had tried to go over the scene last night,
his mind had refused to cooperate, replacing images
of the Old West setting with ones of an apartment in
L.A. Whenever he thought of Carolyn, he saw her
tearstained face as she'd walked alongside Haley to the
ambulance. He'd finally given up and tried for sleep,
but that, too, had eluded him.

He snatched up his car keys and left the hotel room,
then took the elevator to the lobby. Crossing the large
room where he and Haley had exchanged their first
civil words, he glanced up and caught sight of a chan-
delier, dripping in teardrop-shaped crystals and providing elegant, muted lighting. He halted, reminded of
the photo of Haley wearing the diamond earrings.

She'd grown up in a world where privilege was a given, he thought. Yet she'd left it, and from what he knew about her so far, she'd had good reason. Her place was behind a camera or on a stage, not in the executive offices of this hotel.

He made his way out of the hotel to his car, the morning chill chasing at his heels until he'd closed the door and fired up the heater. The car took several minutes to warm, time for Keith to remember Haley saying she'd had to adjust to the colder weather when she'd moved back to Oklahoma.

He put the car into Drive and wondered if frustration at not being in the field of her choice had been the reason she'd left the hotel for the director's position. And if so, how much would it take to get her out of the small theater and back to acting? Back to what was soon to become his world, and by all rights, should still be hers.

HALEY ROSE from her swivel chair and, dragging the long phone cord along with her, found the closest wall in her office to slump against.

"Yes, I understand that, Mother." She rolled her eyes at Brent, who was sitting on the sofa. He shook his head and sorted papers in the open briefcase on his lap. "But Brent's offered to do the interviews with the press. He's on the board of directors and is my assistant. Why do I have to go if Brent will?"

Haley listened to her mother's objections, then sighed and closed her eyes. Her head fell forward, then she flipped her hair out of her eyes. When she did, she saw Keith walk through the doorway of the office, a jeans jacket in one hand, his script in the other.

"Yes, I realize that I agreed to the reception, Mother... yes, yes. I realize that, too." Haley's gaze connected with Keith's, and she mouthed, "I'll be off in a sec." He nodded, then crossed to the sofa.

Haley's eyes followed him as her mother continued lecturing in her ear. There was a small tear at the shoulder seam of his Maverick jersey, she noted, and one of the maroon numbers was partially peeled off from too many washings. She glanced down at his athletic shoes... the same as the ones he'd worn for the cardboard cutout display that had left so very little to the imagination. Then her gaze drifted up to the back pockets of his snug-fitting, pepper-washed blue jeans. One pocket bulged slightly with what Haley assumed was his wallet. He chuckled quietly at something Brent said, then looked back over his shoulder at Haley, catching her inspection.

She cleared her throat and forced herself to look away. "What? I'm sorry, I didn't hear that last thing you... Right, you have a point... Yes, all right." She sighed again. "Yes, I'll be there."

Keith sat down next to Brent, watching as Haley spent the next few moments assuring her mother that she wouldn't back out of the reception at the last minute. She trudged back to the desk and hung up the phone, then dropped to her chair and looked up at the two men. Her eyes only briefly touched on Keith before skittering nervously to Brent.

Brent rose and walked to the desk, bracing both palms on the surface and leaning toward Haley. He spoke in a quiet voice, but Keith, pretending to skim his script, could make out the man's words clearly.

"Haley, you shouldn't go to that reception if you're not ready yet," he advised. "From what you've told me, I'm surprised your mother isn't more understanding. She should know how you feel about publicity."

Haley nodded, then glanced past Brent to her office door. She looked at the nameplate for several moments before saying, "But she's right. Handling publicity for this theater is part of my job. And we both know that my name will draw more attention from the local press than yours."

"But you don't want that."

"It's not my fondest wish, but I have to agree with my mother." She picked up a pencil and began tapping it on the desk. "I can't continue to allow one event from my past to rule the rest of my life."

Brent stood straight but kept his voice low. "I just hope it isn't too soon. I . . . care about you, Haley."

Keith frowned, wishing he could get a look at more than the back of Brent's head. He wanted to see the look in the man's eyes. Had he meant, *As your friend, I care about you, Haley?* Or did his remark have more significance than that? Keith didn't like the pause Brent had put before the word *care.*

"Thank you," Haley said. "But I'll never know if it's too soon until I face it, will I?"

Brent nodded. "I guess. Well, I'll get going." He picked up his briefcase and headed for the door.

"Sorry that took so long," Haley said to Keith as she gathered up her copy of the script, a pencil and a notepad. Her mind still on the conversation with her mother and Brent, she suddenly left the office without a word.

Keith frowned and stood. Where had she gone? Was he supposed to follow her? Wait here?

"Keith?" she called out from the hallway.

Keith went to the door. "Yes?"

"I want to go over this in the auditorium today."

"Oh, okay." He got his script and caught up with her.

"I mentioned that, didn't I?"

Keith smiled and shook his head.

"Oh, jeez." Haley rolled her eyes and pulled a set of keys from the pocket of her short denim skirt. Unlocking a set of wide double doors, she aimed a crooked grin over her shoulder at him. "You're going to wish you'd never signed that contract, Keith. Lots of the people you'll come across in this business are just like me. No left brains to speak of. Logic and organization are *not* our strong suits."

She shouldered open the doors and sashayed through the darkened backstage. Still smiling, Keith took the set of keys she'd left in the lock and followed her in.

The smell of paint and musty costumes was stronger here than in the hallway. Boxes and furniture, piled with small sets and coiled rope, lined the walls, forcing Keith to sidestep his way to the wings. A tall stool seemed to rise up out of nowhere, and Keith nearly tripped over it.

Haley flipped on a stage light that provided about enough illumination for the average bat to find its way around. "Keith, bring that stool to center stage, will you?"

He did as requested and set it down in the small circle of light, then climbed on, figuring Haley would watch from the audience as she'd done that first day. He'd figured wrong.

Her hand went to her hip, stretching her navy T-shirt taut across her breasts. It was the first time she'd worn anything quite so formfitting, and for a moment he was mesmerized.

"Hey, bud. Off my stool." She lightly swatted his thigh with the script.

"Oh, sorry," he said with a chuckle, hopping down.

When she boosted herself onto the stool, her skirt rode up her thighs a fraction. She hooked slim ankles around the stool's legs, and a tiny silver chain caught Keith's eye. A miniature silver charm dangled from her ankle bracelet, one that Keith couldn't quite make out.

His gaze rose, and Keith realized that he'd been caught, just as he'd caught her earlier in her office. Though the light was low, Keith thought he detected heightened color in her cheeks.

"I...want you standing today so we can, you know, work on...your body language, movement." She looked down at the script in her lap. "If your leg starts hurting, just tell me. We'll take a break."

"Right. Where do you want me?"

"Where you are is fine," she said, her voice a little breathless. "Now, the scene I want to tackle is the first one between you and your leading lady. This is going to be a tricky piece of business, Keith."

"How so?"

"The scene portrays an initial sexual attraction between your character and Sarah that overlays the dialogue and action. Ian scribbled a note on my copy of the script that you might be interested in."

Keith moved closer and glanced down at the page. In the margin were several notes to Haley. The one her finger pointed to read,

Highly charged sexual chemistry between characters vitally important here to lend realism in love scene later. Since Sarah adheres strictly to the mores of the day, most of this will be up to Keith's character.

Keith swallowed and felt the same attack of nerves he'd experienced the first time he'd come to the love scene in the script. He'd been assured that the scene would be tasteful and that the nudity was absolutely necessary to heighten the intensity between Sarah and his character. Still, he worried about this scene more than any other. "I, uh..." He exhaled a stream of air and chuckled wryly. "It'll be tricky, all right. I'm not looking forward to doing a love scene."

"You wouldn't be normal if you weren't nervous."

"Have you done love scenes before?"

She smiled. "You forget, I was on a soap. Lots of love scenes on soaps."

Keith knew it was crazy, but felt a twinge of jealousy, nonetheless. He visualized Haley in bed with any number of good-looking actors. He could even hear some faceless director giving instructions. *Put your hands in her hair ... stroke her hip ... pull her closer.*

Shoving his hands into the front pockets of his jeans, he paced several steps away from her. "How did you learn to get over the embarrassment? I mean, I haven't even done the scene yet and I'm already embarrassed."

"Well, the first thing you do is try not to work yourself into a lather before filming even begins." Haley hopped down off the stool. Keith heard her approaching footsteps echo through the auditorium, then felt her hand on his arm. "Relax, Keith. This is going to be difficult enough as it is."

"Okay," he said, but wondered how he was supposed to relax with her hand on his arm. When she dropped it and walked back to the stool, he breathed a quiet sigh of relief. Turning back to face her, he said, "So, what do we do first?"

Perched upon the stool again, she grinned and shot Keith a wicked look. "We get personal."

CHAPTER EIGHT

"PERSONAL?" he asked, then cleared his throat to rid his voice of its raspy sound. "How personal?"

Haley chuckled deep in her throat. "I'm sorry to laugh, but you're really cute when you're tense, you know?"

"Why, thank you so much," he said, grinning as he narrowed his eyes at her. "I can see you're going to be loads of help, coach."

Her laughter faded, but a smile lingered on her lips. "Getting personal *is* going to help you, believe it or not. Because the most basic thing about acting is that to understand the character that you're to portray, you have to understand yourself. *Your* emotions, *your* beliefs, *your* behavior."

His brow creased in a frown.

"Does that make you uncomfortable?"

"No, I think I understand myself pretty well. It's just that..."

"Just what?"

"Doesn't the 'know yourself' theory go against what we did yesterday? We spent the better part of the day analyzing the character, not me. Bringing me into the equation would only muck things up, wouldn't it?"

"No, no. You're the most important part of the equation," she said, then hopped down from the stool, pitching her script on the floor. She took quick steps toward him. "With every character you'll ever play, you'll draw from personal experience. For instance, you've never been married, have you?"

"No."

"But I'd be willing to bet that you've experienced some of the same emotions that a married man has experienced. Happiness, despair, frustration, jubilance. So even if you can't know exactly what it feels like to have made a lifetime commitment, you can honestly portray someone who has by drawing from your own personal storehouse of emotion. An acting coach of mine taught me the Stanislavsky theory. It's called the 'magic if.' He says that you, the actor, should call upon the power of your imagination by asking yourself what you would do if the events and circumstances in the play, or in this case the movie, were actually happening to you, not the character."

"The 'magic if,'" Keith murmured, liking the sound of it.

"Okay. Now I'll tell you how to use that theory to get through the love scene."

Had Haley been blind, she might not have noticed the quick change in Keith. He'd relaxed considerably as she'd explained techniques, but the mere mention of the love scene had him tensing up again. The man was an open book when it came to body language. His shoulders lifted and tightened, and his hands began nervously rubbing the tops of his thighs.

"Ah-ah-ah," she warned, knowing she'd have to keep the tone of the entire lesson light. "We're big people now. We know all about sex and can talk about it without having to spell words or use euphemisms, right?"

His masculine chuckle was deep.

"You think this is going to be easy for me?" she asked brightly. "I never liked doing love scenes myself, bud. And I'm supposed to teach you how? Think how embarrassed, how mortified, I'm going to be instructing you on— What?"

Keith was shaking his head. "You're a good actress, Haley, but you're not that good. No way am I falling for the old 'this is going to hurt me more than it hurts you' business."

"Was that what I was doing?" Her eyes were guileless, but she didn't stifle the laugh that bubbled up from her throat. "Okay, okay. You've got my number. This is going to be more embarrassing for you. I *have* been through it more than a few times."

"Yeah, you're the expert. So how do I get past the embarrassment?"

"You can't, really, Keith. Not completely, anyway. And it's going to be worse in this situation with Ian wanting Carolyn nude."

"You sound as though you don't approve."

"I don't. Mostly because Carolyn's so rattled about it."

Keith grimaced. "She is? I'd hoped that she was a veteran of this sort of thing and that would make it less awkward."

"Nope, Carolyn's no veteran. In fact, I was shocked when she told me about it. She's always been militant about gratuitous nudity."

"Gratuitous? The producers told me that Ian wouldn't use the footage if that were the case. You've read the script—what do you think?"

She shrugged. "I can't tell by simply reading the script. I'll have to see the scene first. And what's gratuitous to one person is absolutely necessary to the next. Besides, I'm biased. I've had to do love scenes. Never completely nude, but I've done them and..."

"Hated them, right?"

What Haley hated was that she'd allowed the conversation to take this path. How could this sort of talk help Keith? Sure, she was opposed to the nude scene, but directing the film wasn't her job. Teaching Keith was.

"No," she said, "I felt awkward, like you said. But I didn't hate them. I felt challenged, in fact. After all, we're talking about the physical manifestation of the most complex emotion of all."

"I never thought of it that way."

"But I'm right," she said, then strode over to him. She climbed back on the stool. "Let's work on the attraction scene first, then maybe start on the love scene. Let's try the 'magic if' and see if that'll help you."

"Okay." He was willing to try anything, even if this lesson was the death of him. Why couldn't Ian have found him a male acting coach? Or even a female coach he wasn't so... knocked out by.

"So," Haley said, crossing one beautifully shaped leg over the other, "if the 'magic if' technique says that you should imagine the events in the scene happening to you, and if expressing your character's inner emotions means drawing from your own ... then guess what we're going to have to do first?"

"Don't tell me," he said. "This is the part where we get personal."

"And they say jocks are slow."

Keith gave her a look of mock annoyance. "I've heard the same said of blondes."

She chuckled then, tucking a strand of her hair behind one ear as she paged through the script. She skimmed the scene, made a notation or two with the pencil she pulled from behind her ear, then looked up at Keith.

"All right. Let's jump right in. Tell me what you like. What's the first thing about a woman that attracts you? And if you say it's a woman's personality, I'm going to have to ask to see your tongue, Keith."

He smiled. "Nah, I won't lie about it. It's a woman's looks."

"More specific, please."

"More specific?" Keith squinted up at the dim stage light, trying to think. He'd never stopped to analyze his likes and dislikes this way. Besides, it was hard to remember specific likes and dislikes when his libido was otherwise occupied with Haley. "It's, uh, I mean, do you want to know features, body parts or what?"

Straight-faced, she answered, "I said the first thing that attracts you to a woman. With men, isn't that usually a body part?"

"Oh-ho. First it's jock bashing, now it's male bashing, huh?"

"Oh, I, um, could have phrased that better, I suppose. Okay, how about—" she tossed her head back, staring up at the light just as he had done "—since physical attributes are the first things on both men's and women's attraction lists, then yes, body parts are what I'm asking for. That better?"

"Yes, I think so. It's just that I don't really have a favorite... I do like certain... but..." He shook his head, then shrugged. "I know what you're trying to do, Haley. You're trying to build up my immunity to embarrassment, aren't you? You figure the more I talk about this stuff so... so clinically, the easier it'll be when the camera starts to roll."

"No, Keith," she said with a light laugh. "I'm really only trying to help. Look, I'll cut to the chase, okay?"

"Yeah, please."

"It always helped me to imagine that I was attracted to the actor I was playing opposite."

"The magic if."

"Exactly. Sometimes it was easy. Sometimes I was attracted to the actor. And sometimes if that wasn't the case, I'd choose something else about the man that I found... stimulating. His laugh, the sound of his voice, even the way he looked at me—my character, that is. So, in love scenes even more than other types

of scenes, the most important thing, again, is to..."
She rolled her wrist, beckoning him to complete the
sentence.

"Know yourself?"

"Yes. Right down to making up a laundry list of
favorite anatomical parts. Yes, it's clinical, but it's an
effective acting technique. And my theory's always
been, hey, whatever gets you through the scene."

Keith nodded. "All right, a list. I can do that."
Moments of silence passed while he thought. He stared
down at his sneakers, then up at the stage light again.
Finally he met her gaze. "With me, it's usually eyes
and mouths first, not necessarily in that order."

Haley blinked, a disbelieving half smile tilting one
corner of her mouth.

"No, really. I mean, I'm a normal healthy guy and
I appreciate a pretty body as much as the next man.
But eyes catch my attention first. You know, shape,
color—" he looked at hers "—how expressive they
are. Take yours, for example."

"Mine?"

"Yes. They caught my attention immediately. Their
color is...hard to describe. Green, but such a light
green, one you don't see very often. And I noticed how
expressive they were that first day. Your eyes are really beautiful."

Haley swallowed. "Thank you." She trained her
expressive light green eyes on a page of the script and
began to scribble. Keith heard her mumbling beneath
her breath, but couldn't make out the words.

"What did you say?"

She shook her head, her pencil still moving. How long did it take to write the words *eyes* and *mouth?* "Nothing," she said. "Just thinking out loud."

"Tell me."

Her shoulders lifted slightly, and she ducked her head. "It's just something I've noticed about you. I had you pegged for a...a leg man. It's just...something I noticed you doing, looking at my legs."

As her voice trailed off, Keith remembered his thoughts from earlier. It seemed to him that she was having as much trouble with this lesson as he was. Or was that simply wishful thinking on his part? His gaze dipped to the body part in question. If there was ever a pair of legs that could sway a man from other preferences, it was Haley's legs. "To be honest," he said, his eyes meeting hers, "I never thought of myself as a leg man until I saw yours."

His words hovered in the silence of the cavernous old auditorium, which almost seemed to be waiting for either of the two people on stage to make a sound...break eye contact...take a breath. They waited moments more. Moments while each struggled with an attraction that had nothing to do with characters in a script and everything to do with two real live people.

Haley's pulse thrummed in her neck. Her breathing grew shallow.

Keith's own pulse picked up speed, and he obliterated the distance between them with four slow steps. Possibilities chased through his mind as he lifted his hand to her face. Was it possible that something could develop from the spark of chemistry between them? Possible that two weeks might be stretched to a month, then longer? Possibilities and wishes and the look of awareness in her eyes made him ignore the voice in his head that warned him this was a line he shouldn't be stepping over.

"Keith, no," she objected. "This would cause problems... we can't—"

"Yeah," he agreed, his gaze on her mouth, "it would definitely cause problems."

Knowing that, but not caring, he kissed her. Once, then twice, his mouth covered hers with soft, butterfly caresses. He felt more than heard Haley's quick intake of breath.

He angled his head and kissed her again, both hands going to her shoulders. With this kiss, he lingered, learning the shape of her lips against his, glorying in the small moan from Haley as he deepened the kiss. He watched her lashes drop before shutting his own eyes and parting her lips with his tongue.

Haley's hands tightened on the script in her lap. *Problems. This will cause problems.* Those thoughts echoed somewhere in the outer reaches of her mind as, sightless, she breathed in Keith's clean scent, felt the wonderful pressure of his hands and knew the firm pressure and taste of the mouth that moved over hers so expertly.

Problems be damned, Haley thought as her insides became liquid. She didn't want the kiss to end. What she wanted, she realized as his large, warm hands slid into her hair, was for him to touch her more. She realized, with no small amount of panic, that she wanted to feel his hands, caressing, smoothing, brushing over her...

She broke the kiss, embarrassment flooding in. Oh, God, had her sex-deprived state caught up with her or what?

"Keith," she said, shaking her head.

"I... probably shouldn't have done that."

Glancing up, she noted his flushed skin, the serious look in his eyes. "Probably not," she agreed quietly.

"We have to work together."

"Yes. That's a... major concern."

"So why did I do it?" he wondered aloud, his hands still in her hair and his heart still tripping out a staccato beat.

"Same reason I didn't stop it, probably. Curiosity. Chemistry, maybe."

"Yeah." He heaved a loud sigh and stepped away, turning his back on her. He shoved his hands into the back pockets of his jeans. "But our curiosity is satisfied now, right?"

Haley focused on the small tear at the shoulder seam of his jersey. As her blood cooled, she told herself he was right. Curiosity was satisfied. With the kiss out of the way, she could go on with the lessons, secure in the fact that...what? That his mouth on hers had fired her senses and made her yearn for more? That his hands on her skin had made her melt?

Problems, she thought again. It had definitely caused problems.

"Right?" he asked again, this time more force-fully. He glanced over his shoulder at her.

"Right," she told him, grasping every bit of will-power she could.

LUNCH, AS IT HAD BEEN the day before, was spent in her office with a sandwich from home and a canned diet drink from the machine backstage. Keith had left ten minutes ago after shrugging into his faded denim jacket.

When she heard the back door to the theater close behind him, Haley rested her forehead on the desk, asking herself how the hell she was going to get through twelve and a half more days of this.

She picked up her sandwich and bit into it. What had possessed her to tell Keith she'd noticed his look-ing at her legs? Where had her mind been? If she'd just kept her mouth shut, there wouldn't be a problem. She groaned and tore off another bite.

Your eyes are really beautiful.

Pleasure stole over her again at the remembered compliment. Though it was unwise to do so, she in-dulged herself in recalling the expression in his eyes when he'd said it. It had been a long time between compliments from men. It had been a long time be-tween *men.*

Not that there'd been many for Haley. She had put her personal life on hold, promising herself the lux-ury of a serious relationship and commitment once she'd "made it." And since the shooting, she'd scaled her love life down even more, going from casual dates to no dates at all.

Two and a half years. No wonder Keith had affected her so strongly. Why, any man saying and doing what he had would have caused the same reaction.

No. The least Haley could do was be honest with herself, she thought, setting down the sandwich. There wouldn't be a problem if any other man had made those remarks, and she knew it. The problem was that Keith had made them.

KEITH HADN'T REALIZED how hungry he was until the wonderful mixture of aromas—burgers, onion rings and chili—met him at the door of Webers.

He stood in line and reached for a bottle of root beer, thinking of how nervous Haley had acted after he'd kissed her. She had tried her best to hide it, but Haley had been as edgy as he had been after their session on anatomy.

Yep, he'd screwed up, all right. By letting his libido act in his brain's stead, he could probably count on the same wonderfully tense atmosphere from here on out.

The line moved forward, and Keith moved with it. Now that he knew just how detrimental to his acting interests any kind of personal involvement with Haley could be, he knew what he had to do.

"HOW WAS LUNCH?"

"Great," Keith said, setting the bottle of root beer on her desk. He put his palm on the top of the bottle.

"This is for you. I found a place that sold great root beer."

"Oh...thank you. You didn't have to do that."

Keith nodded, not affected in the least by the pleased look in her eyes. He noticed the paperwork in front of her. "Do you need to finish that before we get started again?"

"Yes. It'll be just a few minutes. You can take a seat if you'd like," she offered, nodding toward the sofa.

"No, that's okay. I think I'll go back to the auditorium and go over the scene again before we do."

"Oh. That's...fine."

Keith took off his jacket and pitched it on the sofa. "'Kay. See you in a bit." He picked up his script and headed for the auditorium.

On stage, he walked to the stool and sat, then leafed through the script until he'd found the attraction scene. Eyes, he thought, and conjured up Carolyn's image. They'd been brown, hadn't they? Or were they blue?

God help him if they were green.

CHAPTER NINE

CAROLYN GAVE the long-distance operator her call-ing-card number and was thanked for using AT&T. Even before the phone in the condo she shared with Jonathan had a chance to ring, she was chewing her bottom lip and feeling her stomach knot up with nerves.

One ring.

This was crazy. No matter what Haley said, Caro-lyn wasn't prepared to tell Jonathan about the nude scene.

Two rings.

She prayed he wasn't there. It was seven-thirty Oklahoma time, five-thirty in California. If luck were hers, he was still on the freeway, or better yet, he hadn't even left the bank.

Three rings.

The *bank!* Jonathan was a banker, for God's sake! He was never going to understand this! And wouldn't it just do wonders for his reputation at work? It was bad enough that he was living with an actress. He never complained about that, but—

Four rings.

Good, he wasn't there. She'd just wait for the ma-chine to pick up, and she'd leave a message. They would play telephone tag for the next day or so while she came up with the right words.

Five rings. Click. "I'm sorry, neither Carolyn nor Jonathan can come to the phone right now. Please leave a message at the tone."

"Yes!" Carolyn said, then noticed a man frowning at her from three phones down. She doused her smile and faced the pay phone. Coward that she was, she'd chosen to place the call at a phone bank in the hotel lobby. That way she could plead "no privacy" to Jonathan if the conversation began to get heavy.

Beep.

"Hi, honey. It's just me, checking in. I hate that I didn't catch you at home. Guess I'll just talk to—"

A familiar mechanical rattle cut into Carolyn's message, and she shut her eyes. *Oh, no,* she thought, holding in a groan and tightening her stranglehold on the phone.

"Carolyn? Carolyn, don't hang up!" She heard Jonathan's deep chuckle. "I . . . just got home . . . was coming up the walk when I heard . . . the phone."

Carolyn pictured him leaning against the wall beside the kitchen phone, and a shaft of pleasure broke through her panic. She could see his loosened tie, the briefcase at his feet and the suit jacket hooked over one finger. Suits . . . who would've thought that Carolyn would fall so hard for a man who wore suits. "Jeez, Mr. Drysdale," she said, affection making her voice wobble, "you sound like you *ran* all the way from work."

"Nope." He laughed at the nickname she'd stuck him with when she'd first heard what he did for a living. "Just didn't want to miss your call. God, it's good to hear your voice. It's so damn quiet around here."

Her throat tightened. *I miss you, too.*

"I'm gonna remind you of that the next time you run for the volume control on the CD player," she warned playfully. "You, uh, know how you hate it when I play Van Halen at full blast."

"Caro, I miss you so much I don't care if you book Van Halen in our living room for their next concert! When will you come home, sweetheart? Do you have any idea?"

How she loved it when he called her Caro. "Jonathan, I've been gone less than a week. Filming hasn't even started yet."

"What? Why not?" His disappointment was evident, but Carolyn also heard anger.

"Just a delay, honey," she said. "Delays are part and parcel of this business—you know that."

"Yes, I know," he said wearily. "I was just hoping that a miracle might happen and you'd get to come home earlier than you expected. I don't like being separated from you. I'm…not used to it. And I don't want to get used to it."

"Jonathan," she said, irritated that this subject never seemed to die, "we've talked about this before. Separations are going to come more frequently if I have any say in the matter. And not because I want to be apart from you. I want more movies, bigger parts, more exposure." She winced at the word she'd chosen, then rubbed her forehead with her free hand. "I...just wish you could understand. I love you, but—"

"Don't do that, Carolyn." There was a prickly edge to his voice.

"Do what?"

"Qualify your 'I love you's.' I never hear 'I love you' from you anymore. It's always, 'I love you, Jonathan... *but*.' That hurts, Carolyn. I have a place in your life just as long as I'm careful not to crowd the more important part—your career."

Carolyn bit her lip. Their relationship, which had been so good for the first year, had been on shaky ground for the past six months. And she was to blame. Jonathan's banking hours never intruded on their time together. *His* ambition wasn't an issue.

She sighed loudly, dreading his reaction to her newest career move more than she dreaded the nude scene itself. "I'm sorry. I know my career gets in the way of our relationship, but it's...it's who I am, Jonathan. You fell in love with me knowing that."

"Carolyn," he said, the restraint in his voice obvious, "acting is a job. Just like banking. It's no more who you are than banking is who I am." There was a pause. Knowing him as well as she did, she could picture his taking a deep breath and rubbing his closed eyes with the pads of two fingertips. "And yes, your career gets in the way of our relationship, but you might be surprised to know why."

"Why?"

"Not because of the time it takes you away from me, but because it's taking you over, Carolyn."

"Oh, please!" An older couple turned to stare as they walked by. Carolyn lowered her voice. "Jonathan, that's ridiculous. Before you get too deep into your 'pod person' argument, I'll thank you to remember that I've been in this business since I was a kid. I'm no different now than I was as a six-year-old doing commercials with my parents, maybe just a bit more ambitious."

"And this is a healthy thing? You've struggled for too many years, but now when you're finally making a good living, when you're at the point where most people are scaling down and thinking of marriage and families, you're scaling up. You're damn right, I don't understand."

Marriage. Family.

It always came down to that. Carolyn silently cursed her bad luck. In Jonathan, she'd found a man who loved her and wanted marriage and babies. She'd just found him at the wrong time.

"I . . . can't talk about this right now," she said, realizing that she hadn't told him about the scene, but knowing this was no time to break that kind of news.

"Carolyn, we have to talk about—"

"I just can't! Okay? I love you, Jonathan. But . . ." Oh, God, she'd done it again. "I'll call you soon."

"Yeah. Okay." He sounded tired, defeated. "If that's the way you want it, I'll talk to you, then."

Carolyn cradled the receiver, an ache spreading through her chest. An ache that she knew would only intensify as another night without Jonathan dragged its way into tomorrow. What a predicament she'd found herself in. She was on the verge of success in a career for which she had fought like a tiger. Then there was Jonathan. Sensitive, loving, wonderful Jonathan. Sexy Jonathan. *Conservative* Jonathan.

Oh, Mr. Drysdale, she thought, feeling tears threaten. *How the hell are you going to handle seeing me nude on the screen? And how the hell am I going to handle losing you?*

KEITH PASSED over the small Indian tom-toms and red felt cowboy hats, visualizing his poor sister tied to a post and at the mercy of the twins. He nixed the beaded necklaces and tin sheriff badges, predicting how short their life spans would be after the hellions got hold of them. The moccasins were cute, but Angie had told him that the boys were going through a hate-to-wear-shoes stage.

He was on the verge of giving up on souvenir shopping when he saw the sweatshirts. Nostalgia hitched the corners of his mouth into a smile, and he picked up one of the small crimson shirts, shaking out the folds. The words Oklahoma Sooners barely fit across the front. A perfect gift from Uncle "Keef," he decided—matching sweatshirts from his and Angie's alma mater.

He picked out two size fours, then couldn't resist adding miniature Sooner footballs from the next bin. Before he could get to the hotel gift shop's cash register, a man two aisles away came striding toward him.

"You're Keith Garrison! Man, I love the Mavericks."

"Thanks." Keith dragged out the polite smile he reserved for fans, then shifted his nephews' gifts to one arm and shook the man's outstretched hand.

"Boy, oh, boy, the season the Mavs are havin' this year! I'll bet you miss it, huh?"

"Sometimes." Normally Keith wouldn't have minded talking football with a fan. Normally the fact that the fans spoke to you as though they knew you personally wouldn't have been annoying, but he was dead tired this evening. And not in the most charitable of moods. Unlike yesterday, when the hard work had psyched him up, Keith had a headache from the tension that had yet to dissolve between Haley and him. Added to that, his leg ached. Still, he listened as attentively as possible while the man gave a play-by-play critique of the previous weekend's Maverick game.

"Well, better pay for these," Keith said when he finally found the chance, glancing down at the shirts and balls. "It's always nice to meet a fan."

"Oh, hey, it's great to meet *you!* Listen, could I get an autograph? For my son, Andy," the man said before Keith could get away.

"Yeah, sure." Keeping the smile in place, Keith signed the back of a business card he was handed. "There you go." He gave it back to him.

"Thanks. Really good to meet you, Keith."

"You, too."

Moments later he was at the cash register and the salesclerk was ringing up his purchases. He felt a tap on his shoulder and heard a woman squeal, then say, "Keith Garrison! Are you *the* Keith Garrison?"

He closed his eyes briefly, dragged out the same smile and turned. He rolled his eyes and chuckled when he saw who the woman was.

"Hey, Carolyn," he said, the smile becoming genuine.

"Oh, please," she said, pretending to swoon, "please, please, can I have your autograph!"

"Cut it out," he said with another chuckle. "What are you up to?"

"I was out making a call in the lobby when I saw you in here. It was a perfect opportunity to be nosy, so I sneaked in when you were busy signing the man's business card."

"Perfect opportunity to be nosy?"

"Um-hmm. Come on," she said, taking his arm. "Let's go get some coffee."

"Okay."

After the salesclerk had bagged his items, they crossed the lobby. Carolyn led him into the bar.

"I thought you wanted coffee," Keith said, placing his bag on a chair at the table she'd chosen. He sat in the seat next to her and propped his aching leg on the chair opposite him.

"I hope you don't mind, but I need something a little stronger than that."

"Don't mind at all," he said, then studied her as the waitress took their orders, coffee for him, a mixed drink for her. For the first time he noticed that her eyes looked tired and her manner wasn't as bright as it had been yesterday.

"So," Keith said when their waitress had left, "what did you want to know?"

Carolyn shrugged, not meeting his gaze. "I was just going to poke my nose into your progress with the lessons."

"Well, it's only been a couple of days, but I've learned a lot. You were right about Haley. She's no slouch."

Carolyn's eyes brightened momentarily, and her mouth curved upward. "She's a little dynamo. Ask any of our old gang. She was always in the library, researching characters or time periods, always taking another acting course. That's the reason Ian hired her for you, you know. She knows more about the craft, more about our business, than any drama coach on the Coast." Carolyn looked down at her hands. "You must have seen some of Haley's work. She won a daytime Emmy, you know. Ever catch her on the soap?"

"No. As a matter of fact, I only found out she'd been on a soap yesterday. I was watching one of those tabloid news shows—they did a report on stalkers."

Carolyn's brow creased, and she continued staring at her hands as the waitress came with their drinks then left. "I wonder when they'll ever get tired of doing that story," she said.

"Probably when the public gets tired of hearing it. I watched it because the same thing happened to a friend of mine."

Carolyn looked up. "Who...? Wait a minute, you were friends with the football player? Griff somebody...?"

"Patterson. He was a teammate of mine. He's still picking up the pieces," Keith said in a quiet voice.

Keith thought of Haley as he took a sip of his coffee. Though it was probably unwise, he couldn't fight down the need to ask more. "Did they just stop offering her parts or something, Carolyn? I mean, it's so hard to understand why a person with her talent..."

"Yeah, I know," she said, sighing and twirling her swizzle stick. "I don't understand it completely myself. She still had lots of offers and he's locked away, right? And what are the chances that lightning will strike twice, that some other nut case will come after her?" She took a swallow of her drink, then set it back on the napkin, taking pains to center it on the ring of moisture it had left behind. "But the shooting wasn't the only thing involved in Haley's decision to give it all up. She would probably deny it, but she was fighting an internal battle between what she wanted and what her family wanted for her from the day I met her." She looked across the room, watching a young couple who entered the room and took seats at the bar. "A more uppity collection of characters you'll never meet, Keith. They were appalled, simply appalled, that their daughter would choose a profession like *acting*—" she made a sour face and lifted her nose in the air "—over being heir to the respectable family hotel fortune."

"You're kidding."

"Not even a little." She swirled the swizzle stick again. "She never heard a word of encouragement, never got an ounce of support from them. They were always quick with the 'I told you so's,' though. It got to the point that Haley stopped telling them about the parts she'd auditioned for." She shook her head again. "Family's where you go when you've scraped your knees and need a hug to make it better. Haley finally learned that there would be no hugs, no sympathy. Only recriminations."

Keith raised his mug to his lips thoughtfully. It was hard to imagine what Haley's situation must have been like for her. His family had always been in his corner, whether they agreed or disagreed with whatever path he'd chosen.

"The shooting was the final straw for Haley," Carolyn said, reaching up to toy with one of the colorful, jangly earrings she wore. "Her family had been telling her for years that she'd picked the wrong profession. And though she would try to block that out, their lesson came home to her every time she was turned down for a part. Rejection is Hollywood's number-one export—that and ten-minute marriages. No one escapes it completely."

She frowned into her drink, then tilted the glass for another swallow. "When Wharton showed up at her door with his obsession and a gun in his hands, a new ingredient was added to the formula. Danger. All of a

sudden ours wasn't merely a crazy business to be in—
it was a dangerous business to be in. Worse, Wharton
wasn't locked away in prison. He was put in a mental
institution where the possibility of getting out quicker
is greater. Where he could continue to write his letters."

"He's still writing her?"

"Righteo. My agent is Haley's former agent, and he
tells me Wharton's still sending letters to the agency.
After Haley was shot, they hired a detective firm that
specializes in stalker cases to protect her and all of
their other clients. These guys analyze Wharton's letters, keep the agency informed of any changes in his
mental state, and they'll make sure Haley's informed
if the guy somehow escapes or gets out earlier than
expected."

"It's good to know that somebody's taken some
action." With Griff all of the grief was compounded
by the police's inability to do anything until the
woman had actually committed a crime. Maybe things
were changing for the better.

Carolyn shrugged. "Too little, too late, for Haley."

"Do you think she'll ever go back? Maybe the lure
will prove too strong."

"Ian's theory is that she will."

"Ian?"

"He was her first director on 'Forever.' He says the
job at TAT is only the first step." Her smile was cagey.
"And don't think for a minute that he's not trying to
manipulate the situation a bit himself. First and fore-

most he hired her to coach you because of her skill. But he had another motive.''

"Trying to ease her back into the business, is he?'' Keith asked with a grin.

Carolyn chuckled. "And Ian always gets his way. That's the hallmark of a good director. I've seen him make some of the most inflated egos in Hollywood think that they'd won their arguments when all along Ian had wanted it that particular way.''

Keith wondered if he should bring up the love scene that Ian was so adamant about. The nudity did not sit well with Carolyn. Or himself. Feeling tense, he shifted in his chair and glanced around the dimly lit bar. "Something wrong?'' Carolyn asked.

His gaze shifted to her, then fell away. "I was thinking about . . . the love scene.'' He looked her way again, noting the flicker of emotion in her eyes. "Looks like Ian's going to get his way on that, too.''

"There was never any doubt about that,'' she said. "But, hey—'' she flipped her palms in the air "—what're you gonna do, right? We either do the scene or let someone else pick up our paychecks.''

That was putting it in a nutshell. But her attitude didn't help untie the knots in Keith's stomach. "Haley's trying to help, but . . .''

"But you're still nervous about it? That's normal. No amount of coaching's going to help you overcome all the nerves.'' She covered his hand with hers and gave him a smile. "We'll get through it, Keith. We'll just close our eyes and think of England.''

He chuckled. "You don't seem as upset about it as Haley said you were."

She withdrew her hand. "Haley said I was upset?"

"Was that something I shouldn't have said?"

"Oh, no..." She shook her head and shrugged. "It's just that I think Haley's more upset about it than I am. Not that I look forward to it. Love scenes are awkward, and this one... Well, the nudity will make it worse. But Haley feels I'm all riled up about it, when I'm only...a little less relaxed than I would be with any other scene."

Keith eyed her closely, noting that Carolyn put a little too much effort into downplaying her anxiety. "Well, good. It's a relief to know you're more relaxed than I am. I mean, at least one of us won't be terrified."

She placed her hand over his again. "Terrified, Keith? Are you really?"

He grinned. "Well, maybe that's putting it too strongly. But I'll tell you this, I think I'd rather play football with my bum leg than do this love scene."

Silence took over, and Keith reached for his coffee. He peered over the mug at Carolyn, wondering at the thoughtful expression she wore. She tapped her fingertips against her now-empty glass and looked him over as if he were a perplexing algebraic formula.

"What?" he asked, lowering the mug.

"I'm...just surprised. When we first met I...well, this is going to sound awfully 'California'...but I got these vibes from you."

"What do you mean, 'vibes'?"

"Maybe that's not quite the term I'm looking for, but..." She waved a hand and tossed her head, her black hair brushing her shoulders. "It doesn't matter, anyway. I might have been wrong."

"Wrong about what?" She eyed him with obvious reluctance, and he prodded, "Come on. What?"

"Well, I just...felt something in the air between us. Didn't you?" She plucked the swizzle stick from her drink and twirled it between her thumb and forefinger, then caught his gaze with hers. A slow, sensual smile inched across her mouth. "Tell the truth. You did, too, didn't you, Keith?"

Astonishment stole his voice. *She'd felt something in the air between them?* He remembered her being flirtatious that day, but he'd taken it in the spirit that he'd thought was intended. Playfulness. Tongue in cheek.

He swallowed. "Well, actually, I didn't—"

"Oh, come on, Keith," she said, her laugh low and husky...sexy. "Let's get this out in the open. I'm not saying anything is going to come of it, but we can at least be honest with each other, can't we?"

"Oh, well...yes. Honesty is—" His gaze shot to the fingertip she placed on his wrist. Swallowing hard again, he glanced back up.

"Important. Vitally important, Keith."

"Carolyn, I..." He shook his head, wondering how on earth to explain he wasn't attracted to her without looking like a jerk. He liked this woman. He looked forward to working with her. But he didn't feel the chemistry, the "vibes," that she obviously felt. If only the situation were reversed and Haley was the one playing his leading lady, and Carolyn was his coach! "I . . . don't know what to say."

"Let me say it, then."

"No. I don't think it would be a good idea to—"

She held on to his wrist when he tried to slide it away. "Just relax, okay? I'm not going to throw you to the floor and have my way with you right here in the Riverton bar." Her eyes twinkled with amusement even as they smoldered with sensuality. "Actors always fall just a little bit in lust with their leading man or lady. I've seen it happen over and over again in this business. Sometimes relationships grow out of that attraction, sometimes the couple has a short-lived fling." Her eyes dropped to his wrist, and one finger softly rubbed his skin.

"I'm very attracted to you, Keith."

He tensed when her hand moved from his wrist up his arm. She stopped at the edge of the jersey's sleeve, hesitated a fraction of a second, then slipped two fingers under the hem. With a circular motion, she softly caressed him again, her eyes locked on his. Another finger burrowed under the sleeve.

He clamped a hand over hers. "Carolyn, I . . . I just . . ."

She scooted her chair closer to him, leaned closer. Her scent was breezy and fresh. "What, Keith? Stop shaking your head and tell me what."

"I'm just not—"

Her hand moved beneath his, and Keith closed his eyes in misery.

"Haley told me you're a better actor than she expected, Keith. Has she told you that I'm a good actress?"

"Yes," he managed.

"Then you shouldn't worry so much about the love scene, should you? It's make-believe," she said in a sultry whisper. "Just like the conversation we're having right now."

His eyes popped open. Stunned for the second time since they'd come to this bar, he watched openmouthed as she sat straight and pulled her hand from under his sleeve and the expression in her eyes went from smoky and passionate to...well, to platonic. "You mean...you're not... You were only..."

She winked at him and put her hands in the air as if to say "Ta-da!" "Acting. But I made you believe, didn't I?"

"Made me believe?" He barely restrained himself from getting out of his chair and strangling her. "What you did was scare the sh—"

"Now, now, Keith. I didn't mean to scare you. I meant to show you that I know how to turn it on or off in the blink of an eye. From what Haley's said, I know that you'll be able to, too. For your sake *and* mine, don't work yourself into a lather over this scene before we even get in front of the cameras. Just remember that it's make-believe. You and I are going to make an audience *believe* that we're hot for each other."

Keith half groaned, half laughed, and rubbed a hand over his face. "I'm not *believing* what just went on here."

"Oh, but you did." She pushed her chair back, chuckling as she stood. "I pulled you in just as surely as the two of us will pull in the audience, big guy. Bank on it."

She bent and gave him a chaste kiss on the cheek. "I gotta go. You relax, all right? And ask Haley to tell you about a technique called the 'magic if.'"

"She already has."

She nodded. "Good. You know, you're in awfully good hands, Keith. She'll teach you all you need to know."

CHAPTER TEN

Dear Sabrina,

It wasn't you! Goddammit, why wasn't it you? The ad said you were coming back to 'Forever and a Day,' but it was a lie, wasn't it? How could you lie like that! You're not stupid, Sabrina. You had to have known what this kind of deception would do to me! You had to have realized that seeing another person in your place would tear me to shreds! But you went along with the deception, anyway. You purposely hurt me!

I won't believe that you're innocent in this. You could've stopped them from doing it. It's as if you want me to get angry again. You want me to hurt like I did before when you never answered my letters. Well, you should be careful for what you wish for, Sabrina. You might just get it.

Jack

HE THREW THE PEN across the room and buried his face in his hands, the echoes of the other patients' jeers and laughter still in his ears.

He'd been so happy about seeing Sabrina again that he'd told them all about her and him. He'd told them that she loved him and had come back on 'Forever' just for him. Only when her show had aired, it hadn't been her. A few of the others had known it was a different Sabrina. They'd laughed at him. Humiliated him.

Dammit, he wouldn't stand for any more humiliation!

He stored the letter containing his true feelings with all the others, then pulled out a clean sheet of paper. Now was not the time to let his anger interfere with his plans to get out of this place. Retrieving the pen he'd thrown, he started the letter he would send to the agency, the letter that would be returned here for the doctors to evaluate.

A FROWN FURROWED James's brow when he spotted Keith Garrison walking through the lobby in the direction of the elevators. Haley had assured him that for the past two weeks she had merely been giving the man acting lessons, but James couldn't help being disturbed by the man's involvement in his sister's life right now. It was one thing when Haley had left the hotel to work in local theater, but it was an entirely different and dangerous matter for her to be involved in movie work again. God, he didn't want her going back. And if it was in his power to do something about it...

"Mr. Garrison," he shouted, striding quickly to catch up to the man. Garrison stopped, looking in James's direction.

"Hello." James took the last few steps and held out his hand. Garrison shook it, curiosity shading his eyes.

"I'm James Riverton, the general manager here. Just wanted to meet my celebrity guest."

"Oh, yes. Riverton. You're Haley's brother. Good to meet you."

"You, too," he said, smiling politely yet feeling anything but. The man's good looks added to James's uneasiness. He hoped his sister wasn't attracted to the tall, dark and physical type. "You're going to be in town for what... a month or so?"

"More like three or four," Keith answered, wondering why it was of interest to Riverton how long he'd be in Tulsa. When he saw the man's smile slip a bit, Keith's curiosity was stoked. "Why do you ask?"

"Oh, just a bit of brotherly concern, I guess. Haley's schedule at the theater is pretty full as it is. With the lessons she's giving you... Well, I only hope she hasn't taken on more than she can handle." He gave Keith a pointed look. "I'm sure you can understand that I worry about her."

Keith remembered what Carolyn had said about Haley's family having been so adamantly opposed to her career. Was her brother worried about *her*, Keith wondered, or worried more that she was associating with the wrong people... actors? Knowing how much damage her family's "nose in the air" attitude had done in the past, Keith felt the need to take the man down a notch or two.

"Sure, I understand. After what happened to her, you'd rather Haley have as little to do with someone like me as possible, am I right?"

"Well...yes." James's smile brightened. "It's nothing personal, but—"

"Oh, hey," Keith interrupted, giving a false smile and clapping James on the shoulder, "I won't take it personally. Because I don't intend to stay away from your sister."

"But...you..." James sputtered.

"Look, I have a sister, too, Riverton. Mine taught me the difference between 'brotherly concern,' as you call it, and sticking my nose in where it doesn't belong. What you're doing with Haley falls into the second category."

James narrowed his eyes. "You don't know what you're talking about. Her safety is of utmost importance to me. I'm only trying to protect her from having to face the same ordeal again."

"Protect? Or smother? Take my advice, James. You're going to lose her completely if you don't back off."

Moments later, on the elevator, Keith grimaced as he thought about the exchange with James. He probably could have handled that better. He probably shouldn't have been so blunt. But, dammit, didn't Haley have enough on her plate right now without her brother trying to control her life?

She'd certainly been anxious enough today during his lesson. The reception that was being held for TAT tonight had had her in a state. So much so that Keith had wanted to tell her that he would take her to the thing, stay by her side the entire time and use the blocking techniques that the Mavericks' defensive squad was famous for against reporters.

But Keith wasn't going to show up at that reception. No way, no how. It didn't matter that he had an engraved invitation that she'd given him in his hip pocket. It didn't matter that he'd fantasized all the way home in the car about what Haley would wear tonight, how she would look in a dress similar to the one she'd worn in that publicity still. What mattered was that he have as little contact with her outside the lessons as possible.

When the elevator doors opened onto his floor, it occurred to Keith that his decision not to go would please James Riverton no end.

He didn't kid himself that James's disapproval was the only reason that he punched the Lobby button and went in search of a tuxedo-rental shop.

JAMES SNAGGED Haley's arm and dragged her away from the array of silver chafing dishes and platters.

"James . . ." she sputtered, a half-eaten chocolate-dipped strawberry poised inches from her lips.

"I want you to meet Mr. and Mrs. Van Deventer. They're big patrons of the arts."

"Mmm," she said, nodding as she finished off the fruit. She looked up at him as they walked. "Yes, good idea."

James stopped, shaking his head as he slipped a silk handkerchief out of his pocket. He glanced around and, shielding her body with his, dabbed at the melted chocolate on one corner of Haley's mouth. "Gypsies left you on the Riverton doorstep,'' he stated with a chuckle.

''That's what I've always thought.''

He tucked the handkerchief back into his pocket and continued across the ballroom floor, his arm looped through hers as he led her along.

A half hour later, after meeting and talking about the theater with several more couples like the Van Deventers, Haley spotted Dennis O'Kane and his wife across the room. She turned to James. ''You haven't met the owner of the theater yet, have you?''

''No, but I'd like to.''

''Then come on.''

This time Haley led. Her confidence had grown since the reception had begun, and she was aware of something she hadn't noticed about her situation. She was finding a place for herself in the city she'd grown up in. Though she had come back with no prospects for satisfying work, for friends ... for happiness, she was definitely on her way to finding those things. How did the old saying go? God never closes a door but that he opens a window? She'd lost so much when she'd been attacked, but she'd been slowly getting some of it back. Her job was fulfilling. She was meeting new people through the theater. And she couldn't deny that she was happy about the chance to patch things up with her family.

As they neared Dennis and his wife, Haley's gaze was caught by a wide set of shoulders several feet away. She did a double take, also noticing that the man—his back was to her—had thick, straight, russet colored hair. He was tall, muscular and—her eyes slid down to his right hand—was wearing a Super Bowl ring. Inexplicably her heart beat faster.

"See someone you know?"

Haley looked from Keith to her brother. She hadn't realized she'd stopped walking until he'd spoken. "Uh, yes. I think so."

James looked at Keith. "I met him this afternoon," he mentioned, nodding at Keith. "Your football player."

"*My* football player? He's not *my* anything, James. And he doesn't play football anymore. He acts. I'm just giving him acting lessons." Haley wasn't comfortable with the defensive tone she'd used.

"*Your* acting student, then."

"Well, only for a few more days."

"Oh." James tugged at her arm. "Come on. Introduce me to the O'Kanes."

Ten minutes later Haley excused herself and left James with Dennis, his wife, Jobeth, and two other couples who'd joined the group. She told her brother that she wanted to rustle up a drink and maybe sample a few more of the hors d'oeuvres, but that had been less than the truth. The whole truth was that Keith Garrison's presence at the reception was distracting her.

She'd thought the chances of his actually taking her up on the invitation were slight. And she was a little uneasy with her reaction upon seeing him. Her heartbeat had done a positively strange quickstep.

She'd merely been surprised, she told herself. Surprised that Keith would want to spend a Friday night at a fussy black-tie reception. He'd been knocking himself out during their past week together. Haley assumed he'd want to get together with some of the cast members he'd mentioned meeting and go to a sports bar or somewhere similar to relax.

She surveyed the room that was now filled with guests, but didn't see him. He'd probably left, she decided. This type of get-together couldn't be fun for him. Whom would he know here? What would he have to talk about with these people?

Those, of course, were ridiculous questions, and Haley knew it. It wasn't a matter of whom *he* would know. It was a matter of who would know him. The answer to that was ninety percent of the people here. Football fans came from every echelon of society in this country; there would be as many at this party as at a sports bar, most likely. And Oklahomans in particular, she knew, were serious about the sport. Hadn't he been surrounded by a group of people when she'd spotted him earlier?

She accepted a glass of champagne from a waiter and edged her way toward the strawberries again. After dipping three of them in chocolate and arranging them on a small glass plate, she raised one to her lips.

"You must *really* love strawberries."

Haley nearly bit her tongue. She swallowed quickly, then swiveled to find him standing close behind her.

"Keith."

Her breath caught in her throat, and she edged backward two steps. If he'd proved to be a distraction wearing wash-faded jeans and an old football jersey, he was absolutely stunning in a tuxedo. Exquisitely tailored, the black coat hugged his broad shoulders and set off the snowy white shirt beneath it attractively. His ruddy complexion was a wonderful contrast to the shirt. "You . . . surprised me."

"No. This is surprising," he said, pointing to her plate. "How many of those are you going to leave for the rest of us?"

She grinned without a smidgen of guilt. "Are you, uh, enjoying the reception?"

"Um-hmm," he said, raising one of her strawberries to his lips. Haley's gaze followed his hand to his mouth. Distractedly she noticed that his cuff links were onyx.

"How 'bout you?"

"Oh, yes." She looked out over the large turnout. "It was silly to dread it so much, I guess."

"Not really. Not if you feel you had a good reason to."

Haley caught sight of a cameraman for a local TV station. He was across the room, panning the crowd with his camera, the bright light catching Tulsa's high society for this evening's late news. She tried to ignore a flutter of uneasiness and glanced up at Keith. "I thought I did, but it's . . . time to move past all that."

Keith nodded, his every instinct telling him he'd been crazy to come to this reception. Just now when she'd looked at him with that hint of fear in her eyes, his protective instincts had flared. When he'd first laid eyes on her this evening other, more elemental, instincts had been at work. The instinct to snatch her from her brother's arm, for example. The instinct to lead her out of this ballroom to somewhere private. The instinct to repeat the kiss in the auditorium, and more. . . .

God, she was beautiful. She'd left her hair down, the waves in such gorgeous disarray that he wanted to tangle his fingers in it. Her eyes were more intensely green tonight because of the splashes of sparkling emerald in the dress she wore.

He'd been crazy to come, all right. And he was even crazier to stay. But he didn't move toward the door.

"I met the theater owner," he said, grasping for small talk as he watched Haley sip from her glass of champagne.

"You did?"

Keith nodded. "He says you two went to prep school together."

"Yes, we were old drama buddies."

Two people approached the buffet, their eyes on the strawberries. "Excuse us," Keith said, and placed a hand at the small of Haley's back, guiding her away from the food. The satin fabric of her dress felt slick and cool against his fingers. "I know you have hostess duties, but would you mind sitting with me at one of the tables for a few minutes? This bum leg of mine is acting up."

"Oh, of course. You should have said something sooner, Keith."

They cut through the throng of people, Haley chatting with and smiling at guests along the way. She kept the conversations short, hurrying toward an empty table. She pulled out a chair for Keith. "Here, sit down," she ordered.

He sent her a wry look. "It's aching a little, coach. I'm not an invalid yet."

"Oh, just sit down. Do you need another chair to prop it up on?"

"Yes, but I can get it." He sat, then deftly inched another chair closer with the toe of one shiny black shoe.

"You look as if you've done that a few times." Haley lowered herself to a chair next to him, noticing how his jaw clenched. She glanced down and caught his hand slipping under the table and going to the top of his thigh. He slid it to his knee, then massaged it.

"Yeah," he said, his eyes telling her he was in more pain than he would admit to. "I've got the maneuver down pat."

Haley thought of the pace she had set for him over the past week, of the dark smudges under his eyes she'd noticed when he came to the theater each morning. Had that added stress caused him physical pain, as well? she wondered guiltily.

"You know, maybe I've been pushing you too hard this week, Keith."

"No. I can handle it."

"But, your leg... You don't want to put yourself out of commission before filming starts."

"Is this the same woman who told me her lessons would make summer football camp seem like just that . . . camp?" he asked with a grin.

"Yes, but I meant mentally. I didn't think about how that might affect you physically."

"Here," Keith said, sliding her champagne glass toward her. "Wash the guilt down with this."

Haley grinned, then lifted the glass to her lips.

"Do you hear me complaining? You've taught me more in two weeks than I could have learned in six months from anyone else."

Haley shook her head, her lips still curved in a smile. "Thanks, but you're going to find there are plenty of good acting coaches on either coast who can take up where I'll leave off."

None that he wanted, Keith thought. He wanted Haley. He'd been thinking about the need for a drama coach after he finished the movie, but his mind had balked at the idea of being coached by anyone but her. He realized he was intrigued with her on a personal level, but he also appreciated her expertise. And they worked well together. An idea suddenly formed in his mind, and he was surprised he hadn't thought of it before. "I don't want another coach. Why should I even look for someone to take up where you leave off when I already know how good *you* are?"

She sputtered out a laugh. "You can't honestly want to continue with me after the film wraps."

"And why not?"

"Well . . . because, that's why." Flustered, she glanced from his glass to hers and back again. "Because I'm in Oklahoma and you'll be in California, for one thing. Travel expenses and schedules alone—"

"Who says I'll be in California? I have a ranch outside San Antonio." Keith's excitement with the idea grew as the details took shape in his mind. "If I'm lucky enough to get film work after this movie, I'll spend part of my time on location and the rest of it in Texas. That's only one state away from you."

Only one state away. Haley hadn't dared to think past their last day together. He'd be going his way, and she'd be staying here. What more was there to think about? Admittedly she had imagined what their relationship might have been had they met when she was still in the business; her thoughts had strayed in that direction several times, in fact. But she'd certainly never entertained thoughts of continuing as teacher and pupil.

Only one state away. Haley stared at him for long moments, thrown off guard by the glint of intensity in his eyes. "You're...serious about this."

"Yes. It makes as much sense for me to hire you as my private coach as hiring someone in California or New York. I'd be paying travel expenses in any case, wouldn't I?"

"Well, yes...But I don't think—"

"Don't say no until you've had a chance to really think it over, okay?" He covered her hand with his, creating an instant warmth. "Please. Just think it over?"

"I—" She bit her bottom lip, knowing she shouldn't agree to his request but struggling with a longing to do just that. Lord, it was tempting. *He* was so tempting. But as much as she might want to extend their relationship—both professionally and yes, personally—there were so many problems. Schedules, for example, both hers and his. The theater would become more and more time-consuming in the future, and Keith didn't know it yet, but his time would be a precious commodity, too. He was going to be successful in this business, very successful. Haley had become more convinced of that each day she worked with him. And she'd been shocked at one of the emotions it had inspired in her. As she'd watched technique and natural talent meld into one hell of a reading from him one day last week, she'd felt inordinately proud...and inexplicably jealous. Jealous over the fact that he could pursue a career in this business and she... well, she chose not to anymore. Professional jealousy had been the downfall of many a Hollywood couple. And it was more than enough reason for her not to coach him anymore.

"Keith," she said, shaking her head again. "I—"

"Please." He squeezed her hand lightly. "Just...think about it."

"Haley," her brother's voice interrupted them from behind.

She turned to look at him. "Hi, James."

He gazed a moment at their intertwined hands, then focused on Haley. "There's a television reporter

who'd like an interview with you about the theater—'' he glanced at Keith, not bothering to hide his
disdain ''—if you have time.''

Anxiety sprinted through her nervous system,
overriding her puzzlement over James's rude behavior. "Oh...certainly I have the time, but...wouldn't
it be better if Dennis talked to the reporter?"

Her brother pursed his lips. "He asked for you. I
suppose he thinks your face will draw a larger audience.''

Keith shot James a scowl, not at all pleased with the
way the man was talking to his sister. His gaze
switched to Haley, and his heart twisted at her visible
apprehension. "Haley, tell him no if you're not up
to—''

"He asked for you, too, Mr. Garrison," James
broke in. He nodded to the reporter, who stood several yards away, wearing a hopeful look on his face.
"He'd like comments from our celebrity guest."

Keith swore silently, his attention never swerving
from Haley. "Let him talk to someone else if you
don't want to do this, Haley."

"Oh...no, I'm okay." Her smile was meant to be
reassuring, but came out a little on the shaky side.
"Do you mind, Keith? You're a guest at this reception. You're not required to give endorsements."

"Hey, endorsements are my specialty. Come on,"
he said with a warm smile, unobtrusively sliding his leg
from the chair and standing. He helped her to her feet,
then secured her hand in the crook of his arm. "We'll

get this over with, then come back and rock to that harp music," he said, pointing to the harpist her mother had hired. "You think she knows any Creedence Clearwater?"

A grin broke through her nervousness and she squeezed his arm in thanks.

CHAPTER ELEVEN

THE CAMERAMAN WAS young, had hair to his shoulders and wore a black baseball cap with the words Twisted Sister on the front. He'd set up his camera and lights next to a wall in the lobby and was waiting for Keith, Haley and the reporter with a bored look on his face. Keith nodded hello as they approached.

The reporter, all grins and solicitousness, directed Haley to stand facing him in the bright light. "We'll be going live in about two minutes, Ms. Riverton," he said, putting his earpiece in place and reaching for the microphone the cameraman held out to him. "I'll say a few words about your affiliation with the theater, then ask about upcoming productions, the number people can call for box office info, that sort of thing." He turned to Keith. "If you can then step up beside Ms. Riverton when I mention your name, Mr. Garrison?"

Keith nodded and walked out of camera range, stopping next to the cameraman. "Will I be in your way here?"

The young man turned the bill of his cap to face backward, then peered through the camera's eyepiece. "Nah. It's a free lobby, man."

Keith slid his hands into the pockets of his slacks and glanced in the direction of Haley's brother. He was about five feet away, sitting in a plush chair as he kept an eye on the proceedings. Haley's voice pulled Keith's attention back to her and the reporter.

" . . . rather not discuss the shooting," she was saying to the man. "It's not something I talk about."

The reporter frowned. "Not even a word or two about things being back to normal now after your ordeal? Everybody in Tulsa's heard about it. When they see you're living here again, they'll be anxious to know the hometown girl's all right again."

The reporter probably didn't notice the slight strain in Haley's eyes, but Keith did. "Vince, I'm sure you can understand that I'm just not comfortable with that subject. Your audience will see that I'm all right again without having to bring up the shooting."

The man opened his mouth to say more, but whatever it was died on his lips. He put his hand to his ear, then nodded to the cameraman. The frown disappeared, and he lifted his microphone.

"Dan," he said, smiling into the camera, "I'm live here at the downtown Riverton Hotel, which is the site of a reception being held this evening for the Tulsa Actors' Theater group. I have former soap-opera actress Haley Riverton with me. Her fans will remember her as Sabrina Holloway from the popular soap 'Forever and a Day.' She's living in Tulsa now and is the director of TAT. Ms. Riverton," he said, turning to Haley, "you must be pleased with the turnout for the reception."

"Yes, Vince, very pleased." Though anyone else watching the broadcast might not have noticed the waver in Haley's voice, it was all too obvious to Keith. Her composure had slipped slightly the moment the reporter had brought up the soap opera. "Tulsa has always been a very supportive community as far as the arts are concerned."

"And I'll bet you're hoping to see some of that support for your first production at the newly renovated Blake Theater."

She seemed to relax a little when the subject changed to the theater. But her hands were still clenched at her sides, Keith noted with a frown. "Yes," she answered, "our first production of the season is the musical *Oliver!* which will be opening next month."

"And for box-office information, people can call . . . ?"

Haley gave the phone number, and Keith breathed a sigh of relief for her. Though Vince had skirted close to the subject she'd warned him away from, the interview was over now and the possibility of seeing Haley upset seemed unlikely. He took his hands out of his pockets, getting ready to take Haley's place in front of the camera.

"Dan, I also have retired football great Keith Garrison here to talk with us. He's in Tulsa filming a movie and a guest at tonight's reception."

Keith took a step forward.

"But before I bring him over, one more question, if you don't mind, Ms. Riverton."

"Uh, certainly."

"It's been more than two years since you were shot in your apartment in L.A.—"

Keith sucked in his breath, and his gaze swung to Haley. "Son of a bitch," he breathed, watching her eyes widen.

"Any comments on how things changed for you after the attack?"

Keith moved forward, and Haley glanced up at him. Her look warned him not to take action.

"No, Vince. No comment." Her words were curt and delivered with an expression devoid of emotion. Good, Keith thought, still angry as hell at the reporter but glad for her sake that she'd handled the incident as she had.

Her mouth quivering slightly at the corners, Haley took a step away from the man, but he wrapped a hand around her upper arm. "What about the court decision that Wharton wasn't competent to stand trial, Ms. Riverton?" he asked quickly. "Aren't you afraid, with him in an institution and not a prison, that he'll get out sooner? Possibly be a continued threat to—"

"That's it," Keith ground out, catching the cameraman's attention. "Shut it down, pal."

The cameraman's gaze jerked up from the camera. "Keep your voice down, man," the young man mouthed. "The mike'll pick it up."

"I said, shut the camera down."

He frowned. "What are you, crazy?" he whispered. "This is a live feed."

Keith's wrath grabbed Vince's attention, and the reporter blinked nervously at the camera. He placed his hand over his earpiece. "Um, yes, Dan. I'm sorry, but we seem to be having a few technical problems...."

"Your problems are only just beginning if you don't turn off that camera," Keith said through gritted teeth. He put his hand over the lens of the camera and came forward, reaching for Haley. She was shaking her head as if in disbelief, but Keith also saw a storm brewing in her light green eyes. He was glad for it, glad that she was angry and not in a state of despair. "Let go of her arm."

Vince dropped it and stepped back. Keith shielded Haley and the reporter from the camera with his body. "You bastard, she told you she didn't want to talk about it, didn't she?"

The man had the nerve to shove his microphone into Keith's face. With a smirk he said, "We're still live, Mr. Garrison. I take it you want to say something about the stalker incident."

If looks could kill, the slimy little man would have been cold and prone on the expensive carpeting of the Riverton Hotel lobby. "The only thing I'm going to say," he answered, his eyes narrowed with anger as he pulled Haley toward him, "is that no comment means *no comment,* friend."

With that, Keith put his hand over the camera lens again and led Haley away. He was vaguely aware of James crossing their path on his way to the reporter as Keith moved Haley toward the front entrance of the hotel. *Go ahead, Riverton,* he thought, his irritation transferring from the reporter to the brother. *Run over and smooth whatever feathers you're worried I ruffled.*

When he heard James's raised voice, he glanced back over his shoulder.

The bright light had been turned off, and James was glaring at the reporter's face. " ... stepped *way* over the line!" the general manager was shouting.

"Well, well," Keith whispered, pleasantly surprised that James would stand up for Haley at the risk of bad publicity for the hotel. Tucking her closer to his side, he glanced down at her. "Are you okay?"

"Yes," she said, but her voice was tremulous now. She looked up at Keith. "I ... should get back to the reception. Try to explain to Dennis about—"

"No, James will explain. I'm getting you out of here."

"Oh, no," she groaned. "James. He was watching that. He'll be furious at me."

Keith opened a glass door next to the revolving one and led her outside. "I think you're wrong about that." He shook his head at the doorman who approached them, then guided her across the street to his car. "Your brother was reading that jerk the riot act when we left."

"He was?" Haley glanced back over her shoulder at the hotel.

"Yeah." Keith opened the car door for her. "Surprised me, too."

He circled around the back and got in, starting the car and remembering another night when he'd driven her home. As on that other night, she was shaken up, maybe even more so. She sat staring at the dashboard, chewing her lip. And he couldn't tell for sure in the darkened interior of the car, but he thought she might be fighting back tears.

"You going to be okay?" he asked again.

She nodded. "Just take me home, please."

"Do something for me first?"

"What?" she asked, looking his way.

"Sit over here," he said, then patted the bench seat beside him. "Come on. You don't need to be over there by yourself, Haley."

She eyed him and the seat speculatively. Walking into his one-armed embrace when he'd come to her rescue with the reporter had felt good, comforting, somehow. Suddenly she wanted the comfort more than she wanted to avoid the problems it brought with it.

Bracing one arm on the seat back, she scooted next to him and welcomed the warmth of his hand when it captured one of hers.

"You remember the night the woman in the mall wanted your autograph?" he asked, his voice low and gentle as he steered the car onto the street.

"Yes. Somewhat similar to tonight, wasn't it?" she asked, her tone wry as one trembling hand reached up to smooth away hair that had fallen into her face.

"Similar, except that I wasn't aware of what had happened to you two years ago."

Surprised, Haley looked up, watching his profile as the city street lamps threw light over his strong features. "I didn't think there was anyone in this country who hadn't heard about it," she said quietly.

"I've been pretty self-involved for the past two years. What with all the surgeries and rehab and decisions to make about my future. Know how I found out about it?"

"I . . . suppose Ian told you."

"Nope," he said as they came to an intersection. He rested their joined hands on the top of his thigh. "It was one night last week in my hotel room. I was watching one of those sleazy tabloid shows because of a report they were doing on stalkers."

She shivered, but she wasn't sure if it was because of the subject or their sudden intimacy. "People . . . can never seem to hear enough about stalkers, can they?"

"I can't say why other people are so interested, but I was watching because it happened to a friend of mine. Griff Patterson. He's an ex-teammate who was harassed by a stalker—a woman. She's in prison now. Anyway, I was shocked when your picture came on the screen. When I'd driven you home from the mall, your reaction to that woman made me think you probably just had a thing about privacy. But the next night, watching your picture flash on the screen, and then the . . . the clip of them putting you in an ambulance . . ."

Haley tensed, and his fingers tightened around hers. "Well, then I understood . . . completely, I'd thought."

Puzzled, Haley looked up at him again. It was an effort, but she pushed her awareness of him aside and asked about what he'd just said. "What do you mean, you thought?"

He aimed the car at an entrance ramp to the expressway and accelerated. "I understood why that woman's attitude made you crazy," he answered. "And I know why you would ask a reporter not to bring up the shooting. But after getting to know you, having seen your talent, it's...hard to understand how you could walk away from acting so easily."

She was quiet, and Keith cast a careful glance her way, wondering if he'd overstepped the bounds of her privacy. But he'd led the conversation down this path for a reason. Keith wanted to get much closer to Haley, to become personally involved with her.

She sighed and shook her head. "It wasn't easy. I...fought to stay, believe it or not. But I just...couldn't live with the changes."

"Changes?"

"Yes. The press beating a dead horse was really only a minor annoyance compared to the feelings of...I don't know, the mistrust I developed." She felt the car slow and watched Keith turn the steering wheel to take her exit. "It's no way to live, Keith. Where before I was so thrilled with fans who wrote to me or wanted my autograph, after the shooting I suspected everyone who approached me with a pen and pad in their hands. The privacy issue became so much a part of my life that everything I did was affected by it."

Keith remembered it had been the same for Griff. "Like making sure you never went anywhere alone? And not going places after dark?"

She nodded. "But not only that. I had nightmares. Constantly. I still do, just not as often. And I even worried about publicity, exposure of any sort. I didn't want my picture in the paper, or interviews either in print or on TV." She gave a humorless laugh. "Not that there was that much publicity to be concerned with. After I got out of the hospital, I wanted to get back to work. But all the parts I was offered . . ." Her words trailed off, and she shook her head. "More often than not the characters were victims of some kind of violence. Rape, stabbing, gunshot.

"I'd played victims in the past . . . before the attack. And I'd never felt one way or the other about it. But after it happened to *me*," she said, her voice growing more tense and quiet, "after I'd experienced the fear, the pain, the nightmares . . . I just couldn't stomach the thought of bringing those characters to life anymore. I was too close to it. The emotions were too real. And it felt exploitative."

Keith let out a long, hard breath. He turned the car into her apartment complex and drove up to her door, then shifted into Park. For long, silent moments they sat there, both staring at nothing. "The magic if," Keith said, breaking the silence with the lesson she'd taught him. "Imagine the events in the scene are happening to you."

Haley laughed again—softly, sadly. "Boy, was it easy to imagine. You know how I was telling you that there's no substitute for life experience for an actor? Well, I was absolutely blessed with life experience, wasn't I? I knew firsthand what it felt like to be terrorized, helpless. I knew the mind-numbing fear. And the pain. I had learned what physical pain was all about.''

Keith was sure it was unconscious on Haley's part when she gripped his hand tighter, when she pressed closer to his side. Nevertheless, he was thrown off balance by the sheer force of the emotions her actions elicited. He wanted to wrap his arms around her and shield her from the pain she spoke of. Yet entangled with protective urges were carnal urges. The hand he held was small, soft, feminine. The warmth of her body beside him made him want to touch more of her.

"In the hospital, I actually tried to tell myself that I could benefit from the experience. But instead of building character," she went on, her voice growing stronger, "it began to take me over. I...was... It's hard to explain.''

Keith lifted their entwined hands to his mouth and brushed a light kiss over her skin. Meant to console, the gesture heightened his all-too-inappropriate desire. "I think I understand" was his hoarse reply. "You said you couldn't trust as easily, or play the roles—"

"No, not just that." She lifted her gaze to his, her eyes clouded with an emotion that Keith couldn't decipher. "Spirit. Do you remember asking me who or what had broken my spirit?"

"Yes.''

"More than talent, I had a strong spirit, Keith. I was tough as nails. And I knew it. Even at twenty-one," she said. "I had so much drive...determination, so many dreams. They were big. I wanted big things—TV, stage, screen.

"It's what kept me going in the face of rejection after rejection. My family didn't know that about me. They'd preached an ongoing sermon about the ills of the life I'd chosen, always sure they'd get to me with 'no one can survive the constant rejection, especially you, Haley.'"

"They were wrong."

"Yes. Or so I thought." She looked away, but before she did Keith saw the quick change in her expression. Her mouth tightened and misery shaded her eyes. Keith's heart ached for her. "Until the shooting changed everything. Until all of my drive and determination buckled under the weight of emotional turmoil."

Her voice was hollow, and she directed her gaze at the apartment door. Keith felt her begin to tremble and drew her closer. When she spoke next, he could hear the sobs that had gathered in her throat.

"All my strengths were gone, Keith. I... had nothing left of the old me...the strong me...to fight with. And th-the last project that my agent—he wanted me to look at a television script for a movie of my life. They wanted to call it *Dreams of Glass*. Glass," she said, "because it's so easily shattered."

"Oh, Haley," he said, his eyes closing.

"Yep. That was the working title." Her free hand came out of her lap to swipe at a tear. "I... couldn't stay after that. I knew it was over then. My dreams *were* shattered. When you're so s-screwed up emotionally, such a basket case that you can't even...can't even play yourself?''

He shifted sideways on the seat and pulled her into his arms. Her tears wet his white shirt, and he wished in a way that he'd never brought the subject up. "How could you expect to be able to do that so soon after it happened?" he said, his hands in her hair and his mouth close to her ear. "How the hell could your agent be so insensitive? To come to you with an idea like that—"

"Good ratings" was her whispered reply. Her breath was warm, and he could feel it through his shirt, the vibrations of her words speeding the blood through his veins. "Stalkers were and still are topical...in the news. I was in the news."

And right now, he thought, she was in his arms. He'd imagined her there, but the circumstances had been much different. In his fantasies, tears weren't falling and comfort was the furthest thing from either of their minds. He tightened the embrace, breathing in the spicy scent she wore, and found his fantasies had been long on lust but short on substance. Reality, where he held Haley as she cried out her loss, brought his heart, his emotions, into the equation.

Closing his eyes, he turned his head and kissed her hair. He felt her body tense. Slowly she leaned back in the embrace, lifting her gaze to his.

"This feels..." She gave a shaky laugh, the streaks from her tears visible even in the low light of the car's interior. "It feels too good."

A grin touched one corner of his mouth, and he rubbed at her tracks of mascara. "Too good?"

Her gaze flicked down to the hands that had somehow found their way to his satiny black lapels. She could feel the strong beat of his heart through the two layers of fabric.

"Yes," she said, sniffing. "After that reporter, it feels good to talk about what happened to me, and it feels good to cry about it with someone who might understand . . . but . . ."

"But what?" he asked, knowing what was coming.

"But, this—" she lifted one hand and waved it helplessly "—feels *too* good, Keith."

"That should tell us something, shouldn't it?"

She swallowed, then removed her other hand from his chest, jerking her eyes away quickly. "Problems," she whispered. "It tells me we're in for big problems."

His hands were still in her hair, and he nudged her to look back up at him. "No. Not if we handle it right. And you and I, we've handled our share of problems in our lives, haven't we?"

At that, Haley gave a wry chuckle. "Are you forgetting how I just handled that reporter back there?"

"Give yourself some credit, Haley. I would have simply dropped him where he stood. You were completely in control. Now, come on," he said, wanting to defuse the situation—temporarily, at least. He drew his hands from her hair and opened his car door, reaching for one of her hands. "Invite me in for coffee. We'll talk about the movie, or anything else you want to talk about.''

Haley's eyes widened, and her lips twitched in a smile as she slid out after him. "You're not pushy or anything, are you? First I tell you there'll be problems if we . . . we . . .''

"Get involved?" he supplied, shutting the car door then matching his stride to hers.

"Right." She reached into a discreet pocket in the black dress and pulled out a key. "Then you're inviting yourself in for coffee."

Her hand was on the doorknob when Keith touched her arm.

"I am pushy," he said. "And I do want to get involved. But most of all, I don't want you to be alone right now."

CHAPTER TWELVE

HER APARTMENT LOOKED as if it had been decorated in California and shipped to Oklahoma. Thick sand-colored carpeting covered the floor, and to the side sat a contemporary wicker sofa and chairs. Their fabric cushions were brush stroked in a range of blues, with light and dark shades of coral thrown in. Accent pillows patterned in seashells were scattered around, and on a wicker étagère more seashells were displayed—big ones, tiny ones, some in shapes and colors Keith had never seen before. Pieces of driftwood, several starfish and a set of small brass palm trees adorned other shelves. Haley saw him looking over her collection. She set her key on a table. "I brought the ocean with me," she said. "No way was I leaving that behind."

Another thing she'd had to give up, Keith thought. California, with its ocean, a place she'd obviously come to love. He watched the beautiful dress shift and shimmer as she disappeared through a doorway to what must have been the kitchen, then he loosened his tie and unfastened his collar button. Glancing around the room again, he noticed a large painting on the wall depicting a storm at sea. He walked closer and studied a small boat that was being pummeled by the wind and waves. Had she picked out this painting before the attack? he wondered. Or after, when its symbolism would have called out to her?

He heard her clattering around in the kitchen, opening and closing cabinets and drawers, then turning on water. Moments later came the sound of the sputters and drips of a coffeemaker.

There had been so many more reasons behind her leaving than he'd imagined. He'd been ignorant to suppose that fear for her safety alone had chased her back home to Oklahoma. And more ignorant to hope that time might have proven a source of healing. Two years later she still bore the emotional scars. And people like the reporter at the reception would likely chew on that particular bone for some time to come.

In the kitchen Haley wiped down counters and eyed the coffeemaker. Noticing a stain on the counter, she decided suddenly that it needed scrubbing, and opened the cabinet under the sink to get cleanser. A delay tactic, she knew, but she needed to think. God knew, she hadn't considered the consequences of her behavior in the car. She should have kept her distance—emotionally and physically. Like a child she'd ignored the potential consequences; she'd only wanted what she'd wanted.

Too good. It had all felt too good.

She continued her attack on the stain, wondering why feeling good had to be such a crime. For two years now her life had been a study in sweeping up the shattered pieces, then painstakingly trying to glue all the slivers and shards back into place. Wasn't it time that she started indulging in the feel-good aspects of life again?

Haley put away the cleanser and rinsed out the rag, then took a cup and saucer out of a cabinet.

"Can I help in there?" Keith called out from the living room.

"No, I've got it. I'll be out in a minute."

Haley pressed a hand to the quivering muscles in her midsection. For heaven's sake, the mere sound of his voice made her stomach quake! She'd tried since that first day to relate to Keith's attributes on a professional basis. But she realized now that it had been an exercise in futility. He affected her on a physical level, a personal level, more than any man she'd ever met.

After that statement he'd made at the door, she should have immediately applied both palms to his broad chest, shoved him into the hall, then locked the door behind him. Yes, that's what she should have done. But she hadn't wanted to. She'd wanted, in fact, to second his statement with one of her own. *I don't want to be alone tonight, either. And, yes, I want an involvement with you.*

And why not? the selfish part of her demanded to know. What was so wrong about...wanting him? He was gorgeous, intelligent, fun, and he looked as sharp and sexy in a tuxedo—make that anything he wore— as any male model. And most of all, he'd listened to all of her reasons for running away and hadn't judged. She'd had shoulders aplenty to cry on after Jack Wharton had destroyed her happiness, but not one of her family or friends had restrained themselves from passing judgment on her decisions. Her parents and brother had thought her foolish to try to resurrect her career after leaving the hospital. They'd expounded on the safety issue, the sanity issue, the money issue, with a vigor that had rivaled their preaching when she'd first left Oklahoma for the West Coast. Carolyn and Ian and all of her other actor friends had been just as vehement when she'd made the decision to leave. Keith had simply listened. Then he'd held her when the tears came.

She heard his footsteps and glanced up just as he entered the room and casually propped himself against the door frame. He'd discarded both the bow tie and the jacket, and had rolled up his shirtsleeves, exposing brawny forearms. He was, Haley thought as she attempted to pour the coffee, absolutely gorgeous.

"How're ya holding up?"

"I'm much better than I would have been if I'd had to face being alone right now," she admitted, and gave him a small smile. "Thank you . . . for staying."

"Believe me," he said, his lips curving, "I'm glad to do it."

"How do you take yours?" she asked, nodding at the coffee.

"Like that. Black." He dropped his hands from the door frame and stepped forward, brushing the sleeve of her jacket with his arm when he reached for the cup. "Aren't you having any?"

"No, it'll only keep me awake. I don't think I'll need much help doing that tonight." She led the way into the living room, taking a seat on the wicker sofa and kicking off her high heels. She saw the jacket he'd neatly draped over a chair, noting the plaid bow tie that peeked out of a breast pocket.

Watching him seat himself on the sofa, Haley suddenly remembered a scene from "Forever." Sabrina and her love interest had been out on the town. A love scene, one that had been dubbed the soap's "steamiest ever," had ensued once the couple had returned to Sabrina's apartment.

During much of the filming of that scene, Haley had been annoyed, supremely frustrated at the many takes because of awkward body positionings, zippers and buttons that had refused to cooperate, and a sheet that had a terminal case of the dropsies, continually slipping down to reveal the strapless body suit she'd been wearing.

She hadn't been annoyed with the finished product, however. It had indeed been steamy. Watching it later, even Haley was almost convinced that she and the actor had been made for each other.

Haley knew what her imagination—make that her *glands*—were up to. Reminding her of that particular scene, nudging her to compare the circumstances with tonight, it was pushing her toward a decision that her intellect told her was wrong.

"I like your ocean," Keith commented, his gaze taking in the room as he lifted his cup to his mouth. Haley watched him blow on it, take a sip, then blink when the steam from the coffee rushed into his eyes. "I've done the same thing with my place in Texas. Decorated it with all the stuff I love about that part of the country. Lots of Old West memorabilia and the like."

"Your place...in San Antonio?"

"Yeah. But even though I lived in an apartment in Texas during the off-season, I was in hotels the rest of the time. When football was over for me, I decided to buy a home. Looking at this," he said, indicating her decor with a nod of his head, "makes me think I must have missed San Antonio more than I knew. You should see the house. Looks like that ranch house from *High Chaparral*. It's outside the city on about twenty-five acres."

"I didn't figure you for a home owner. In fact, much as we've spent the past two weeks in each other's back pockets, I don't know much about you at all." Haley gave herself the thumbs-up on that one. Get to know him better. Don't jump into something before you know him better.

"True," he said, taking a sip of coffee, then placing the cup and saucer on a glass table beside the sofa. "Okay. I used to play football."

Haley grinned.

"And I'm going to be in a movie."

She widened her eyes, appropriately impressed.

"And, let's see ... Oh, here's something good. I'm an uncle."

"Oh, then you have brothers ... sisters?"

"One sister. A twin sister, in fact. And my nephews are twins. Two of the most...*active* four-year-old boys you'll ever meet. They call me Uncle Keef," he said, his smile full of the pride of a doting uncle.

"That's cute," she said, chuckling.

"Don't let appearances fool you." He raised one hip and dragged a wallet from his back pocket, flipped it open to a picture and he handed it to her. "They *are* cute, but they're also terrors."

"They couldn't be," she objected, examining their angelic smiles. She saw a resemblance to Keith in the reddish hair and big brown eyes, but their sweet little faces were shaped more like the woman in the picture opposite theirs. She turned the wallet around and lifted it closer, bringing the sharp scent of new leather to her nose. "Is this your sister?"

"Um-hmm. Angie."

"She's beautiful."

"Thanks. I've always thought so." He laughed softly and moved next to Haley, taking one side of the wallet in his hand. "Look here at this picture," he said suddenly, flipping through several pictures of the twins from infancy on up, until he came to one of a little girl in braids. It was Angie, Haley figured; her hair was bright and her features almost identical to the twin boys'. But on her face was the most forlorn expression. Keith explained, "She hates this picture. I keep it just to gig her."

"How mean," Haley said, playfully butting his shoulder with hers. "She looks so sad."

"She was. It was taken on the first day of kindergarten, when some brain trust in enrollment thought twins should be separated to make them more independent. Angie sat in the corner and cried the whole day."

"That's terrible. What about you?"

"Me? Well, I didn't sit in a *corner* and cry. I sat at my *table* and cried. Took me forever to live down the wimp image."

Haley laughed, saying, "It's awfully hard to believe you were ever called a wimp, Keith Garrison."

"Well, crybaby was the exact term, and it got even worse when Mom went storming up to the school with this picture. She got us put in the same class and made sure we weren't separated until junior high."

"That's a sweet story. Are you and your sister still close?"

Keith grinned, nodding. "Not like back then. We were joined at the hip at that age. In high school we double-dated a lot and even wound up going to the same college together. She's staying at my house with the boys right now."

"Oh?"

"For the duration of filming. Her husband's out of the country on business for a couple of months, and she felt she'd be safer at the ranch. I got a fancy alarm system and hired a guard service while I'm out of town," he explained. After letting Haley look at several more of the boys' baby pictures, he folded his wallet and angled forward, replacing it in his hip pocket. His shoulder brushed hers.

With the brief contact, Haley's gaze met his, then fluttered away. "So, you'll, um, go back to San Antonio after the movie's wrapped?"

"Um-hmm. That's home." He looked at her. "And only about an hour's flight from here."

Haley knew by the sudden seriousness of his tone that he wasn't mentioning flight time for conversation's sake. Mere inches separated them. One of his hands rode the top of the sofa, close to her shoulder blade, and the other rested on his thigh. His intent expression went hand in hand with the tone of his voice.

"Keith...about the lessons," she said, breaking eye contact to stare at the étagère across the room. "I...realize that you'll be only an hour's flight away. But still, it wouldn't be very...sensible, do you think?" She plucked at the fabric of her dress, pleating it with her fingertips, all the while feeling a forbidden awareness of him. "I mean, I understand there'd be the distance problem with any coach you hired, but... I never intended for this arrangement to be anything but temporary—just the two weeks that Ian contracted me.

"And you'll want someone who's more experienced to continue your lessons with," she added. "I was fine when you needed only to relearn some of the basics. But you're also going to need more advanced techniques one of these days, and I'm not sure I'm equipped for that."

He shook his head. "I'm completely satisfied that you're equipped to teach advanced techniques. From what I've seen so far, and from what people like Carolyn and Ian say..." Keith's words trailed off, and he frowned, noticing Haley's sudden disquiet. "What?" he asked.

"Carolyn and Ian don't seem to understand that I'm perfectly happy as a theater director," she said tersely. "Did either of them suggest to you that I would be a good choice as a permanent drama coach?"

"No, that was my idea. Why, would it bother you if they had?"

Yes. A great deal, Haley thought. But she didn't know which reason bothered her most. The fact that her friends, after two years, still refused to accept the fact that Haley wouldn't consider acting again? Or was it because, deep down, she'd wanted the idea to have been Keith's? The former was the reason she chose to voice. "I had trouble convincing them I was doing the right thing when I left L.A."

"Seems to me you did the only thing you could do." His voice was gentle, soothing.

"It's...nice to have someone understand." She glanced at him. "Can you also understand that it's...difficult even being a theater director? Makes me...miss acting at times. But missing it now and again, I can handle. I love what I do too much not to."

It was on the tip of Keith's tongue to say "You're too *good* at what you do not to. That's why I want you for my coach," but he knew this was not the moment to pressure her. Instead, he asked, "But being theater director is as close to this business as you want to be?"

She took a deep breath, nodding. As near as he was, she was finding it more and more difficult to forestall the idea that she should continue as his coach. "Don't cheat yourself, Keith. You're going to need professionals around you who are...*devoted* to this business, not someone like me who would rather forget it even exists. And you lead a high-profile life-style. You saw me with that reporter tonight. I'm not comfortable in those situations anymore, even when I'm not being asked questions about the shooting."

Moments of silence ticked by, then Keith surprised Haley by touching her cheek, tilting her head toward him and gazing into her eyes. "Reporters? My high profile? We're not talking about lessons now, are we?"

Haley lowered her lashes, blocking out the sight of her reflection in his amber eyes. She couldn't block out the thought of what he'd said earlier. *I'm pushy. I want an involvement.*

"Come on, talk to me, Haley. You found it easy enough a few minutes ago when we were laughing and bumping shoulders and looking at pictures of my family."

"Okay. I—" The feel of his fingers on her skin made coherent thought almost impossible. Dangerous, dangerous man who made her want to follow her heart's lead. "You're right," she whispered, plucking at the dress again, "we aren't talking about the lessons now."

"Look at me . . . please?"

Reluctantly she raised her gaze to his. The look in his eyes was similar to the one he'd had that day in the auditorium. Without thinking, she blurted out, "If you're going to kiss me again like that day on stage, I won't be able to think straight."

He smiled, a lazy, masculine smile. "That's all it would take? A kiss?"

"Well, it was a pretty good kiss."

"Yeah. For me, too." His voice was husky. "I want to kiss you again. You know that, don't you?"

Her mouth dry, her eyes locked on his, she nodded.

"Is that so terrifying?" he asked. "You look as if you think I'm going to clip you behind the knees and fall on top of you."

That brought a shaky laugh. "No, I'm not afraid of that."

"Good. Because I won't. I've learned a lot about you tonight, and part of it is that one of the most difficult things about the past two years has been convincing people the decisions you had to make were yours. Not theirs."

How was it, Haley wondered, that her longtime friends and family members hadn't understood, but his man whom she'd known only two weeks did? "Yes," she said quietly.

His fingers glided lightly from her cheek to her hair. With his thumb he traced the shell of her ear, his fingers sifting through the strand of hair behind it. "Earlier tonight, on the way here, I thought, 'Time's short. If I'm going to get anything started with this woman, I'd better get on with it quick-like.' Then you told me about all that's happened to you in the past two years. So what do you think I'm going to do about us, knowing that?"

"Give up on us, do the movie, then go back to Texas?"

He chuckled. "Not a chance."

"Somehow I didn't think so."

"But do you want that, Haley?" He twisted a long strand of her hair around his finger, watching the curl instead of her eyes. "Because if you told me you did, I would. I wouldn't like it, but... you've been pushed and prodded by too many people. I wouldn't do that to you. And," he added, taking a deep breath, "that approach is risking failure." His eyes met hers. "I don't want to risk failure with you."

She shook her head. "Oh, Keith..."

"What? What does 'Oh, Keith' mean?"

"It means... Oh, I think it means I'd rather you just clip me behind the knees and fall on top of me."

He smiled, then shook his head.

She twisted to face him fully, then looped one palm over his raised arm and lightly traced the contours of his strong, rugged jaw with the other. "I'd rather you not be... so... so appealing. Or honorable or understanding or such a good kisser. And I'd rather you not be only an hour's flight away."

"Because... ?"

She swallowed. "Because I like all those things about you so much. And I don't want to risk failure, either. And it scares me, this decision."

He turned his head, catching her off guard by nuzzling a warm kiss into the palm of her hand. "No reason to be afraid," he breathed against her sensitive skin. "Just call it. If you want me to leave right now, I will."

He hadn't kissed her, but she still couldn't think straight. Which seemed to suit her heart just fine. God, how she was tired of making sacrifices.

"Stay," she heard herself whisper.

CHAPTER THIRTEEN

"STAY?" ELATION...relief...desire. All pumped through his blood as he lowered his head to capture her mouth with his.

As if to tell him she wouldn't go into this blindly, she kept her eyes wide open and her spine stiff and straight as he tasted her lips once, twice, then a third time. Her hands went to his shoulders, and Keith felt her tense fingers grip at his shirt.

He quietly spoke her name, still keeping his kisses chaste when what he wanted was something completely different. But just because she'd told him to stay, he realized, just because *he* was thrilled to his socks about it, didn't mean she was completely convinced she'd made the right decision.

He thought about backing away, about trying to talk out her anxiety with her, but there was no way in hell he could do it. Not now when his senses were crowded with the smell, the feel, the taste of the woman who had driven him to distraction in one form or another ever since he'd first met her. He angled his head and kissed her again, thinking, anxious or not, unsure or not, Haley would come to know how right she'd been to ask him to stay. He knew it because he'd never felt such rightness before with any other woman.

He cradled her head, his thumbs caressing her nape, her hair like a waterfall of rustling silk over the backs of his fingers. "Haley, open your mouth," he urged in a whisper, then waited three anxiety-filled beats before she bestowed him that gift.

His tongue swirled in, and Haley's eyes slid shut. Yet good as it felt, as much as it made her heart quicken, she couldn't seem to shake the uneasiness that accompanied those sensations.

He lifted his head, and her eyes shot open again. "What?" she asked, her nerves as brittle and fragile as a sand dollar.

He didn't answer. He simply took his hands out of her hair, then braced them on his knees, and...looked at her. The look was completely undecipherable. Anger? No. Frustration? Maybe a little.

Then she saw it. The glint of humor in his eyes. He lifted the hand that wore the Super Bowl ring and slid it beneath her knees. He placed his other hand on her shoulder and shoved lightly. She gave him a quizzical look as she slowly fell backward, her head coming to rest on a seashell pillow.

"What are you...?"

He grinned and made an exaggerated clipping motion at the backs of her knees before covering her body with his.

Haley laughed into the front of his shirt, the tension slowly ebbing from her body. "You think you're a real funny guy, don't ya?"

"Yes," he answered immodestly. "And... I've still got it," he bragged, then huffed a breath of hot air on the surface of the ring, buffing it on his shirt.

It felt natural to loop her arms around his neck, natural to smile into his eyes. "What, were you afraid you'd lost all that athletic prowess being off the field for so long?"

He gave her an off-center grin. "Actually I was more worried about a whole different kind of prowess."

She caught his meaning easily. "The kiss."

"Yeah. The kiss."

"You know, you might be better off starting something with someone who isn't so neurotic. One minute I think, 'That's it, I'm tired of living my life on the basis of something that happened in my past,' the next, I have qualms. The kiss was—" she looked up at him and rubbed his lower lip with one thumb "—just as fantastic as the one at the theater, Keith."

"Yeah?"

"Yeah," she assured him.

"Good. Then I'm going to do it again. You're just nervous, coach, not neurotic. You might try a technique I use. It's called the 'magic if.'"

His lips descended, and this time Haley met them with a smile. No tension. No nerves. Well, maybe a few nerves. But she found herself responding to him easily. Too easily. Excitement, arousal, were embarrassingly quick. But then, she thought, the entire night had been leading up to this moment. From the second she'd spotted him at the reception, her thoughts had been guiding her in this direction. It must have been the same for him because when she arched closer, grazing his chest with her breasts, a groan issued from his throat, and the kiss became reckless, deep and hungry.

She gloried in the feel of him, his wide shoulders, the damp hair at his nape, the slightly rough feel of his chin abrading her skin. He left her mouth and traveled down to the sprinting pulse in her throat, and all the while his hands were wreaking havoc with her senses. They caressed every bit of bare skin he could find, then trailed down to her waist to touch, to stroke, the skin that was still clothed in satin.

He rested his forehead against hers, his hands just below her breasts.

God, this woman, he thought. *Everything she is, I . . . like. The way she looks, feels, smells. The person she is.*

But there was more. There was every reason to believe that he could fall in love with her. So easily, so damn easily. "Haley," he said, his voice gritty and his breathing fast, "this doesn't feel too soon to me, but if it does to you . . . Do you . . . want me to go?"

She made the mistake of looking into his eyes. Lord, abstinence did destroy brain cells. "No."

One kiss tumbled into another and another. She'd lost touch with that part of her mind responsible for reasoning and logic. Her eyelids closed at the exquisite sensation of his first touch upon her breast. Through the fabric of her dress, his fingers stroked her gently, reverently, extracting a small sigh of pleasure from her. His hand smoothed a path up to her shoulder, then he tugged at the bolero jacket she still wore.

Lucidity hadn't escaped her completely, she discovered, because the image of her scars flashed on a screen in her mind's eye. They were the reasons she would never again wear a strapless dress like this one without a jacket to cover her shoulders.

His knuckles found the first one, and Haley started, her eyes coming open. His gaze locked on hers, calm and steady, then slowly and with infinite care, he touched the small star-shaped scar. Emotion shone in his eyes. "Are there more?"

"Yes. One next to it," she answered in a halting whisper, "and one . . . here." Covering his hand with hers, she guided it to the scar between her breasts, the one that lay within a quarter inch of her heart. She pressed his fingertips against the fabric that overlaid the welt.

"God, Haley. So close." He pressed his lips to the one on her shoulder. "That night . . . the one when I saw the report about you," he whispered, "I couldn't get to sleep that night. Couldn't lose this . . . anger I felt." He laid a tender kiss, brief and heart stirring, on the still-pink welt. "That should have told me, huh? That there'd be more between you and me than lessons."

Haley's throat tightened, curbing speech. It was fortunate, because she had no idea what to say. She'd assumed she would face intimacy with a man again one day, and she'd been concerned about baring the not-so-pretty reminders of what had happened to her.

But Keith had obliterated those concerns. Her heart swelled; she was unaccustomed to seeing her scars in any light save a bad one.

"Oh, Keith..." she murmured, finally finding her voice. "I...fought feeling this way about you...I really did."

"Me, too," he admitted. "Me, too."

He worked earnestly at divesting her of the jacket. Haley sat up, helping him, then watched through a fevered mist as he pitched it on top of his jacket.

The fine lines of strain on his forehead were impossible to miss. As was the bold proof of his arousal against her thigh. "Keith," she whispered as raindrop-soft kisses were scattered on her cheeks, her nose, the corner of her mouth, "should we...discuss a couple of things?"

"Like...?" His breathing unsteady, the thump of his heart heavy against hers, he captured her hands and drew them back up around his neck.

"This...sofa, for starters." She closed her eyes, needing a clear head if she were to get through the next few moments.

"It's nice," he said hoarsely. "But—"

"A little...uncomfortable for someone your size?"

He sat up, scooping her into his arms in Rhett Butler fashion. "Where to?"

"That way," she directed, pointing. It hit her that she'd never been carried this way by a man, not without cameras recording it and a director choreographing it. She liked it, she decided. A lot. What she didn't like, what was probably more uncomfortable for her than the sofa was for Keith, was the next subject that needed to be addressed. She cleared her throat and took advantage of being held this way by burying her face in his neck. "There's, uh, one other thing."

"What?"

"In that...wallet you showed me?" She wished for instant sophistication or the clinical mien of a sex-education teacher. But having neither was no excuse these days. These were the nineties, after all, and being candid wasn't merely admirable—it was essential. "The...one with the pictures of nephews? You wouldn't, uh, also happen to have...?"

He said nothing at first, then Haley thought she felt him smile. They reached her bedroom, but Keith didn't immediately set her on her feet. Instead, he reached into his back pocket and brought out the wallet. "Yes, I do."

He lowered her gently to the bed and came down beside her on one hip. Extracting the foil packet, he placed both it and the wallet on the bedside table.

"Is there...anything else?"

"No," she answered quietly, a hesitant smile curving her lips. "Just this."

She came into his arms then, her beautiful mouth stringing kisses that heated, kisses that tortured, along his jaw. He felt her hands fist in the material of his shirt, then she dragged it free of the slacks. Keith fell to his back, amazed at the level of his desire. It was stronger than he'd ever felt for any other woman. When she'd unfastened the studs and spread the material wide, he brought her to lie atop him, and thought, *Just this . . . just this . . . just this . . .*

His fingers tangled in her hair, and their lovemaking took on speed and fervor. Clothes were dispensed in quick, jerky motions, and hands roamed the skin that was bared. Her dress was hurriedly unzipped and slipped off her body. His pants and briefs were shucked and kicked off the end of the bed. Hose and panties—both black, both lacy, and both designed to annihilate a man's control—were skimmed away, baring her pretty legs, the legs he could never get his fill of looking at, the legs he wanted wrapped around him . . . soon.

"Haley," he said gruffly, touching, stroking, kissing to his heart's desire. "So beautiful."

He made her *feel* beautiful. And his mouth on her breast, tugging, suckling, made her ache. *Keith,* she thought, *please now!*

He fulfilled her silent wish by reaching toward the bedside table, then coming back to her and settling between her legs. He framed her face with his hands, looked into her eyes with an expression of need and passion that stole her breath away, then moved to kiss her mouth. His first thrust brought a moan of pleasure to her lips, and she wrapped her legs around him.

"God, Haley," he said in throaty approval as he put his hands on her legs, smoothing his palms from the tops of her thighs to her knees. "It feels just...just as good as I knew it would."

With his words, she was lost to everything save the feel of his moving inside her, hard and sleek, and the fast beat of his heart next to hers. When she tightened the embrace, Keith's groan rent the air. His thrusts came quicker, deeper.

Haley closed her eyes and saw him as he'd looked earlier tonight. At the reception, when he'd teased her about the strawberries...with the reporter, when he'd shielded her from the camera by putting his hand over the lens...on her sofa, when he'd told her that he wouldn't risk failing with her.

Then release came and her thoughts dispersed, flung like stardust fragments to the far reaches of heaven.

COMING AWAKE SLOWLY, Keith blinked and turned his head on the pillow to watch Haley sleep. Her hair was an absolute mess. Several strands of it covered one eye, a clump of it was tangled in the fingers that rested on the pillow next to her, some was flattened beneath her cheek. Keith grinned and traced one long strand from her ear to where it stopped in a curl at the top of her breast.

He raised himself up on an elbow and propped his head on his hand. Her bedroom was painted in shadows, and a look at his watch told him that morning was still a couple of hours away. Good, he thought, slipping down the sheet that partially hid her breasts from view. He wanted the time to savor the pleasure of lying in bed with her and to look his fill at her sleep-flushed skin.

He hadn't had the chance to do much looking last night. When their lovemaking had ended, when their breathing had slowed and their bodies had cooled,

Haley had subtly made it known that she wasn't quite relaxed enough with him to shed all inhibitions easily. When he'd pulled her body flush with his to celebrate the afterglow of lovemaking with quiet words and gentle caresses, just as they were drifting off to sleep, she had carefully extricated herself from the embrace. When he'd awoken moments ago, he hadn't been surprised to find that several inches of space separated them on the bed.

He hadn't been surprised, but he had been disappointed. Coming from a family who had taught him early the pleasure of physical closeness, of touching and hugging and kissing, Keith had never known any other way to be. When it came to making love, he was big on falling asleep with a woman in his arms. He had particularly looked forward to that experience with Haley. Their joining had been breathtakingly quick, with not enough time spent on leisurely exploration. Keith had hoped to remedy that the next time they made love, but until then, he at least wanted her wrapped around him as they slept.

He saw the scar between her breasts. His finger lightly touching it, his mind winged back to all she'd told him in the car last night. Her fear, loss of trust, the roles she was offered after the shooting, her family's attitude.

Her family. So unlike his. Maybe her reticence, the distance she'd put between them after they'd been as close as a man and woman could be, had less to do with being relaxed than it did with growing up in a family such as hers. A family that probably spent far too little time touching, holding and cuddling.

Haley awoke to the feel of large hands gently pulling her toward a solid, warm, masculine body. Before she could panic, her sleep-dulled mind reminded her of the goings-on in this bed last night. A lazy grin formed on her lips, only to be replaced with a grimace when she felt her hair being pulled. "Ow."

"Here," she heard Keith say, his voice a low, muffled rumble near her ear. "You're all caught up." He disengaged her fingers from her hair.

"Oh, no," she said, scrambling fully awake with images of crushed curls and bangs that stood straight up as she tried to rake the mass of hair out of her face. "I must look—"

"Beautiful."

She glanced up into his eyes. His dark, half-slumberous, wholly gorgeous brown eyes. Beautiful? Her? No, he was the beautiful one. From his mussed russet hair to the slightly sandpapery feel of his jaw, to the muscular legs that were at this moment looped around hers, he was one beautiful man. And a man who had made her *feel* beautiful last night. As well as protected. For once, she'd suffered no nightmares.

"Oh, Keith," she murmured. His hands were moving over her back, then down past her hips to cup her buttocks. The kisses he bestowed to her throat, her shoulders, the tops of her breasts, were morning warm and made her arch toward him. "We didn't make a mistake last night, did we?"

"No," she heard him say, then felt his lips at her waist...lower. His mouth covered her intimately, and Haley's eyes closed against her will. "It was no mistake, coach."

"YOU READY for this, cowboy?" Carolyn asked. She held a plastic cup bracketed between her palms, alternately blowing on the hot chocolate it held and taking quick, tentative sips.

"This might shock you, but, yes, I am." Keith flipped up the collar of the long rider coat he wore and pulled his black Stetson lower on his forehead. A cold snap had hit the Tulsa area last night, and the shooting schedule had been rearranged to take advantage of it. On this, their first day of filming, the love scene was to have been first, but the weather gave Ian the opportunity to shoot an exterior that was scheduled for later. The gunmetal gray sky and the low temperature had provided the director with the desired shots. They'd spent all morning on what would amount to about two minutes of actual movie, but Ian had been thrilled with it. And also thrilled that they could still get to the love scene after lunch.

Lunch break being nearly over, Keith, Carolyn and the limited number of crew members who would be allowed on the closed set were milling around outside the cabin that had been built as Carolyn's character's home.

Keith put his hands in the pockets of the scratchy overcoat and grinned at Carolyn's apparel. The long, mud brown skirt and high-necked muslin blouse were an odd match to the bright purple down coat and insulated gloves she wore to keep warm.

"How 'bout you?" He scuffed the ground with the pointed toe of one dusty boot. "You told your banker about it yet?"

Carolyn looked up from the steaming drink to meet his gaze. Her anger was apparent in the way her mouth pinched in at the corners. "Well, you and Haley must be getting awfully chummy for her to have told you about that."

He nodded and said carefully, "Our last few lessons've centered on this love scene, Carolyn. I could sense that something about it was giving her grief. And she didn't just offer up that information—I had to drag it out of her."

Carolyn seemed to relax. But only a bit. "Why should my situation be giving her grief?"

"You know why. She's told me how close the two of you were in California. And so did you, for that matter. She cares about what happens to you."

Carolyn skirted the subject by grinning and giving Keith a speculative look. "Just how chummy *are* you two getting? Haley's pretty closemouthed with the personal stuff, no matter how hard someone might try to drag it out of her. She must be feeling somewhat closer to her drama student these days." Her grin broadened into a full-fledged smile, and she nudged him with an elbow. "Any particular reason why, Keith?"

Even if he'd wanted to keep quiet about his and Haley's blossoming relationship, he was sure he'd sabotaged his attempts with the stupid grin he couldn't hide. But there was no help for it. Ever since their first night together, the grin was a constant with him. He merely had to think about Haley, and there it was.

In the four days since he'd brought her home from the reception, they'd been together as much as Keith could manage it. There had been those last couple of lessons, her play practices that she'd tried unsuccessfully to shoo him away from, dinners together—either at her place or at restaurants he'd wanted to try out. And then, of course, there had been the nights. In her bed, in his at the hotel. God, the nights. Keith spent a lot of time when he wasn't with Haley imagining more nights with her. Imagining every night with her. For a long time to come.

"Oh, ho, ho. Let me see this face." Carolyn took his chin between her thumb and forefinger. "I know this look. I've seen this look before. It's *luuv*."

Keith chuckled, and shook his head. "Let's just say that...given time..."

Carolyn was still zeroed in on his expression, and she hadn't let go of his chin. "Now, Keith. This is not a look of caution I'm seeing. This is definitely a *luuv* look. Come on, seriously. Tell me, because I care about her, too."

"Okay," he said, realizing that although Carolyn's voice never lost its teasing note, she was concerned about her friend. "Seriously? You're right. Something is going on. We've only known each other for just over two weeks, but I—"

"Wait a minute. Is this requited or unrequited or... what?" she asked, her eyes suddenly bright.

"Well, what there is of it...I mean, so far...that is..." Keith heaved a sigh of frustration as he tried to define what his and Haley's involvement actually was. Everything was still so new between them, and to try to categorize or label their relationship was not only difficult, but it scared him somewhat. Deep inside, he felt that he and Haley had the makings of something more than a temporary, for-the-duration-of-filming fling. But it worried him to think about what would happen once the film wrapped. His heart was on the line here.

"It's not *luuv* yet, okay?" Even though it felt a lot like that to him, it was too soon to say what it meant to Haley. "But whatever it is, I'm pretty sure it's requited. But listen, Haley isn't—"

"Well, all right!" Carolyn set her cup on a wooden railing and nearly tackled Keith, hugging him enthusiastically. A crew member walking by teased them with a good-natured "Come on, guys, can't you wait till we get the film loaded?"

"Oh, Keith," she said, ignoring the man's remark, "this is fantastic!"

"Now wait a minute, Carolyn." Keith pulled out of the embrace, righting the hat that she'd knocked askew. "I think it's a bit early for congratulations. Especially as far as Haley's concerned. I... feel like I sort of dragged her kicking and screaming into this thing, and..."

"I won't say a word about it to her, okay?" She held up her fingers like a Boy Scout. "Don't forget, I know Haley pretty well. She was never one to jump into anything without lots of soul-searching. I imagine she is feeling pretty shaky about this 'whatever it is.'" She took a deep breath, then smiled again. "So I'm fully aware that my running over to her house to discuss wedding plans won't help matters. You don't have to worry about that. But I can be excited about it, can't I?" Still beaming, she squeezed Keith's forearms.

He gave her a narrow look. "Just why *are* you so excited about it?"

"Because," she said, reaching for her hot chocolate again, "other than the fact that I'm not exactly devastated about her getting tangled up with someone in the business...this is the first thing I've seen her do in the two and a half years since Wharton that involves some risk. It's as if she has an imaginary map she's been following, 'the road to a normal life.' And any side path, any out-of-the-way scenic route that might lure her away from that all-important, boring, careful highway...well, until now, she just wouldn't risk it."

Remembering Haley's distress about everyone's disapproving of her decisions, a small frown creased the skin between his brows. "You said she was careful before the shooting. Stands to reason that she'd be twice as careful after something like that. And by the way, taking that boring highway, as you call it, was not completely her choice. I'm sure you know about the parts she was offered, the script her agent brought her, *Dreams of Glass?*"

Carolyn's lips stretched in a slow smile. "I like this. I do like hearing you jump to Haley's defense. You're in deep, aren't ya, cowboy?"

Keith rolled his eyes and gave a frustrated laugh. "Yeah. Yeah, I am, but—"

"Good. You're the best thing that could happen to Haley. Not only are you tall, dark and athletic," she said, sighing in the same swooning manner that his sister often used, "you'll make Haley realize what she's missing. She won't be able to handle the envy. She'll just have to act again."

He shook his head. "Carolyn, Carolyn, you don't get it. My being in this business is not a good thing, it's a big sticking point. You think envy will serve as some kind of catalyst to send Haley back to Hollywood. I think it could ruin whatever chance we have to develop something strong, something that will last. She's dead set against going back, Carolyn. And you know what? I'm not so sure she's wrong."

Carolyn didn't say a word for several seconds. Then she laid a gentle hand on his sleeve. "Keith, if I sound like a stage mother gone ballistic, it's because I love Haley, all right? Do I remember what a hard time she had after the shooting? Yes, vividly. Do I know how difficult it would be for her to try again, to put up with the publicity, to wait out all the crap roles? You bet I do. But I also know that deep in her heart of hearts, acting is what she wants to do. And if this thing between you two happens to evolve into love, then you,

Keith, are going to know where I'm coming from. You'll understand that acting may not be what she *needs*, but it's what she *wants*. Come on, you know what it feels like to want something bad, don't you?''

"Yes, I do, but—"

"Here you are," Ian broke in, approaching Keith and Carolyn. "We're ready for you now."

Keith saw the flash of panic in Carolyn's eyes, then the quick mask of professionalism she tried to cover it with. But Carolyn's panic made him realize that thoughts of Haley had been put on the back burner and the subject of Carolyn's banker, Jonathan, had taken center stage. She still probably hadn't told Jonathan about the scene. Keith thought about what she'd said concerning wants and needs as he followed Ian and Carolyn to the cabin, wondering what the outcome would be for Carolyn. She was going after what she *wanted*. He hoped for her sake that it would also be what she *needed*.

"Roll camera."

"Rolling."

"Speed."

"And action."

Seated at the head of the bed, her back pressed to the spindled iron headboard, Carolyn lifted shaky fingers to the lacy collar of her blouse. She wet her lips and gazed into Keith's eyes. He stood just shy of five feet away, one bent knee resting on the wedding-ring quilt, one boot planted on the rough plank floor. His hip was pressed against the bed rail, his hands loosely at his sides.

"Sarah. You shouldn't do this," he said. "Not with me."

Carolyn held her gaze steady with Keith's. Her fingers continued to tremble as they moved down the front of her blouse. She swallowed, then unfastened the last button and tugged the blouse from the waistband of her skirt. "Only with you," she whispered.

She stood and walked slowly to face him, then reached for his hand and brought it to her cheek. "Only with you," she said again, and guided the hand downward over her throat, then just inside the collar of the blouse.

"And cut! Perfect, perfect, Carolyn." Ian strode forward and stood beside the two actors, pushing up the bill of his Madeira cap. "That'll be the last take for that sequence. I think we've got all the angles we're going to need. Carolyn, you were right on with the shaking fingers, the quiver in your voice. Just what I wanted." He sent a look over his shoulder at Keith. "You, too, Keith. Great stuff, great stuff. Roberta," he said, motioning the director of photography over, "get your gaffer in here. I want one of the kick lights moved to the head of the bed."

Roberta nodded, then left. The first assistant director stepped up to take Roberta's place. "You want makeup?" he asked.

"Yeah." Ian turned back to Carolyn and Keith, putting a hand on each of their shoulders. With an exhaled breath and a grin that was meant to be reassuring, he said, "Okay, here we go, kids. I'm going to clear the set of every single body that isn't absolutely necessary. I want you two just as comfortable as I can get you. Now, we've gone over the choreography already, but if you have any questions, anything you might want to discuss before we roll...? No? Let's go for it, then.''

Ian gave Carolyn's shoulder a gentle squeeze. "You okay?''

"Hey, piece of cake," she said with a shrug and a smile. But she made the mistake of looking at Keith, whose expression said he knew she was lying. He knew that the shaking fingers and quivering voice had been no act. She looked away, uncomfortable with the expression in those dark eyes; it reminded her of the way Jonathan looked at her when he knew she wasn't being honest with herself.

Ian gave Keith a couple of pats on the arm before moving to the other side of the set. Carolyn heard him say "Clear it" to the first assistant director, and then the AD's louder command, "Clear the set!"

Avoiding eye contact with Keith, Carolyn sat down on the edge of the bed. Cindy, a short, dark-haired woman, came striding up and placed her makeup case and a white terry-cloth robe on the bed next to Carolyn. She gave Carolyn a warm smile. "We meet again," she joked, referring to their makeup session of only an hour or so ago.

Carolyn returned the smile but couldn't summon up the same amount of warmth. Her insides had begun to swim, and a headache threatened. She breathed deeply, focusing her attention on the array of makeup tubes, palettes and brushes Cindy was fussing over.

"You know, I'm such an old movie buff. I just love all of your parents' work," the woman commented as she shuffled through one of the trays. Glancing up, she studied the exposed portion of Carolyn's chest for a moment. "Turn more this way, please. Yeah, good. Oh, and you'll need to take off the blouse and camisole. I've got a robe for you right here. And Mr. Garrison, I'll need you out of the shirt in a minute."

"Sure," came his voice from behind Carolyn.

With fingers that shook more than they had for the cameras, Carolyn parted the blouse and shrugged out of one sleeve. Keith's hand clamped lightly over the still-clothed shoulder. "Carolyn..."

She shook her head and closed her eyes as if that would chase away the image of Jonathan's pained expression that clouded her mind.

"Carolyn, it's not too late," Keith said quietly.

But it was.

CHAPTER FOURTEEN

Dear Sabrina,

I've had time to calm down. I still think you did a terrible thing by leading me to believe you were coming back to "Forever," but I can forgive you. None of us are perfect, are we?

I admit that I was wrong to get so angry at you just because of one mistake. I was just so disappointed when I didn't get to see you. You can understand that, can't you? I hope you've forgiven me for it, like you forgave me for hurting you before I was put in this hospital.

You know, it's odd. Since I've been in here the desire to see you in person again is stronger than it ever was. But maybe that's not so odd. Maybe it's true that absence makes the heart grow fonder. In my case it's true.

All my love,
Jack

"So, THEN, UP DRIVES this truck full of chickens."

"Chickens?" A smile lit Haley's eyes, and she turned from the take-out sacks she was busy with at her kitchen counter.

"Chickens," Keith said with a laugh, then sidled up next to Haley and reached into one of the bags. As he found the french fries, his brows lifted. He had three of them in his mouth before Haley could grab them away from him.

"If you could wait a minute, I'll get you a plate," she said in mock annoyance.

"I'm starvin'," he groaned. And it was the truth. This had been the second day of filming. Like yesterday, it had been twelve hours long, ending at six-thirty this evening. Keith had hurried back to the hotel, showered, dressed in a sweater and jeans, then headed for Haley's apartment. He hadn't eaten since noon.

He looped an arm around her neck and pulled her close for a deep, satisfying kiss.

"If you were that hungry, you wouldn't keep kissing me. You're keeping me from getting this food on the table."

He pretended to think that over for a few seconds, then shook his head and swooped down for another kiss. "Nah, I'll never be that hungry."

Haley laughed and scooted out of his reach, opening a cabinet and getting out plates. "Finish the chicken story."

"Oh, right. The chickens." He followed her to the small dining area, carrying two of the sacks. They sat and began taking out the food. "Supposedly the prop master had wanted live chickens for the scenes outside Sarah's cabin. So it was the set decorator's job to order them from a poultry farm for an exterior we'll shoot next week."

Haley nodded, then took a sip of her root beer. "But they came today?"

"Yeah," he answered, laughing again. "But it wasn't just that they came on the wrong day. It was how many of them came. You've never seen so many chickens."

"How many were supposed to be delivered?"

"A half dozen or so."

"And a truckload came?"

"Um-hmm." Keith took a huge bite of his cheeseburger, chewed and swallowed. "And before the set decorator could get to the truck, the man with the poultry was already unloading all these birds."

Haley laughed, picturing the mayhem of a set deluged with chickens. She'd seen some strange things happen during the filming of a movie, but never that. "You weren't in the middle of a scene or anything, were you?"

"Yes. We were several yards behind the cabin when the truck drove up to the front."

"Bet the sound man went crazy when he heard the truck," Haley commented, her eyes dancing with amusement. "Engine noise is not something you want in the background of an 1800s period piece."

"He did react rather violently now that you mention it. He jerked his head up and said, 'What the hell is that?' Then he yelled, 'Cut! Cut!' which always gets Ian's attention in a hurry."

"I can just see it," she said, grinning.

"That's not the best part." Keith took a big drink of his shake, his eyes twinkling. "By now, Ian and the rest of the sound crew, all of us really, start to hear all this chicken noise, you know? Clucking and wings flapping. Then the chickens start trailing around the cabin toward us. And everyone looks at the prop master, who then glares at the set decorator, who gets this really sick look on his face.''

"Oh, no. What did he *do?*''

"Well, you have to have met this guy to get the full effect. He's from Brooklyn and has the worst gutter mouth you've ever heard. Anyway, he goes running toward the truck, screaming obscenities and trying to herd the chickens back around the cabin. We were all just slack jawed, sort of stunned. Then we heard him yell *Stoopid!* This place is friggin' *stoopid* with chickens!' We all lost it then.''

"How in the world did the truck get past the gate?''

Keith shrugged. "Somebody said something about typos on the call sheet. The date and number of poultry needed was wrong.''

"That's too good,'' she remarked, then stole a couple of fries off Keith's plate. "You know what would be funny? I should call up Ian at the hotel and make clucking noises when he answers.''

"Very mature, Haley.''

"I know, but that's how it is on a set. Very juvenile. There's always a practical joker or someone cracking everyone else up with dumb jokes. It relieves the tension.'' She put her chin in her palms. Then, her eyes bright with humor, she launched into an anecdote similar to his—but with a dog, not chickens—from her days on the soap.

When their laughter had faded, Keith was hit full force with the realization of how much he'd missed her all day. He reached across the table and took one of her hands in his. "Come here," he said, then tugged her out of her seat and onto his lap.

"I thought you were starving." She glanced pointedly at his half-full plate.

"It can wait." He plucked two french fries out of her hand, dropping them onto his plate.

Then he took her mouth with his in a kiss that went quickly from tame to torrid. His hands went roaming. They glided up her denim-covered thighs, then stole under the ribbed hem of the sweatshirt she wore. A masculine sigh of appreciation was breathed against her lips when his hands found her lace-covered breasts.

"How can I want you this much all the time?" he asked in a rough whisper, one hand snaking around her back to unhook her bra.

"Mmm. I don't know." She closed her eyes, resting her forehead against his. "I'm just awfully... glad you do."

He chuckled quietly and stroked her nipples with his thumbs. "Yeah... it does seem like you're rather glad right now."

She rubbed her thigh against his arousal. "You're not exactly depressed yourself, bud," she remarked dryly.

Keith laughed, then brought her mouth back to his. "God, I love being with you," he said between kisses. "I love this mouth... this body... I love—" He stopped himself from verbalizing the emotion that had been on the tip of his tongue and foremost in his mind for the past several days. "I love . . . being with you," he repeated.

But his pause had not gone unnoticed. Haley's hands tensed on his shoulders, and she looked away when Keith tried to kiss her again. "Our food is going to get cold," she said a little too brightly. He could have kicked himself for the slip.

His hands slid down to her waist. "Haley," he whispered urgently. "Come on, talk to me. Look at me."

When she did, he could clearly see the panic he'd caused. She exhaled heavily and raked a hand through her hair, then laid her head on his shoulder. "Keith, it's . . . it's too soon. We shouldn't be . . . can't be feeling anything more than . . ."

"Anything more than what, Haley?"

"Oh . . . I just don't know. I don't want to call it lust, because it's much more than that. But to call it what you almost called it . . ."

"Love?"

Keith felt her muscles tighten again, and shook his head, more than a little annoyed that the word should cause her so much anxiety. He speared his fingers into her hair and lifted her head, forcing her to look at him. Placing a tender kiss on her lips, he asked, "What's so frightening about that word? And don't give me the 'too soon' argument again, because it doesn't wash with me. You said that what we have isn't just a simple case of lust, and I agree. But whatever name we put to it won't change the fact that it exists.

The feeling is there. And it's a strong feeling with me or I wouldn't have *almost* said it, would I?''

"That's just it. Why is it so strong? This...quickly, I mean."

"Why shouldn't it be? Because we haven't had time to really get to know each other? How did you put it the other night? We've been in each other's back pockets pretty much every day for almost three weeks now, and not for just an hour here or an hour there, but for the better part of those days. We might not know each other as well as some couples do, but we probably know each other better than others. Haley, time isn't what has you running scared, is it?"

She swallowed, her lashes fluttering down. "No. Or, at least, it's not the main thing that has me scared," she whispered. "I've just...had to give up so much in the past couple of years. Whole parts of me that I once thought I couldn't live without. Don't you see? I don't want to feel that...that *strongly* about something or someone again. I'm not sure I can handle any more disappointment."

"And why would that have to happen?" He knew why she felt it did, but wanted to get it out in the open. Then and only then, he thought, could they move past it and get down to the business of a future together.

"It's obvious, isn't it?" Her expression was pained, but Keith wondered if she was aware that her fingertips were moving in gentle, loving circles on his shoulders. "I do everything I can to distance myself from my former life, and who do I pick to fall for? Not only are you about as high profile as they come, but you're going to be even bigger in movies than you were in sports.''

The look he gave her was one of supreme doubt.

''Oh, trust me on this one,'' she told him.

His heartbeat had quickened and his blood had surged when she'd said she had fallen for him. And he wasn't about to let their circumstances get in the way of that. If he had to pull out of his contract today, he would. But Keith didn't think that would be necessary. ''Even if you're right, who says we can't work out the details to suit us? We're not the first couple to have conflicting professional lives. You don't want to be in the limelight? I'll do everything I can to make sure my personal life remains personal. You want to distance yourself from that whole circus? Actors can and do live outside the glare of publicity all the time. It's just a matter of refusing to let the press drag you into it.''

Haley laughed, the sound harsh and devoid of amusement. ''Like when a reporter grabs your arm and demands a comment from you on a two-year-old story that's likely never to die?'' she asked, sarcasm threading her words.

''Exactly like that.''

Whatever answer she'd been expecting, Keith thought, it hadn't been that one. She gave him an ''I can't believe you just said that'' look.

''You did refuse to answer the man. You said 'no comment' and stuck to it,'' he pointed out in a quiet voice. Raising his hand to her cheek, he brushed her skin with the pads of his fingers. ''I know it upset you.

It upset me to see you go through it. But you got through it, didn't you?"

"Well . . . yes, but I—"

"Want a guarantee that it'll never happen again?" he asked with as much gentleness as he could muster. "I can't give you a guarantee, Haley, you know that. But you can't know that it won't happen, anyway. With *or* without me."

He was right, of course. Haley could find no argument with anything he said. But still, she couldn't help but quake at the thought of wanting something so badly only to have it taken away from her. If she'd learned one thing from her ordeal, it was that the higher you reached, the farther you had to fall. She couldn't stand the thought of Keith's becoming one more shattered dream for her.

"I *do* love you," he murmured. "Which doesn't mean I'm asking for anything more from you right now than just being with me. Just give us a chance, Haley."

He was right about something else, as well. Just because she was afraid of putting a name to an emotion didn't mean it didn't exist. Love. She'd been falling in love with him since that day in the lobby of the Riverton when he'd asked to see her tongue so he could tell if she was lying. Since he'd looked at her with that vulnerable expression in his eyes when he'd requested her help so as not to "fall on his ass" with this movie. Since he'd first kissed her on that stage, telling her that he'd never been a leg man . . . until he'd met her. Since he'd shielded her from the lens of that TV camera.

With him. With him. It was her heart's desire to be with him.

Weary of the fight, Haley covered his hand with hers and guided it to her mouth. His eyes closed and a rush of expelled air came from his lips when she placed a soft kiss in the center of his palm. "I do want to be with you," she whispered.

He stood abruptly, holding her tight against his chest. "Haley" was all he said, his warm breath close to her ear as he propelled them both to the bedroom. She wound her arms around his neck and hooked her ankles around his waist.

They fell to the bed, mouths joining and hearts thudding wildly. Passion rolled over them with the swiftness, force and beauty of a tidal wave. And when the tide had receded, when at last they lay still and quiet on Haley's bed, Keith remembered the last words she had said before he'd brought her into the bedroom. *With you.* They made him think back to the scene that had been shot yesterday.

He tilted Haley's chin up with a finger, and she opened her eyes. Her lips, kiss swollen, lifted at the corners in a lazy smile. He leaned forward, kissing them again. "You haven't asked about the love scene."

"Nope," she said, still smiling. "I found out I'm not the professional I thought I was."

"Don't tell me you got jealous."

"Okay, I won't."

He grinned. "There's no need for you to be, you know. With the crew and the lights and camera, it's kind of difficult for a guy to get . . . *glad,* if you know what I mean."

Haley swatted his arm, then sighed when he lifted her torso and trailed kisses from her collarbone to the top of her breasts. "Could I please . . . not hear about this right now?"

"Besides," he continued, his voice infused with laughter as he blatantly ignored her request, "did you know that they put body makeup all over Carolyn? It is the worst tasting stuff I've ever—"

"You are such a jerk," she said fondly.

CAROLYN WRAPPED herself in the plush robe the hotel provided, then squeezed the excess moisture from her hair with a towel. She had used the last bit of energy she'd had left after the twelve-hour day of shooting to get back to the hotel and into the Jacuzzi. Now if she could work up the enthusiasm to drag herself out of the bathroom and to the bed . . .

Somehow she did, then dialed room service and reached for the TV remote.

Ah, the life of a glamorous actress, she thought, turning on the TV. She angled up from her reclining position on the bed and stuffed two pillows behind her, groaning at the pain in her backside from being astride a horse all day.

But as sore as her rear end was, and as achy as her shoulders and arms were becoming from gripping reins for hours on end, today had been a treat compared to yesterday. She would take physical abuse over mental anguish every time, she decided as she flipped through the TV channels.

An announcer's cheerful voice caught her attention, and Carolyn dropped the remote on the bed, choosing to watch a television tabloid show until room service came.

But the show wasn't as diverting as she might have hoped. Thoughts of the love scene returned. Strangely enough, the embarrassment hadn't been quite as sharp as she'd expected. Keith had been a sweetheart, distracting her by cutting up between takes. He'd cracked her up, once crossing his eyes, once complaining—for her ears only—that her body makeup tasted awful. He'd helped her the most, though, by delivering one hell of a fantastic performance. And that had speeded things up. Yes, Ian had asked for more than one take from each angle. But on the whole, the scene had been shot in what might just go into the books as record time.

Now all Carolyn had to worry about was telling Jonathan. And that was what was causing her the most mental anguish. She tried to imagine a scenario in which the love of her life would frown for a moment, then take her in his arms and tell her that he loved her, no matter what. But that, she knew, was pure fantasy.

She heard the announcer mention Haley's name, and Carolyn's eyes shot to the TV set. She raised herself up on her elbows, winced, then focused in on a publicity still of Haley. Oh Lord, she thought, expecting yet another in the long line of stalker stories. But instead, the story detailed something of a skirmish that had taken place a week ago in the lobby of the Riverton Hotel between Keith and a Tulsa news reporter. Carolyn's eyes widened in surprise as she watched footage that the Tulsa reporter had obviously given over to the tabloid program. First there was Haley, smiling and talking about the Tulsa Actors' Theater, then all of a sudden the reporter was grabbing her arm and asking about the shooting.

Carolyn's hands doubled into fists. "Sorry bastard," she muttered. Then she blinked when the screen went dark, obviously from someone's hand covering the lens of the camera. That's when she heard Keith's voice, calling the reporter the same thing Carolyn had called him seconds ago. "Well, I'll be damned," she said aloud. "Keith Garrison to the rescue."

Two thoughts sprang immediately to mind. The first being that Keith's actions in that hotel lobby would probably garner more publicity for his first movie than doing every talk show on the circuit. The second was that if Haley let Keith get away, Carolyn would personally kick her little ass all the way to the Pacific and back.

The announcer was back on the screen, giving the usual details surrounding the shooting, then adding a remark alluding to a personal connection between Haley and Keith, "the star of Madeira Production's current film being shot in Tulsa, Oklahoma." She went on to supply her audience with information about Keith: his sports background, product endorsements and the ranch outside San Antonio, Texas, that he'd purchased recently.

Shaking her head and smiling, Carolyn clicked off the set. *Keith Garrison,* she thought, *I like your style.* He *was* the very best thing that had happened to Haley Riverton in a long time. She just hoped that Haley wouldn't screw things up with the guy. Carolyn knew how easy it was to do just that.

A sharp knock on her door sounded, and Carolyn got up, groaning and rubbing her backside as she made her way across the hotel room.

"Room service?" she asked, her hand on the knob of the still-closed door.

"No," said a familiar male voice. "It's Jonathan, Carolyn."

CHAPTER FIFTEEN

Dear Sabrina,

How much control do you think I have! Don't you even care how many sacrifices I make, what I put myself through for you, for us? It's been hard enough with you never answering my letters, but I'd gotten used to that. After all, you never answered them before they put me in this prison—they can call it a hospital or institution, but you and I both know it's really a prison.

Then you and the soap opera pulled that crap about you coming back on the soap! Was it fair to trick me like that? To get my hopes up, then to pull the rug out from under me that way? It hurt me, but even then I forgave you, Sabrina. That's how devoted I am to you. Devoted and forgiving.

But now you're cheating again, humiliating me! And you don't care how public you make it, if the whole world knows about it! I go along, play the games these son-of-a-bitch doctors want me to play, just so I can convince them it's okay to let me out. All for you, for us to be together once and for all. And you throw it in my face!

I'm warning you. There's only so much of this

I can take. I'm only human, you know. I thought
you had learned that after what happened the last
time.

                                                    Jack

TEARS IN HIS EYES, Jack slid the letter into an envelope, then clasped his head in his hands. He wanted
her to *read* this one, wanted to send it to Tulsa Actors' Theater so she'd know what she'd done to him.
Maybe then she'd suffer as much as she'd made him
suffer. God, twice! She'd done it to him twice now!

One time he could forgive. But not twice.

Lifting his head, dashing the tears away with the flat
of his hand, he wrote the agency's address on the envelope. She needed to know that she was destroying
him. Deserved to suffer.

But good sense filtered in. No, he'd danced to the
doctors' tune for too long to ruin it all now. They'd
told him yesterday—before he'd seen that goddamn
report on the television show—that he was being
moved sometime this week to another facility. A satellite, they'd called it, for patients who met the crite-
ria for the conditional-release program. Jack knew he
couldn't afford to make a mistake now. Not when he
was this close to getting out. If not from the release
program, he thought, then sooner. Maybe on the way
to the next prison they'd be sending him to.

He took the letter out of the envelope and started
writing a new one. One like the others he'd sent to the
agency.

"I HATE TO SAY I told you so..." Ian said, his tone superior as he smiled down at Haley.

"Yeah, right. I can tell it's just killing you." Haley pulled a gloved hand out of her pocket, brushing back a lock of hair that had blown into her eyes. Looking across the set, she watched Keith hold out a hand to help up the actor he'd just "shot," then turned back to Ian and added, "He *is* good. Isn't he?"

Ian made a notation on a clipboard that an assistant had handed him, then gave it back. "For the amount of experience he has? Yes. Very. But I think he should continue with the lessons. Has he talked you into being his coach on a full-time basis yet?"

Haley narrowed her eyes at the director. "You think you're really crafty, don't ya?" She looped arms with Ian, the grin on her face belying the perturbed look in her eyes. "Two weeks, Haley. I'm only asking for two weeks," she singsonged.

"Hey, that's all I get paid for. What you two work out after that is none of my business."

"I say again, Yeah, right."

Ian chuckled, then gave the word for the crew to begin shutting down for lunch. The principal actors, directors and important technical people began drifting toward the area the caterers had set up for breakfasts and lunches several yards away. Ian and Haley—he had invited her to the set to watch the gunfight sequences—followed suit. Out of the corner of her eye, Haley saw Carolyn walking with Keith and another actor.

"I'm not going to deny that I had an ulterior motive for hiring you to coach him," Ian said. "Sure, I'd
like to see you more involved in the business again.
But I invited you here today to show you the main
reason I wanted you, to witness the results of all your
hard work. He's come a long way in a very short time.
You did a fantastic job."

Ian's compliment warmed Haley's heart. "Thank
you. But I can't take all the credit," she said, her eyes
lighting on the man who deserved most of it. At that
exact moment, Keith glanced up from the conversation he was having with his fellow actors, catching
Haley's gaze. He smiled, tipping his cowboy hat to her
gallantly.

Haley laughed, waving.

"According to Carolyn, things might be getting serious between you and Keith," Ian commented as they
continued walking.

"Yep, they are." And Haley didn't feel anxious in
the least about admitting it. Since the day of Keith and
Haley's talk in her apartment a week ago, she'd refused to worry anymore. She'd thrown out her panic
and concerns like old clothes that no longer fit, and
had simply reveled in her profound good luck at having found a man like Keith Garrison. It felt good, all
that reveling. That, and the very simple pleasure of
sharing her happiness with friends like Carolyn and
Ian and Brent made Haley feel . . . well, happy again,
the happiest she'd been in a long time.

James hadn't been thrilled with the news, and his
attitude had dampened Haley's joy somewhat. But

she'd reassured herself with the thought that James would eventually come to accept her relationship with Keith. Or maybe not. After all, he'd never accepted her being an actress. Whatever the outcome, Haley hadn't allowed his frosty remarks to upset her. She'd simply told him he should grow up and face the fact that she would not allow him to choose the man she fell in love with.

"... deserve a finder's fee?"

Ian's voice cut into her thoughts, and Haley looked up at him. "I'm sorry, what did you say?"

"I said, don't you think I deserve a finder's fee?"

"No way are you getting any of that money back." Haley shook her head, laughing. "A kiss is all you'll get," she decreed, lifting up on tiptoes and planting one on his cheek as they came abreast of the tables.

"And don't think I'm not grateful for it." Ian pulled out a bench and sat down beside her, nodding at Keith when he approached and seated himself on Haley's other side. "I'm afraid I won't be getting many from Carolyn in the future."

Haley turned from Keith, who had just given her a warm hello kiss, then put his cowboy hat on her head. She frowned at Ian. "You're not having creative differences or anything, are you?"

"Are you kidding? You know Carolyn. Once the camera rolls, she becomes the consummate professional." Ian took a bite of a roll. "I was overjoyed when she was cast as Sarah. But I'm afraid that the love scene may have caused some problems in her personal life."

"Oh, no, she finally told Jonathan, did she?"

Keith spoke up. "Jonathan flew into Tulsa. Carolyn just told me this morning."

"He's here?" Haley asked.

"*Was.* Last week." Keith looked at Haley. "She told me it was a very short, but not very sweet, visit. And when the movie wraps, she's going to be moving her things out of Jonathan's condo."

"Oh, I knew this would happen," Haley said with a moan. She glanced down the table at her friend, noting that Carolyn sat apart from everyone else. And since the cameras weren't rolling at the moment, Carolyn's true emotional state was written all over her beautiful, delicate features. Her complexion was pale, and her eyes were downcast. Her full, sensual lips were unsmiling, tight at the corners. The expression she wore was one Haley had seen on Carolyn's face only once in the entire time they'd been friends. It was the same dull sorrow that had been present in Carolyn's eyes when Haley had awoken in the hospital after the shooting to find her at her bedside.

Haley set down her spoon and took Keith's hat off, handing it back to him. She made to rise from the bench, to go to her friend, but Keith put a hand on her arm.

"Maybe you shouldn't," he said gently.

"She needs a friend right now," she countered.

"But maybe not the friend who warned her this would happen."

Haley sighed, sitting down again. "You're probably right. But I hate to see her this way."

"So do I." He laced his fingers through Haley's and gave her hand a light squeeze. "But give her a little time. She's really torn right now. From what she says, she's got a decision to make. You know how hard that can be, right?"

"A decision? Are you saying she's thinking of quitting acting? Giving it up for Jonathan?"

"No," Ian said. Haley swiveled to look at him. "She has to get her priorities straight," he explained, a slightly guilty look on his face. "As much as I might have wanted her for the part of Sarah, I didn't think she'd sign the contract because of the nudity. I tried to talk her out of it, Haley. But she convinced me that she *had* to have the part...no matter what. Now she's come face-to-face with the 'no matter what.' She's probably wondering just how important the part was, after all."

Ian was a good friend, but Haley couldn't help feeling a bit annoyed over his part in all of this.

"Haley, if it hadn't been this nude scene, in this movie," he said, obviously sensing her irritation, "it would have been the next one or the one after that. I've only recently realized it, but she's been on a fast track toward self-destruction ever since what happened to you, only instead of taking the usual Hollywood route of drugs or alcohol, she's done it by throwing herself into her work, making success *the* most important thing in her life."

Haley shook her head, thinking how ironic it was that while she had run away from acting after the shooting, Carolyn had chosen the opposite scenario.

Life's short, play hard, she remembered Carolyn quoting from the sneaker commercial. Haley might not have embraced the philosophy as Carolyn had, but she could understand her friend's credo. They'd both had a premature brush with mortality. "But this Jonathan," she began, "is he so straitlaced he can't stand the thought of *his* woman showing a little skin on the screen for a few minutes?"

Ian smiled down at her. "When did you get so liberal?"

"I didn't. I wouldn't have signed the contract. But, in Carolyn's defense, wasn't that her decision to make?"

"Yes, it was," Ian answered. "But I know Jonathan. By Hollywood's standards he is conservative, but even so, it was Carolyn's rebellious streak and smart mouth that brought him to his knees in the first place. From what I know of him, I'll bet he didn't object to the nude scene because of straitlaced ideals so much as because of worry about what Carolyn's doing to herself."

"And, Haley," Keith put in, slipping his arm around her waist, "breaking things off with her might be just the thing to make her stop and look closely at what she's doing."

She nodded and blew out a breath, picking up her spoon again. Then she looked down the table at Carolyn. "Maybe. But she looks so heartbroken. I hope it's not really over between them."

"Yeah," Keith said, then gave her waist a squeeze. His lips curved in a hint of a smile, and he gazed down into Haley's eyes with a look she'd become familiar with in the past week. "But if they really love each other..."

Haley smiled back at him. "They'll work out the details," she finished for him.

"Yeah."

Ian crumpled up his paper napkin and tossed it down beside his plate. He nudged Haley with his elbow and gestured with a nod toward the young man who was loping up with messages in his hand. "Have I got these people trained or what? Ever since the chicken fiasco, you couldn't get them to bother me during a shoot even if the woods around here were burning down. I told them that anyone short of the ghost of Jack L. Warner had better not get past that gate if they're not on the call sheet, and that I wouldn't take messages until I'd had my last bite of lunch."

Haley chuckled, placing her napkin on the table. "Hope there are no typos on the sheet."

"There aren't. I check it myself every morning now. What have you got for me?" he asked the rather nervous young man.

"Well, there were these three messages for you, and this one from one of the producers," he said, handing him a slip of paper. "And this one's for a Haley Riverton, but I couldn't find that name on my list."

"That's me," Haley said, reaching for the message. Her eyes widened when she saw who it was from. She'd thought it would be from Brent, who was holding down the fort at the theater today. But the name at the bottom of the page was Sy Rosenberg, her former agent. *"Very important, call me immediately."*

Haley looked up from the telephone number she used to know by heart. The wording was so similar to the messages she'd gotten from Sy in the past whenever he had a part for her, Haley could assume only one thing. "Ian Ferguson," she accused playfully, "what do you know about this? The lessons were one thing, but you'd better not be in cahoots with your old buddy Sy. Not if you know what's good for you."

Ian's face was puzzled. "What are you talking about?"

"Did you or did you not tell him about me coaching Keith?" She gave the director the slip of paper, watching as he read the message.

"Well, it might have come up," Ian said, a guilty light in his eyes.

"Just as I suspected." She took back the paper, creased it in half and put it into her coat pocket.

Keith looked at the two of them with a questioning grin. "Since I'm implicated in your private joke, can I ask what it's all about?"

Haley pulled the paper back out, showing it to him. "Sy used to always word messages exactly this way when I'd gotten a part. I think that Ian and Sy have been doing some plotting behind my back."

"Nope. No plotting, I swear," Ian said, chuckling. "I may have said something about the lessons, but I did not suggest that Sy go looking for work for you."

"But you wouldn't be exactly crestfallen if Sy took your information and ran with it, would you?" she asked, arching a brow.

"No." He pocketed his own messages as he rose from the bench. Leaning down, he returned the kiss on the cheek Haley had given him earlier. "I would dearly love to see you through the lens of one of my cameras again, Haley Rivers."

Ian left then, and Haley shook her head, smiling. "He's a case, isn't he?"

Keith looked up from the message. "Who, Ian? Yeah." He looked down at the message again, wondering if Sy's message really was in reference to a part for Haley. And if that were the case, was there any chance that she might be interested? "Are you going to call Sy back?" he asked as casually as possible.

"No, I'm just not ready." She touched his hand. "You understand that I might never be ready, don't you?"

He nodded, but felt disappointed.

"Hey, by the way," she said, changing the subject, "do you know how proud I was watching that gunfight this morning? I didn't see any of your moves coming down Sixth Avenue."

Keith grinned, his disappointment fading. He picked up his fork and held it like an award. "I'd like to thank my mom and my dad, my third-grade teacher, Mrs. Hornbeck, who always believed that I'd be a star someday, my producer and my director. Oh, and last but not least, my acting coach."

LATER THAT AFTERNOON Keith shut the hotel door behind them, locked it, then grabbed Haley by the waist and swung her into his arms. After a long, delicious kiss that had Haley's knees threatening to buckle, he suggested in a throaty voice, "Take a shower with me."

"You're not too tired after a long day of hunting down outlaws?" she teased.

"Uh-uh." He trailed kisses down her neck, and his hands made quick work of her coat. Tossing it aside, he starting walking her backward in the direction of the bathroom. "Never too hungry, never too tired. I've told you that."

"Yes, indeed you have," she said, her fingers at the buttons of his shirt even as he was scooping her up to carry her the rest of the way. "Have I ever told you how much I enjoy being carried like this. It's sooo Rhett—"

The phone rang, interrupting her words and causing Keith to hesitate for a moment. But only a moment.

"Don't answer it," Haley urged.

"Sounds like a plan," he agreed.

KEITH WAS STILL toweling off, and Haley was tying the belt of the robe the hotel supplied when they heard the loud knock on his door. He groaned, wondering who the hell it was. He wanted privacy, complete and utter privacy, until his dawn wake-up call.

"You think it might be Carolyn or Ian?" Haley asked.

"Might be," he answered, grabbing a robe of his own. "I'll get rid of them, then order us up some room service. Sound good?"

"Sounds good." She lifted her face for a kiss, sliding her hands into his wet hair.

"Ooh, I'm worn-out," he complained as he pulled himself away from her.

"From chasing outlaws all day," she stated, laughing when he shot her a lascivious grin over his shoulder. She watched him pad barefoot out of the bathroom, his broad back filling the doorway. Sighing, she looked up and caught her reflection in the mirror. Her eyes widened and she snatched up the comb that lay next to the sink, attacking the wet snarls with a vengeance.

Moments later she heard the raised voices of Keith and another man. The other voice sounded familiar. When she heard her own name, she frowned and set down the comb, leaving the bathroom.

Her brother stood just inside the door, and his angry gaze went from Keith to Haley. He took in her appearance, then smirked. "Well. Guess this is the first place I should've looked for you," he said.

Haley's temper swiftly flared. She looked at Keith, who stood a foot away from her, his hands propped at his waist and his face crimson with anger. "What the hell are you doing here?" she asked her brother. "And before you answer that, you might remember what I told you before. This is *my* life to conduct, baby brother."

"And you're doing such a bang-up job of living it," James gritted out. "When the hell were you planning on answering your messages? Or the phone?"

"What are you talking about?"

Haley had never seen her brother so agitated. He threw his hands in the air. "God, Haley. I've called the theater and your apartment. I even rang this room every fifteen minutes. But I guess you weren't able to hear it in the shower, were you?" He directed a scathing look at Keith.

"Look, Riverton—"

"No, Keith," Haley cut in, embarrassed by her brother's behavior. Good Lord, he was acting like an irate father. Thank heaven her real parents were taking an extended vacation in Europe! She could only imagine their reactions to her life choices if even James was behaving so protectively. Well, it had to stop. Now. "Let me handle this," she said. "James, I'm through with your keeping tabs on me as though I were a three-year-old. If you need to talk to me, you can wait—"

"No, I won't. Because whether you believe you can handle your own life or not, you can't. That was clear the day you ran out to la-la land and made yourself a goddamn target for every lunatic in the country."

"James! What has gotten into you? I won't stand here and listen—"

"Oh, yes, you will!" he shouted, then his gaze rocketed to Keith. He stabbed the air with a finger. "And if you give a damn about her, you'll make her listen!"

Keith's brow furrowed in a deep frown. Her brother's anger verged too much on panic for it to be attributed to normal brotherly concern about his sister's love life. Keith gathered Haley to his side. "What's this about, Riverton?"

"Finally!" James dragged a hand through his normally perfect hair, then closed his eyes, swallowing. "Haley, he got out. Wharton. And they don't know where the hell he is, only that he's left California."

The news hit Keith like a swift kick to the gut. Haley's body stiffened, and she gasped quietly. "How... they let him...? But they... they were supposed to warn me..."

"They didn't *let* him out—he got away. Four days ago. Some brain trust decided that he should be moved to a satellite hospital for patients in some sort of conditional-release program and—"

"Conditional release!" Keith exploded.

"Yeah. I said the same thing when her agent—" he threw Haley a heated look "—who didn't get an answer from her today, called me. He told me Wharton was making such quick progress that they decided he was ready for this... satellite hospital. Sy said his letters to the agency had been less frequent and had stopped threatening Haley. He didn't want to upset you by mentioning them before. But the letters he *didn't* mail to the agency told the real story. They found a bundle of them in his room. That was after he knocked out his escort to the other hospital with the man's own gun."

Haley gasped again, and her palm went to her mouth. Keith watched the blood drain from her face, felt her begin to tremble.

"Here. Sit down, baby." He led her to a chair, his insides churning. After getting her seated, he rested a hip on the arm of the chair and put his arm across her shoulders.

"So why wasn't she notified sooner?" he asked James.

James shook his head, disgust in his eyes. "It's been one bureaucratic screw-up after another. Sy says hospital officials tried to locate Haley in L.A. first. That was *two stinking days* after Wharton got loose. Hell, the idiots didn't even notify the police until the third day! It was the police who finally had the sense to call your agency. And that was at five o'clock on the third day. They left a damn message on the agency's answering machine! By the time Sy got the message this morning, it was ten o'clock our time. Then Haley decided to ignore the message." James rubbed his forehead and closed his eyes. "I'm...sorry, Haley. I shouldn't have come down on you like that," he added, his throat convulsing. "I just can't...believe that this is happening again. I won't *let* this happen again."

Keith silently seconded the emotion. "It won't," he said, then asked, "How do they know he's left California?"

James dropped wearily into a chair opposite Haley's. "Well, he stole a car in L.A. They found it abandoned in Wichita Falls. They think he was responsible for a hold-up at a liquor store in L.A., as well. So he's got money...and he has a gun. And probably another car."

Keith tightened his hold on Haley's shoulder.

"But...he doesn't know where I am," Haley said in a shaky voice, knowing that it was wishful thinking. The city of Wichita Falls, Texas, was very close to the Oklahoma border. And only four hours from Tulsa.

James leaned forward, taking her cold hands in his. "Honey, Sy says there's a good chance that he does. In one of the last letters Wharton wrote, he went on about 'Sabrina' cheating on him. Your agent thinks that he might have seen that television report about a week ago." He released a deep sigh. "It mentioned where you were living and your involvement with TAT."

Haley squeezed her eyes shut, not believing that the nightmare was starting all over again. There was no escaping him, she thought, fear tightening her chest. She thought of how many times she'd berated herself for looking over her shoulder, expecting to see Wharton stalking her. Of how she hated the fact that her fingers still shook every time she had to go through a stack of mail. She thought of the nightmares about Jack's return. She had thought herself unduly paranoid. She'd been wrong. There had been every reason to be paranoid. "So," she whispered, "he could be in Tulsa right now."

James nodded and began gently rubbing her hands between his. "But this time we know. This time I can protect you, honey. I've got armed guards all over this hotel already. If I have to, we'll lock it up until he's found."

"No," Keith said, his own protective instincts flaring up. "If he knows she's in Tulsa, I want her out of town. Out of the state." Then he got up and, not listening to any of James's arguments, went to the phone and dialed Ian's suite. He spent several moments explaining the situation to Ian, then walked back to Haley and James. "Ian's going to film around Carolyn's and my scenes for the next couple weeks. I'm taking Haley to my place in San Antonio."

JAMES SHUT the hotel limousine's door, then leaned in through the car window to give his sister another kiss on the cheek. "You call me the minute you get to San Antonio, okay? And then again when you get to the ranch."

"I will."

He looked past her to Keith, who held his sister's hand in his. "Thank you," he told him.

"There's no need to thank me."

"Yes, there is." He stepped back, and the limousine pulled out of the underground hotel parking garage and into Tulsa's downtown traffic.

James walked back inside the building, not aware of the man wearing dark glasses and fatigue pants who had been standing behind a large column...not aware that his voice had carried easily across the hard surfaces in the cavernous underground lot.

CHAPTER SIXTEEN

"GET SOME SLEEP," Keith said softly, giving her a kiss and covering her travel-weary body with the Zuni-patterned comforter. Haley held his hand in a death grip when he tried to rise from the water bed's side rail.

"I'm not tired," she lied. Survival instincts and the fact that she'd been numb with shock when she'd heard Wharton was out again might have prodded her to come with Keith, but that shock had worn off during the flight from Tulsa, and she'd realized that it had been the height of selfishness to drag him into this.

And not only him, she thought with a shudder, looking at the closed bedroom door. His sister and her children were behind two other bedroom doors in this house.

"I'll be back just as soon as I've explained to Angie why we're here. I need to call James, too."

Haley scrambled up in the bed. "Keith, get her to take the boys away from here, okay? I don't want—"

"Hey, now," he said with a quiet smile, "they're as safe as you are now. No one but you, me, James and Ian knows you're here, remember?"

"But he will. He'll find out."

"Haley, lie back down. Come on now," he said in a firm voice, his hands pressing her to the bed. "Now listen to me. I know you're afraid, but there's no reason to be. And if it'll make you feel safer, I keep a gun on the shelf in that closet over there," he said, pointing. "But you're not going to need it. He's not going to find you. You get some sleep." He kissed her forehead. "I love you," he said at the door.

I love you. His timing couldn't have been worse. Haley buried her head in the pillow and let loose with the tears she'd been holding in for hours. She cried for all the misery she'd caused her brother and parents. And the fallout of misery that Jack's first attack had caused her friend Carolyn. Then finally, she cried for herself, knowing now that she must break up with Keith, but not knowing how she would find the strength to do it.

Keith woke her a half hour later. He slipped under the covers and gathered her into his arms. "I told you he wouldn't find you, love. James says the Tulsa police found a car they suspect Wharton stole after he abandoned the one in Wichita Falls."

"In ... Tulsa?"

"Yes." His embrace, strong and warm, tightened. "They'll have him in custody, then back on a plane to California, before you know it."

Keith refrained from causing her undue fright by not telling her the rest of the news he'd received. That the police had found the stolen car in the underground parking garage at the Riverton Hotel.

"NO WORD YET?" Angie asked, pouring a cup of coffee for Keith and bringing it to the dining-room table.

"No," Keith answered. "The Tulsa police have had her apartment, the theater, even the Riverton, staked out for the past week. No sign of the son of a bitch yet."

Angie squeezed his shoulder. "They'll get him," she said. "It's just a matter of time."

"Yeah, I know." Keith rubbed his eyes with heels of his hands. "I know. But how much longer will Haley be able to take this?"

Gazing sightlessly through the large glass window that looked out on his backyard pool, Keith thought about the toll this situation was taking on Haley. It gave him a good idea what it must have been like for her after the shooting. Since arriving at the ranch, she'd become more distant and introspective by the day. And had the memory of all they'd shared before Wharton's escape not been so indelibly etched into Keith's heart and mind, he might have wondered if there had ever been more between them than the acting lessons. She shied away from any kind of physical closeness. Forget making love— Haley stiffened at his touch, tensed in his arms when he held her at night.

Would it change when the ordeal was over? Or would he lose Haley? An outside force of this magnitude could ruin any relationship; one like it had even destroyed Griff's ten-year marriage.

"You know the old saying," Angie remarked, and Keith looked up at her. "That which does not kill us only makes us stronger. I don't know her well yet, but

I do know that she's been through this once before. I think she's stronger than you know."

All my strengths were gone, Keith. There was nothing left for me to fight with.

She'd said those words to him on the night of the reception. If that was true, if the first attack had taken all that away from her, what did she have to fight a second battle with? "I think I've lost her, Ange," he said, burying his face in his hands.

HALEY JOLTED awake at the noise of the bedroom door being opened. She came clumsily to her knees on the bed, remembering instantly where she was by the way the water bed mattress pitched and yawed beneath her. One carrot-topped head peeked around the slightly opened door, and Haley let out the breath she'd been holding. It was only one of the twins. No, both of the twins, she saw when a second red head came into view.

She dragged a still-quivering hand through her hair, then scooted back beneath the comforter. The gown that Angie had lent her was long, but transparent enough to be inappropriate for the company of four-year-old boys.

They barged in as if they owned the place, which transformed Haley's initial fright into amusement. In the week she'd been here, the overly exuberant, "active"—as Keith had called them—nephews had been a bright spot for Haley. And just two more aspects of Keith, she thought with an ache, that she would miss terribly.

"Haley," Brian said, bumping his stomach against the padded rail, then falling forward to bury his little face in the comforter, "does Uncle Keef know you're on his bed?" he asked in a muffled voice.

"'Cause you could be in *deep* trouble, you know," Barry pointed out, then gave his brother a ninja chop. "Get off the bed, Brian."

Brian reared up, returning the chop. "No, you!"

"No, you!"

The chops and kicks and ninja battle cries were flying now, and Haley held in a laugh. "Guys," she whispered. "Guys, you're going to wake your mother up."

"She's already awake," Angie stated in a firm voice from the doorway. Her eyes narrowed as she bore down on the two warriors. "You two were told to let Haley sleep, weren't you?"

"Uh-oh," Haley said when the boys looked in her direction for help. She shrugged and put her hands in the air, palms up.

They ran toward the door before Angie could get hold of them. "We were just tryin' to tell her about swimmin' on the bed," Brian said, fleeing.

"There is *no* swimmin' on Uncle Keef's bed!" Barry added as he escaped.

Angie gave Haley an apologetic look. "I'm sorry if they woke you."

"No," she said with a chuckle, "I was already awake. They're so cute," Haley added in their defense.

"Yes, aren't they, though," Angie said through gritted teeth.

"No, really. They're probably a handful for you, but a lot of that's due to the fact that there are two of them, don't you think? With two little minds working, there's double the trouble for them to get into."

"I don't know," Angie said with a tired shake of her head. "I was a twin and didn't find as much trouble as they do. Now, their Uncle Keef? He was a whole different story. I tell him all the time that they inherited all that rambunctious behavior from the same place he got it."

Haley's good humor disappeared, and she threw back the covers, climbing out of bed. She made a quick trek to the dresser for jeans and a T-shirt. "Is he . . . out checking on his horses or something?" she asked, her back to Angie.

Angie held in a sigh at Haley's strained tone. Every time she tried to draw Haley into a conversation about Keith, Haley retreated. Though she'd always tried to keep her nose out of her brother's business, it tore at Angie's heart to see the woman Keith was in love with keep him at arm's length. Her brother would be heartbroken if Haley broke up with him once the stalker was caught, she thought.

She closed the distance between them and put a hand on Haley's shoulder. "Haley, what can I do? Can you talk to me about it? Maybe that would help."

Haley choked back a sob. What would help, she thought, was if Angie weren't so sweet and kind to her. If her sons weren't precocious little heart stealers. If

Angie would stop adding memories of Keith to the store Haley already had. Haley didn't think she could stand one more memory that would soon be bitter-sweet.

She cleared her throat. "Thank you. You're very kind. But . . . I'll be okay."

"All right," Angie said slowly. "But if you need to talk . . ."

"Thank you."

Angie sighed and turned for the door. Remembering Keith's message, she stopped. "Keith wanted me to tell you that he's gone into San Antonio for an hour or so."

"Okay." Haley didn't look up from the stacks of clothes. "Thank you."

"You wouldn't want to come swimming with me and the boys a little later, would you? That's the great thing about San Antonio weather and heated pools. You can swim all year round."

Haley gave her a wan smile. "I . . . think I'll pass this time."

After Angie left, Haley had a bite or two of break-fast, watched a boring "infomercial" on TV in Keith's den, then finally decided to read for a while to pass the time. But reading didn't distract her enough to keep her mind away from the goings-on in Tulsa. She'd called James shortly after Angie and the twins had headed out for the pool. He'd said that Brent was handling everything at the theater just fine, and Dennis had found a director to fill in for her for the play until Wharton was found.

Until Wharton is found, she thought, *until Wharton is found!* Dropping the book on the floor beside her chair, she squeezed her eyes shut. Dammit, why hadn't they found him! Where was he! How long—

The twins came barreling into the den at that moment, their hair and bodies soaked and their little feet slapping watery footprints on the carpet.

"Hey, hey," she said, looking up with a laugh. "Does your mom know you two came in without drying off?"

They came to a skidding stop in front of her. "Yes," Brian said, nodding once. "She's the one who told us to."

Haley arched a brow. "Are you sure?"

Barry put his hands on his hips. "She wants us to give you a message."

"Okay," Haley said, figuring Angie had probably told the two to dry off first, but playing along, anyway. "What is it?"

Barry concentrated for a moment, squinting his eyes, then said, "She said, call 911. Who's Sabrina, Haley? The man out there wants to talk to Sabrina."

"Sab— What did you...? Oh...oh, God, no." Haley jumped up from the chair, racing out of the den and into the dining room. The sight she saw through the window chilled her blood.

Oh, God! The nightmare had caught up with her!

Jack Raymond Wharton, his face mottled red and his hands waving as he shouted something, stood only five feet away from Keith's sister. He wore fatigues like before, but this time he also had on an army-surplus-type jacket. Haley swallowed the panic that had risen in her throat, then groped frantically for the cordless phone on the table.

"Nine-one-one. What is your emergency?"

"I...there's a man...he's out...outside...and he has a gun—" Haley couldn't see one in his hands, but knew it was probably in his coat pocket. "He was stalking me and—"

"Ma'am, your address, please."

"Oh, it's...God, outside San Antonio somewhere!" Her gaze snagged on a utility bill next to the phone, and Haley grabbed it. She read off the address to the operator. "Please...send the police."

"Ma'am, stay on the l—"

Haley switched off the phone and ran back into the den. "Boys," she said, hauling the two of them into her arms, then running with them for the far end of the house. "I want you to...to stay in your room, okay? Will you do that for me?"

Frightened, Brian asked, "What's the matter? Why are you cryin', Haley?"

"Are we p-punished?" Barry asked.

"No, no. Everything's...all right." She nearly tripped over toys that were strewn on their bedroom floor. "I just want you to stay in here until Uncle Keith gets back." She set the boys down, her mind working furiously. Spotting their Teenage Mutant Ninja Turtles videotape, she could have shouted for joy. "You can watch the Turtles, okay? Promise me," she said, fumbling with the TV and VCR, "that you'll stay in here...you stay and watch, okay? Please."

"All right!" Barry said, sitting down with his brother in front of the set. Brian looked over his shoulder at her, his little auburn brows still veed in a frown.

Haley gave him a reassuring smile. "It's okay. Everything's...fine." He turned back to the set. Putting her trust in the fact that the boys usually couldn't be dynamited from the spot when the Turtles were on, Haley shut their door, then ran the length of the hall to Keith's bedroom. Adrenaline racing through her, she flung open a closet door and stood on suitcases, searching for the handgun he'd told her was there. When her fingers felt the cold steel of the barrel, Haley closed her eyes, shoving back the terror. Wharton would *not* hurt the boys, and he would not hurt Angie!

She tore back to the dining-room window, desperately trying to come up with some kind of plan. When she spotted Wharton again, her stomach twisted painfully. He had a gun in his hands now. It appeared as though Angie had tried to lead him away from the house—they were several feet farther from the back door than they'd been earlier. Her breathing labored and her heart thudding against her ribs, Haley looked toward the boys' room and sent up a silent prayer that they wouldn't come out. She swallowed once, then went to the back door, opening it.

Wharton jerked toward the source of the noise.

"Angie, run! Get out of here!" Haley shouted, raising the gun to chest level. Though tears blurred her vision, she could see that Angie was still frozen in place. "Get out of here!" she screamed again.

Wharton never saw Angie dart around the side of the house; he never moved. His eyes were riveted on Haley. "Sabrina," he said, then began slowly walking toward her. "Sabrina. Sabrina."

Sabrina . . . Sabrina . . . Sabrina.

The name echoed in her mind. Sabrina had been a victim, but she, Haley, was not. Suddenly she was angry, angrier than she'd ever been in her life.

"No!" she shouted. Wharton's steps halted, and he lowered the hand with the gun. "If you're going to do this to me again, you're going to know that my name is not Sabrina! I'm Haley. Understand? *Haley!*"

His face became suffused with hatred. "You brought this on! You've done it to me! You cheated on me! So I came here to—"

"Think about it, Jack," she said, anger and adrenaline still pumping through her. "I've done nothing to you. You victimized me! But this time I'm not helpless. And I refuse to be victimized by you again! Never, Jack. Never again!"

Her words set him off, and he raised his gun. But he was too late. Haley saw his intent and her fury was like lightning, flashing through her. She felt the kick of the gun in her hands when she pulled the trigger, then saw his gun fly into the pool as he fell to the concrete.

KEITH THREW open the door of his Blazer and hit the ground running. His heart in his throat, he dodged county sheriff units with their blue-and-red light flashing and the crowd of law-enforcement officers, nearly losing it when he caught sight of the ambulance in the side yard.

"God, no!" he rasped, then raced to it. She'd been right; the maniac had found her here. And Keith hadn't listened! He got to the back doors of the ambulance at the exact moment the paramedics were lifting a gurney into the van.

Keith's breathing became shallow, and his knees nearly buckled. Haley wasn't lying on the gurney. Jack Raymond Wharton was.

He grabbed a paramedic by the arm. "Anyone else? Was anyone else hurt?"

The young man shook his head. "There are a couple of ladies inside who aren't exactly steady at the moment, but they weren't hurt."

Keith let go of the man's arm, life pouring back into his body as he vaulted past the officers milling around his pool. One looked up and called out, "Mr. Garrison? If we could talk to you, please?"

"Yeah, in a minute." He didn't stop until he heard the rowdy sounds of his two nephews coming from his den. He swallowed back a sob. The noise they made had never sounded so sweet. From the doorway of the den he saw the two of them straddling the arms of one of his chairs, huge sheriff hats on their heads as they rode the pretend horses. Two deputies sat nearby talking with Angie and Haley.

Angie saw him first and rose from the sofa. "Oh, Keith," she murmured, launching herself into his arms.

Keith's hold on his twin was tight. "Thank God you're all right. I'm sorry. So sorry, Ange," he said into her hair. "This...was supposed to be a safe place. I'm sorry."

"No, no." Her tears wet the front of his shirt. "You couldn't have known. I'm just...just so glad you're here now. I—" She leaned back to look into her brother's eyes. "I was so afraid, but Haley— Keith, she was a wonder. She was the one who called 911, got the boys out of harm's way, found your gun..."

"My gun?"

"The one you told her about." Angie took a deep breath, shaking her head. "Wharton came up on me when the boys and I were swimming. I sent them in to tell Haley to call the police. I kept telling him that...that Sabrina wasn't here, thinking I could make him leave or at least stall him until the police got here. I didn't think she would come outside. But she faced him down, Keith. She drew his attention away from me. And...she was the one who shot him." Angie glanced at Haley, who was still talking to the deputies.

"Good Lord. Is he dead?" he asked slowly, jarred by the news that Haley had been the one to put Wharton in that ambulance.

"No, she hit him in the shoulder. He'll survive."

Keith shut his eyes, hugging his sister to his chest again and feeling ashamed that he'd wished someone dead. But he did. He wanted the man and his insanity out of his and Haley's lives forever. He wanted to push back time a couple of hours. He wanted the gun in his own hands. He wanted...Haley. But he had painful doubts that things would go that way now. Because Jack Wharton was still in the picture. "Is she okay?" he asked.

"I...don't know. She's been so quiet, Keith. But strangely she's also calm. She only cried up until the moment she shot him. Not a tear since." Angie stepped out of his embrace. "Talk to her. I think she needs you."

Keith hoped with everything inside him, with heart, mind and soul, that that was the case. But when Haley's gaze finally lifted and her eyes locked with his, he knew his hopes were about to be dashed. Her expression was calm, as Angie had said, but the deep sorrow in her eyes told the real story. And that story, he realized as he felt his heart shatter into a million pieces, held no happy ending for them.

He stood frozen in place, his throat convulsing when she murmured something to one of the deputies and rose from the sofa. With slow steps she moved toward him. When she reached Keith, she lifted a hand to him, but dropped it before he could take it in his. "Haley," he said, his voice like sandpaper.

"I'm...sorry."

"No. Don't—"

"Yes." Her gaze left his to seek out his nephews. "They...could have been hurt. I didn't want...someone else hurt," she whispered. "Your family..." Her lower lip began quivering.

"Haley, don't. It's because of you that they weren't."

She bobbed her head once, whether in agreement with what he'd just said or not, Keith had no way of knowing. "If I hadn't been here..."

"But you were. Because I wanted you here," Keith said roughly. He wanted so desperately at the moment to clasp her in his arms, but he had to know that it would be for more than just the moment. "I'll always want you here. I love you."

"I...found out something today. I'm...not the victim I thought I was. And I won't ever allow myself to think that again." Her voice was delicate, but winding through it was a new thread of strength. "I'll do whatever I have to do to live the life *I* want. And what I want in it most of all is you. But there'll be so many...obstacles. So much that you'll have to put up with. And I have to know...how far are you willing to go for me?"

He closed his eyes and dragged her into his arms. "How far is forever?"

She cried then. Her first tears since she'd shot the man who had stalked her. She burrowed closer to him, the heavy sobs racking her body. Release, Keith thought gladly as he tightened the embrace and laid his cheek atop her head. She'd needed this release for two solid years.

Long moments later, when her sobs subsided, when she raised her head and looked up at him, her eyes were red and the tears had left tracks on her beautiful face. She lifted a hand to wipe at her cheeks, but Keith stopped her. He leaned down and kissed her, first one cheek then the other, then her mouth. "You were so brave," he whispered. "So strong."

Her lips curved in a half smile, and she shook her head. "No. That was the survival instinct kicking in. What's going to take bravery is facing tomorrow and the next day and all the others that make up this forever you're promising. Are you sure? It's a long time, Keith," she said, her voice quavering a bit. "And it'll be filled with so much—"

"Love," he finished for her, his fingers gently stroking her brow. "And fun, and arguments, and great sex...and babies," he said, smiling at the thought. He nodded toward his nephews. "Maybe twin babies."

She smiled and gave him a speculative look. "Great sex, you say?"

"Oh, yes."

Her smile widened, and she hugged him close again. "I'm holding you to it."

EPILOGUE

"STOP FUSSING. You look gorgeous." Haley slipped on her satin heels, and walked the length of the lavish Riverton suite she and her husband of six months had taken for the weekend. He had every reason to be nervous tonight, but if he didn't stop tying, untying and retying his bow tie soon, there'd be nothing left of the narrow strip of plaid cloth. "Here," she said, reaching up to brush his large hands away, "let me."

"Gladly." He scowled at the ceiling while Haley worked with the tie, his hands now busy fiddling with his cuff links. "I hate these things."

"What? Ties? Or movie premieres?"

He grinned. "Since this is the first premiere I've been to, I'd say it's the tie."

"Would you, now?" Finished, Haley smiled up a' Keith, amazed anew that she was actually married to this devastatingly attractive man. She supposed tha it would become easier to believe with time. But the again, her life had changed so much in such a shor period that she wondered if she'd ever get used to it all They'd married two weeks after the incident witl Wharton at Keith's ranch, then had flown back t Tulsa for Keith to finish the movie. And for her to giv notice to Dennis at the theater and pack her belongings for the move back to San Antonio.

"You've been a wreck all day," she said. "I don't think all that anxiety was due simply to the fact that you'd be wearing a bow tie tonight."

"You're right," he admitted, "I'm nervous as hell about tonight. I'll be glad when it's over."

Haley grinned and grabbed his hands to put a halt to his fidgeting. She placed them at the small of her back and settled in close against his chest, her champagne-colored silk bodice brushing his snowy white shirt.

"You're going to be a hit. I predict two thumbs up," she said, holding hers in the air.

He chuckled. "You wouldn't be just a tad prejudiced, would you?"

"Not even a tad," she assured him with a serious expression. "This is my professional opinion you're getting, Garrison. I allow no personal biases, no prejudices . . . no . . . Keith . . ." Her words trailed away as he began to chain kisses down her neck.

"Not even last night?" he whispered against her skin.

"Not even—" Remembered images floated in. Fevered, intense, passionate images of the night before. "Well, maybe some of that stuff at the last," she allowed.

She felt his smile on her collarbone. "Only the stuff at the last?" he asked.

"Okay, okay. Maybe a few of the things at the beginning, too. And possibly some—not all—of the business in the middle."

He raised his head, duplicating her serious expression of moments ago. "It's good to have a completely unbiased opinion."

She rolled her eyes at his teasing, then rested her cheek on his chest. "Carolyn called while you were in the shower. She and Jonathan have just arrived."

"How's she holding up?" Keith asked, his tone concerned.

"Are you asking about the pregnancy or the fact that Ian kept the nude scene in?"

"Both."

"Well, she's on cloud nine about the baby, says she and Jonathan can't wait until it's here. And as far as the nude scene's concerned—" Haley leaned back, looking up at her husband with eyes that twinkled "—she said that Ian's going to regret leaving it in. He definitely won't have the baby named after him now. She also told me that she's had some of our old friends in Hollywood start the rumor that she had a body double for the scene—most people won't realize it would have been virtually impossible to have used another actress. Now all she'll have to do is deny the rumor in interviews and nobody will believe her."

"Clever woman," Keith commented with a laugh. "I'm relieved that Carolyn and Jonathan were able to work things out. Ian was right about him, after all, wasn't he? It wasn't the nudity he was so hot about, was what Carolyn was doing to herself."

"Yes. Thank God she realized it before it was too late. That break in filming when we left Tulsa for your ranch came at a pretty opportune time for her. She was able to fly out to L.A. and patch things up with Jonathan."

"So how do you think Jonathan's going to take seeing his wife in that scene tonight?"

Haley shrugged, then stepped out of the embrace. "Probably the same way I'm going to take it seeing my husband in that same scene. It won't be easy." She reached for his hand, lacing their fingers together. Placing a soft kiss on his knuckles, she looked deeply into his eyes, trying to convey the emotion in her heart. "But I'd bet he's willing to put up with a bit of difficulty here and there. It's a small price to pay when you love someone."

"I love you, too," he said gruffly, giving her hand a gentle squeeze.

"I know." She knew it because she'd been witness to the price Keith paid on a daily basis. Her ordeal hadn't ended just because Jack Wharton had been locked away in a Texas prison. Keith had been there to hold and comfort her through the renewed bout of anxiety and nightmares after the second shooting. He'd supported her decision to consult a therapist to help get her over some of the rougher spots. He'd tenaciously protected her from reporters who had hounded her for interviews those first few months after the second encounter with Wharton. And when she'd finally felt it was time to grant that first interview, Keith had been there, holding her hand tightly in his, as she'd answered the questions. Her answers, Haley had hoped, might be of some help to others who found themselves in the situation she'd been in.

Had that interview taken place only a month ago? It seemed as though it had been during another life-time. Indeed, it all seemed to belong to another life-time.

Smiling, feeling the excitement of Keith's big night scuttle back in and push all other thoughts to the background, Haley looped her arm in his. They walked to the door, locked it behind them and made their way to the elevator. Keith pushed the button and looked down at Haley with a grin.

"What are you grinning about?"

"I was just thinking that you look as beautiful in silk as you did in red running shoes and black tights." At her frown, he explained, "Don't you remember the day we first met? You had annihilated my ego at the theater, then came over to talk to Ian. We shared this very same elevator that day."

"Oh, that's right," she said, stepping onto the elevator with him when it opened on their floor. "I'd almost forgotten."

"I'll never forget it," he said.

"The way I slammed you?"

"No. The way you looked in those tights."

She smiled, forever grateful that his acting skills had needed polishing. When the elevator doors slid closed, Keith leaned against the back wall much as he had that first day. He put his arm across Haley's shoulders.

"If it's true that *I'm* the real looker in this couple," she mentioned, glancing up at him, "then I should profit from that, don't you think?"

"Oh, I should say so," he replied, his eyes lit with humor.

"I'm glad you agree. Then you won't argue when I ask for top billing in that romantic comedy you've been pestering me to do with you."

Speechless, Keith stared at her. He'd been certain that it was too soon to ask, but he'd loved the script. And he'd loved the idea of playing opposite her in it. And he'd carefully approached her with it, not daring to "pester" her about it. "Such greed," he said, finally finding his voice. "But greed is a good sign," he added, and with a huge smile, he wrapped her in his arms. "A very good sign."

HARLEQUIN SUPERROMANCE®

HARLEQUIN SUPERROMANCE WANTS TO INTRODUCE YOU TO A DARING NEW CONCEPT IN ROMANCE...

WOMEN WHO DARE!
Bright, bold, beautiful ...
Brave and caring, strong and passionate ...
They're women who know their own minds
and will dare anything ... for love!

One title per month in 1993, written by popular Superromance authors, will highlight our special heroines as they face unusual, challenging and sometimes dangerous situations.

Dive into a whirlwind of passion and excitement next month with:
#562 WINDSTORM by Connie Bennett
Available in September wherever Harlequin Superromance novels are sold.

WW

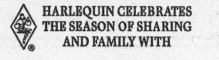

Calloway Corners

In September, Harlequin is proud to bring readers four involving, romantic stories about the Calloway sisters, set in Calloway Corners, Louisiana. Written by four of Harlequin's most popular and award-winning authors, you'll be enchanted by these sisters and the men they love!

MARIAH by Sandra Canfield
JO by Tracy Hughes
TESS by Katherine Burton
EDEN by Penny Richards

As an added bonus, you can enter a sweepstakes contest to win a trip to Calloway Corners, and meet all four authors. Watch for details in all Calloway Corners books in September.

Harlequin is proud to present our
best authors and their best books.
Always the best for your
reading pleasure!

Throughout 1993, Harlequin will bring you
exciting books by some of the top names in
contemporary romance!

In August,
look for
Heat Wave by

A heat wave hangs over the city....

Caroline Cooper is hot. And after dealing with crises all
day, she is frustrated. But throwing open her windows to
catch the night breeze does little to solve her problems.
Directly across the courtyard she catches sight of a man
who inspires steamy and unsettling thoughts....

Driven onto his fire
escape by the sweltering heat, lawyer Brendan Carr
is weaving fantasies, too—around gorgeous Caroline.
Fantasies that build as the days and nights go by.

Will Caroline and Brendan dare cross the dangerous
line between fantasy and reality?

Find out in HEAT WAVE by Barbara Delinsky...
wherever Harlequin books are sold.

BOB4